A LOVE UNDONE

D0061532

This Large Print Book carries the
Seal of Approval of N.A.V.H.

A LOVE UNDONE

AN AMISH NOVEL OF SHATTERED DREAMS AND GOD'S UNFAILING GRACE

CINDY WOODSMALL

CHRISTIAN LARGE PRINT
A part of Gale, Cengage Learning

GALE
CENGAGE Learning·

Farmington Hills, Mich • San Francisco • New York • Waterville, Maine
Meriden, Conn • Mason, Ohio • Chicago

GALE
CENGAGE Learning·

**THE LIBRARY OF CONGRESS HAS CATALOGED
THE THORNDIKE PRESS EDITION AS FOLLOWS:**

Woodsmall, Cindy.
   A love undone : an Amish novel of shattered dreams and God's unfailing
grace / Cindy Woodsmall. — Large print edition.
    pages cm. — (Thorndike Press large print Christian fiction)
   ISBN 978-1-4104-7147-5 (hardcover) — ISBN 1-4104-7147-0 (hardcover)
   ISBN 978-1-59415-516-1 (softcover) — ISBN 1-59415-516-X (softcover)
   1. Amish—Fiction. 2. Large type books. I. Title.
  PS3623.O678L68 2014b
  813'.54—dc23
                                      2014028762

Published in 2014 by arrangement with WaterBrook Press, an imprint
of Crown Publishing Group, a division of Random House LLC, a Penguin
Random House Company

To Bobby Miller,
a rare and remarkable man who loved
our niece with noble honor and gentle
strength and did so during the
heartwarming times as well as the
heartbreaking times. Although you are
now dwelling on this planet without the
love of your life, Tammy's love and faith
continue to reach out to you through the
dogwood tree that defies all science by
blooming year round as a concrete
reminder that regardless of how it feels,
nothing can separate us from the
love of God.

1

Rosanna peered out the kitchen window, trying to see through the sheets of rain. What was taking her husband so long? Had the wheels of his rig gotten buried in mud somewhere? After days of hard rain, the ground was saturated. Or was her very social husband simply visiting with his brother, thinking he had more than enough time to get Rosanna to Viola Mae's house?

Rosanna glanced at the clock. Viola Mae had called two hours ago, thinking her labor may have begun. Perhaps it had, but from her experience as a midwife, Rosanna was pretty sure Viola Mae's first child would take all night and perhaps half of tomorrow before entering this world. And that was *if* Viola was actually in labor.

Nevertheless, the young mom-to-be had to be seen tonight. Rosanna drove herself when the weather was good or even half-decent, but her easygoing, supportive husband insisted on driving her whenever there was snow, fog, or heavy rains. If Rosanna's examination indicated Viola Mae was in labor, Rosanna would stay the night, and her husband would return home.

She wished, and not for the first time, that the Amish in Winter Valley weren't so cut off from the rest of the world. The serenity of living in northwestern Pennsylvania couldn't be beat, but there wasn't a clinic or doctor in the valley, and after her *Mamm* passed away, Rosanna was the only midwife in the region. When at twenty years old Rosanna had given birth to her first child, her own Mamm had delivered the baby girl, declaring the little one would also become a midwife. That was nineteen years ago, and Jolene was many wonderful things, but a midwife was not one of them.

A thud pulled Rosanna's attention to the happenings in the room. A book had fallen from the kitchen table. Her three school-age children were sitting around one end of the kitchen table, homework spread out in front of them as Jolene helped. Four-year-old Hope sat at the table with them, but she wasn't in school yet. She liked homework hour, though, and Jolene had her close to reading and writing already. But the child who required the most help was Ray. After

8

his near-fatal accident three years ago, no one had believed he'd be able to attend school at all — no one except Jolene. Rosanna's chest tightened with anxiety when she considered how difficult an adjustment Ray would have when Jolene moved out of state.

The light aroma of cooked celery hung in the air. Dozens of jars of freshly canned goods filled half the kitchen table. She and Jolene had made good use of the last three days of rain, finally catching up on their canning of September's produce, especially the overabundance of celery for Jolene's wedding. They'd planted more potatoes than ever before just for the wedding feast, but they didn't need to can those. Her eldest child, the one Rosanna couldn't get through a day without, would marry and leave the state in a few weeks. Was Rosanna doing a decent job of hiding the grief she felt? As for her daughter, she was so excited to embrace her future she could hardly sleep.

Where had all the days gone between giving birth to her and giving her away to be wed?

Jolene glanced up from the mounds of papers and looked out the kitchen window. "Is that his rig coming down the road?"

Rosanna couldn't tell, not yet. But she did notice her lone and beloved dogwood, the one her husband had given her as a wedding present. Most of its red leaves had been beaten from the branches, and it'd been looking rather puny the last few years. Would its roots survive such a drenching? At the end of last winter, she and Jolene had cut a few shoots from the tree, hoping to grow new trees before this one died. They should've started that years ago when the dogwood was still healthy.

"It's *Daed.*" Jolene recognized his rig before Rosanna.

She didn't have to ask Jolene to finish helping with homework or to get supper on the table. If Viola Mae wasn't in labor and Rosanna returned home in a couple of hours, the kitchen sinks and counters would be spotless. Maybe the floors too if Jolene and her siblings got into another soapsuds battle. They loved those, and the upside was that the floors had to be mopped dry when they were through.

But on the nights when their Daed wasn't home by eight, Jolene would put her sixteen-year-old brother in charge, and she'd retreat to the phone shanty to talk with Van Beiler for hours. Jolene's loyalty to her brothers and sisters had a clearly marked line when it came to Van. Once he was home from work or arrived for a date or visit, he came first. Rosanna supposed that was how it should be, especially since Jolene was mere weeks away from her wedding. And when he'd said he thought the best place for them to live was in Ohio near his parents, Jolene hadn't hesitated for a second. She'd said that as long as he was by her side, she could live anywhere and survive anything. Later Jolene told Rosanna that Van wanted to move there to support Jolene's desire to do artwork. Painting and drawing scenery and animals and people weren't considered idolatry by the bishop in that district. Van was perfect for Jolene, but did he have to take her to Ohio?

Rosanna bit back her tears. Was it this hard for every mom whose child moved far away? She tried to focus on the bright side of today. "Despite the rain it will feel good to get out. Except for church the Sunday before last, I haven't been off this farm in weeks."

Jolene picked a pencil off the floor. "If you feel cooped up, you should've gone out with Van and me the other night like we asked."

Rosanna clicked her tongue at the absurdity of that idea — her on a date with them. It was ridiculous, but the invite had tempted her and made her feel loved.

Van would make a wonderful son-in-law. He was thoughtful and kind, and he and Jolene were so good together. Rosanna had absolutely no doubt they'd make a strong family unit. Van was older than Jolene, and she had been in love with him since he'd moved here to work in his uncle's blacksmith shop when she was fifteen. But Van hadn't noticed her until two years ago. To hear him tell it, he wasn't interested in finding somebody. A girlfriend came with too many responsibilities for his liking, especially since he was still a teen. Then one day he'd barreled out of his uncle's blacksmith shop hurrying to grab lunch at the nearby bakery, and he saw Jolene trying to open the door to the bakery while balancing a basket of pastries. He said she'd owned his every thought since.

Rosanna had never seen a man as much in love as Van was, so she couldn't begrudge him for taking Jolene to live elsewhere. Since Jolene had never really been allowed to paint, maybe she'd give it a try and decide it wasn't that important to her after all, and then she and Van would move back.

A mother could only hope.

The door banged open, and her husband walked in carrying a large package. His blue eyes held the same zest for life she'd fallen in love with more than twenty years ago.

She put her hands on her hips. "Benny Keim, what have you done this time?"

He grinned. "A surprise for Jolene. But first" — he held up the gold, shiny box — "cookies."

"Benny." Rosanna frowned. "Not before supper."

He walked over to her. "But I need to distract them." He raised his eyebrows up and down. What did he have up his sleeve?

"Fine."

He kissed Rosanna's forehead, and then he pointed at Jolene. "You stay put."

Jolene grinned and pointed at the floor. "Won't budge." But she looked quizzically at her mom, and Rosanna shrugged, feeling a tingle of excitement.

Her husband set the box on top of the homework papers and opened it. "Only two cookies for each of you until after supper."

Benny returned to Jolene and unbuttoned his coat, revealing a brown paper package about the size of a flat shoebox pressed against his chest. He held it out to her. "It's not for anyone to see except you."

Jolene kept her back to her siblings and opened it. Before Rosanna could see what it was, her daughter's eyes filled with tears,

13

and she engulfed her dad. *"Denki,"* she whispered.

Rosanna's heart sang, but she hid all joy from her tone. "Well, let's see what he's done this time."

Jolene released him and let Rosanna peer over the brown paper. Paintbrushes. While she was hoping her daughter wouldn't like to paint and would talk Van into returning here to live, Rosanna's husband was encouraging her to paint. "I can't believe you."

Benny put an arm around her shoulders. "She's been obedient all these years, Rosie. We couldn't have asked for a better daughter. Let her enjoy the gift."

He was right, but it was so hard to let Jolene move that far away. He released Rosanna and touched the paintbrush with the longest bristles. "When I ordered them, the lady on the phone said they're the very best."

Jolene shook her head. "No, they aren't." She hugged him again, tears trickling down her cheeks. *"You're* the best."

Benny grinned, his face red from the fuss Jolene was making over him. "Well, we'd better go before Viola Mae's husband passes out from panicking."

Rosanna opened her special kitchen drawer, lifted the false bottom, and waited as Jolene put the contraband next to a few forbidden photos of the family. Jolene's radiant smile warmed Rosanna's heart. This time next month Jolene would be married and finally living under a bishop who would allow her to discover if she had a gift for creating artwork. That thought would bring Rosanna a lot of comfort when she desperately missed her daughter.

She put on her coat, and before long she and her husband were in the buggy, lumbering toward the next town. It'd be nice if she weren't the only midwife in this area who could help deliver babies. Maybe one of Rosanna's other daughters would enjoy such fulfilling work. Torrents of rain fell from the sky, and she was grateful her husband drove her in foul weather and never complained that birthing babies was an interruption to their home life.

Memories of yesteryear filled Rosanna's heart. When Jolene was little, they'd played dolls, snuggled while reading, attended church, and caught fireflies. By the time she was three, they began to welcome new babies, tend the garden, and end the day playing simple board games. As she grew, they sang while canning goods for winter, sewing clothes for the little ones, and washing mountains of diapers. Jolene's childhood days had rolled in and out day after day.

As much as Rosanna tried, she had never learned how to grab hold of even one day and make it stand still. In what seemed like a blink of an eye, Jolene's school days were behind her, and at fourteen she began to work for the local bakery. Not long after that she'd shared her greatest secret just with Rosanna — her dream of one day marrying Van, if only he'd notice her. He'd moved to their district at seventeen years old to apprentice under his uncle, and all the teen girls had their eyes on him. Especially Donna Glick, Jolene's most ardent competitor since they were schoolgirls.

The rig wobbled hard, and she was pulled from her yesterdays, feeling sudden concern for today. The rains fell harder the farther they went. Could her husband see the lines on the road? She couldn't.

Benny gripped the reins tightly. "We have to turn back." The alarm on his face assured her there were worse things than letting a new mom deliver a child without a midwife.

She nodded.

But before he could turn the rig around, something hit one of the wheels, and the rig jolted hard and then seemed to float several feet.

What was happening? Rosanna's head

spun, and nothing seemed to make sense. Why was Benny pulling back on the reins but the rig continued to move?

Their carriage struck a yellow sign with the symbol for a river, and the rig floated right past it. "We're in the river!" Her husband's scream pierced her heart.

The rig tipped, and water rushed inside. Benny's strong hands pulled her out.

The world became a blur of muddy snapshots. Branches of trees overhead. Debris floating downstream with her. Gray raindrops hiding the sky.

2

Two weeks later

Jolene stood at the kitchen sink, her hands in sudsy water as she stared out the open window. Rays of golden light spread across green fields with patches of brown, dying grass. The dark silhouette of almost-barren trees reminded her of ink art from one of her books. The weather was tranquil, just another beautiful fall evening before sunset.

The serenity of it contradicted their reality. The heavy rains were long gone, leaving two deaths in their wake. Viola Mae had given birth to a healthy son at four in the morning, delivered into the hands of a shaky mother-in-law. Mom and baby were fine. But it had taken a rescue team four days to find the bodies of Jolene's parents.

Then the Amish community had put two caskets in the ground. Since that day a week ago, whether awake or asleep, Jolene continually saw Amish men holding on to ropes as they stood on each side of the grave, lowering two pine caskets into the ground.

Jolene's vision blurred, but she was used to her eyes brimming with tears these days. The world felt huge and gray, as if she could become lost in the vastness of its fog, and yet the air itself seemed to press in on all sides trying to squeeze the breath right out of her.

Warm hands rested on Jolene's shoulders. "Jo." Van's lips were near her ear. She tried to answer him, but the more days that passed, the harder it was to respond to the world around her. She'd been strong for her siblings at first to help guide them through the process, but now her strength seemed gone.

Was the bishop right? Would her parents expect her to accept the decision her uncles had come to?

Van squeezed her shoulders reassuringly. "We need to talk before the others return."

It couldn't be time for that already. She looked at the clock. How were the hours slipping by into nothingness? At her request Van had sent home all her Amish relatives, friends, and church leaders earlier today. She, Van, and her siblings needed to talk among themselves before tonight's meeting.

Tonight. The thought of it stole her breath

— if she was actually breathing. Nothing felt real. Absolutely nothing.

"Kumm." He eased her away from the sink, and she watched as dirty water and melting soapsuds fell from her hands and plopped on the floor. "Leave it." He guided her toward the kitchen table.

Her siblings were there, each in a chair. Had he called them to gather, or had they been sitting at the table while she'd been at the sink *not* washing dishes? Their eyes were fixed on her. Jolene's heart thudded. She'd dreaded this chat to try to separate their emotions from the honesty of their needs so she could understand what was best for them in the long run.

Jolene sat looking at her five siblings — Josiah, Michael, Naomi, Ray, and Hope. Van moved next to her, ready to speak for her or to her as needed.

Twelve-year-old Naomi cleared her throat. "What will happen to us?"

Jolene intertwined her fingers, noticing how wet her hands were. It seemed odd how grief magnified little details while blocking out the big things. She was keenly aware of the damp smudges her hands were making on the table right now, but she couldn't recall what they'd eaten for dinner . . . or if she'd thought to provide drinks.

Ray climbed into her lap. Since he was eight years old now, Mama had said he was too big to sit in Jolene's lap anymore, but at the moment he felt as tiny and frail as a kitten. Was that feeling God's way of letting her know how Ray felt? Hope moved to the side of Jolene's chair, and Jolene shifted Ray to one leg and put Hope on the other.

They were orphans now, and by the looks on her brothers' and sisters' faces, they were well aware of what that meant. After a few years would Hope remember their parents? Would Ray have more than scattered memories of them?

Jolene licked her lips. "Your uncles have offered a plan." It wasn't one she liked, but what could she do about it? Her siblings would be separated, living with different uncles. Their uncles had large and growing families, and they felt they could take only one child each — with the exception of Uncle Pete. He had all sons so far, and he and his wife were willing to take both Naomi and Hope back to Indiana with them. But the fog engulfing Jolene wasn't thick enough to keep her from seeing how awful that plan was.

Van drew a deep breath. "It won't be possible to stay together, but if we can, we'll give you say-so concerning which uncle you'd like to live with."

Her siblings gasped, and all except sixteen-year-old Josiah burst into tears.

Jolene's face flushed as her feelings of helplessness changed to anger. What was Van thinking to blurt that out? After much discussion among themselves, her uncles and the church leaders thought it was the only solution to "the situation," but Jolene had not agreed to the plan. When did a family, its hearth and home and loyalties, become no more than a *situation*?

A vision of the pine coffins being lowered into the ground circled to the forefront of her thoughts again, and she knew the answer — when the ones who had created the family died.

Josiah rapped on the table, and Jolene looked at him. "This is the plan — to divide up what's left of us like a litter of puppies?" He studied Jolene, his tender heart evident in his eyes, but he seemed confused by her willingness to consider what her uncles and the church leaders wanted.

She lowered her eyes, looking at the smudges of water on the table. "It's a plan made by good people who love us."

Van slid his hand over Jolene's. "It's okay if you're not ready to accept your uncles' offer yet, but it isn't as if there are a lot of choices, Josiah. At your age I doubt you can begin to understand what it takes to feed, house, and raise a family like this."

Did Van hear himself?

Jolene pulled her hand from his. "Do not talk about us as if we're cattle that need to be rebranded and sold at auction."

Van nodded. "Sorry. I don't mean it that way. You know I don't."

Fourteen-year-old Michael glanced at Josiah before turning to Jolene. "Why can't we live here with you and Van?"

Was she really supposed to marry next week? She couldn't find one familiar thought or feeling. How could anyone marry in such a state? "This house is a rental and not one Van and I could afford."

"We don't own it?" Ray asked.

She shook her head. Her parents actually owned very little, but Mama had always said it's what owns your heart, not what you own, that matters. Mamm had given birth to all her children under this roof, but Jolene couldn't see any way they could hold on to it. But couldn't she and Van hold on to the children? It'd be a really tight fit, but they could make do in the carriage house apartment in Ohio with all her siblings, couldn't they? Had Van really considered the possibility? All she could recall was his guidance on what he needed her to do. Perhaps they needed to talk about what *she* wanted.

"Josiah, would you take the children upstairs and read to them?" Had they finished *Charlotte's Web*? She'd begun it with them the night her Daed didn't return. When Viola Mae's husband had called the phone shanty around eight thirty that night, Jolene had been on the phone with Van. So she'd switched over to see who was calling, thinking it might be Daed saying that he'd been held up talking with the dad-to-be and that he'd be home soon. He often stayed with Mamm and visited with the expectant Daed. But it hadn't been her Daed on the line. That's when she learned that her parents hadn't yet made it to their destination. It should have taken them forty minutes at the most to arrive at Viola Mae's, but they'd been gone more than three hours. When Viola Mae's husband called back at midnight to say they'd never arrived, Jolene knew . . . but she kept snuggling with her younger siblings, who would fall asleep and wake, asking for Mamm and Daed.

Jolene should remember if they'd finished the book in the following days, shouldn't she? As much as she loved that book, the words had been meaningless to her as she filled the hours reading aloud, giving the children some small reprieve from their new reality.

Josiah nodded and stood. She kissed Ray and Hope on their heads and sent them off. Josiah waited for the younger ones to go up the stairs. "I vote no to separating us" — his eyes filled with tears — "if it matters what a sixteen-year-old thinks. I'm willing to do all I can to keep the little ones together. Not for me or you, but for them."

Van propped an elbow on the table and rubbed his forehead. "You're a good man, Josiah, and I've wrestled with those same desires since the day we learned your parents died, but taking on that responsibility is no life for Jolene or you."

Josiah dipped his hands into his pockets and stared at the floor, probably trying to gather his thoughts. Their dad often teased his oldest son that he was as scattered as hayseed shooting out of a spreader, but Daed promised him he would produce a bumper crop in due time. Would he? If he did, would Jolene see it come to fruition? Their uncle in Ohio wanted Josiah to go with him. Josiah lifted his head. "Maybe our response to this tragedy isn't about *us*. Or how to piece it together so we can be as happy as we would've been if our parents had lived." Josiah stood straighter, looking his sister in the eyes. "Maybe we were given life and are in this family for *their* sakes."

Jolene's heart felt as if it had stopped beating. How did a person of so few words say something that profound? As the eldest Keim daughter, was she put in this place for such a time as this? She nodded at her brother. "Maybe so."

He went upstairs.

Van turned to her. "Jolene, you're not thinking straight. How could you be? You need to trust me when I say it's too much to take on. Hope could easily need to live with us for maybe twenty years." He stood and began to pace. "You've made great strides with Ray, but everyone has known since the day he was struck by lightning that he could end up needing to live with his parents for the rest of his life." He paused. "What about us? We'll start adding our children into the mix within a year or so of marrying. We can't do what you're considering, Jo. I'm telling you that spiritually, emotionally, physically, and financially we can't."

A hint of beautiful, warm light filtered through some of the fog, and she had a fleeting moment of clarity. Was his insistence on the decision she needed to make the cause of some of her confusion? "*We* can't, or *you* can't?"

"*We.* One hundred percent, Jo." He closed the gap between them. "We are in this together. But there's no time to prepare ourselves emotionally to take this on, not with the wedding next week."

She couldn't believe the words that came to her, but she let them flow from her unchecked. "Then we need to postpone the wedding."

He nodded. "A few weeks or months might help. It would give us time to get everyone situated."

"Can't we talk about keeping them together?"

"Jo, that's all we've been talking about."

Was it? While she'd gone through her days in shock, he'd been a constant support, showing his love for her and his grief over her loss, but he'd also assured her at every turn that she needed to follow the guidance of her bishop and her uncles.

A knock on the door interrupted them, and a moment later Uncle Calvin and Aunt Lydia walked in. They spoke a greeting, as did each of the men in the procession of uncles and church leaders who also entered. The last person to come in was an unfamiliar, middle-aged *Englisch* man.

After Lydia asked Jolene and Van if they needed anything, she went to the kitchen sink and began washing the dishes Jolene had left. Calvin moved to the empty seat next to Jolene. He rubbed her shoulder as he sat, but he didn't say anything. What could he say? Make silly small talk or assure her that everything would be fine? Of all her uncles, he was the most like her dad, and during the meetings she found herself watching him for clues of what she should do. But for the most part, he'd been quiet and stoic.

The church leaders and her other uncles had definite opinions about what had to be done, and they seemed weary of walking softly around her now that their minds were made up. She tried not to take it personally. They had families and businesses to get back to. But she was grateful that Calvin had not let them bully her into agreeing before she was ready. Despite having eight children of their own, he and Lydia had asked to take the one child no one wanted — Ray.

The men filled the chairs, and some remained standing. There was no small talk, and Lydia didn't offer to make coffee or bring them a slice of cake. The group was short on protocol and tradition these days.

"Jolene and Van," — Calvin motioned to the Englisch man — "this is Douglas Piedmont. He's a guardianship lawyer who's here to help us know what we can and can't do. So any questions we have, we can ask him."

The men began to talk softly, reaffirming which child would go where and what furniture went with each child and discussing how to get out of the long lease her dad had signed on this place.

As their voices mingled into an indistinct mumbling, Jolene prayed. What should she do? She looked at Van. Would he stay by her if she chose to keep her siblings with her? If she lost him, she'd lose the life she had been dreaming about for the past four years. And she'd probably have a nervous breakdown, whatever that was.

Rambling thoughts swirled inside her brain, but Josiah's words returned to her: *maybe we were given life and are in this family for their sakes.*

She tapped Calvin on the forearm, and he motioned for the group to be quiet. "What do I need to do to keep my siblings with me?"

An uproar followed — some men saying that she was dead wrong and that the children would pay the price and some

29

complaining that a young girl shouldn't have this kind of say.

But the lawyer held her gaze for several long moments. "Actually" — he clicked his pen, staring at her until the men became quiet — "it's a viable question. You'd have to go before a judge and prove you're a suitable guardian. You'd need a steady income, an affordable place to live, and home visits by the court — all of which I'd help you set up without cost."

Was this stranger on her side? Aunt Lydia grabbed a dishtowel and dried her hands as she crossed the room and stood beside her husband.

Calvin glanced at her before he leveled a look at Jolene. "No one expects this of you. Don't let a false sense of responsibility cause you to take on more than you should. But if it's what you want, I'll back you in it."

Lydia put her hands on her husband's shoulders. "*We* will back you in it."

Is this why Calvin had been so quiet? Was he unwilling to hint that she should keep the siblings together and unwilling to support her giving them up?

"You would need to stay in state with your siblings, at least until the courts are satisfied about your capabilities."

She focused on the lawyer. "I don't know a place where we could afford to live."

Calvin nodded, frowning. "This house belongs to Old Man Fisher two districts over. He's cantankerous, but maybe he'd give you a bit of leeway, at least until we can figure out something else."

Lester Fisher scared her, reminding her of the irritable grandfather in the book *Heidi*. Try as she might, she'd never won the man over, not even a smile. Even his children and grandchildren avoided him. "It's worth a try."

"Keeping your siblings is a monumental task," the lawyer said. "They're traumatized and scarred. Grown adults struggle to help children cope with this kind of loss, and you're only nineteen." He tapped his pen on the yellow paper with its blue and red lines.

"Jo, please," Van pleaded. "They need to be in a home with two adult parents, not a teen sister and her twenty-one-year-old husband." His voice trembled.

Fresh pain seared her as she realized where this conversation was leading. He hadn't wanted a girlfriend because of the responsibility. She'd been surprised when he'd asked her to marry him, thinking he'd wait a good five years or more, but he'd said he loved her too much to wait.

Oh, how she didn't want to lose him.

A door slammed, rattling the kerosene lanterns on the kitchen table. The sound had come from upstairs, and she sat perched, listening, ready to run or relax based on the next few seconds. A thud echoed. And another. And another, each harder than the previous one, and she raced up the steps. She glanced in her bedroom. *Charlotte's Web* lay on the floor. Its spine faced the ceiling, looking as if it'd been dropped there. The rocker where she often sat while reading swayed back and forth. Her bed was crumpled where the younger ones should be sitting or lying on it while Josiah read to them. Muffled voices floated from somewhere, and she knew her destination. "Ray?" She hurried into the boys' bedroom.

Michael, Naomi, and Hope stood in the middle of the room, eyes large and focused on the closet.

"Kumm on," Josiah whispered at the closet door. He shifted the kerosene lantern in his hand. "Don't do this, Ray. Not now."

Ray sobbed — short, muted noises, probably crying into a blanket or pillow. Jolene's heart broke. She knocked on the closet door and tugged. "Ray." When she encountered resistance, she recognized the pull of Ray's suspenders, a favorite trick of his for securing the closet door when he wanted to be alone. She leaned her head against the frame. Whether together or apart, how were any of them going to survive their loss? Choking back tears, she had an urge to sing their parents' favorite song. The lyrics wobbled as she began. "What a Friend we have in Jesus, all our sins and griefs to bear. What a privilege to carry everything to God in prayer."

Her siblings joined her. "O what peace we often forfeit, O what needless pain we bear, all because we do not carry everything to God in prayer."

How many evenings had they sung that song as a family before dispersing to go to bed?

The suspenders ricocheted against the door, and she knew he'd either lost his grip or released them. When she opened the door, Ray was sitting against the wall at the back of the closet. His flashlight sat upright on the floor, illuminating the small room. He looked tiny and overwhelmed as he held his favorite stuffed toy in one hand, probably what he'd been sobbing into, and a bat in the other. He'd knocked five or six holes in the wall with the bat before sinking to the floor in a heap. This image pretty much summed up her youngest brother when he was overwhelmed — a childlike gentleness mixed with the occasional destructive outburst. But he never lashed out at or near people. She sat next to him.

He curled against her. "I'm sorry. I know that was wrong. I didn't —"

She ran her hand over his silky hair. "It's going to be okay, Ray. It doesn't feel like it to any of us right now, but it will be. Can you trust me on that?"

He held on to her tightly. "What will happen to us?"

She wished she knew. "We will stick together." But she was a girl facing adult tasks, and it terrified her. Would her brothers and sisters be more scarred in the long run if her best efforts to do them justice were pitiful?

He gazed up at her, and she saw relief overtake his grief for a moment. "Together? Really?"

A knot formed in her stomach, but she put on her best parental face and smiled at him. "Together."

His eyes filled with tears. "I'll do my best to be good. I promise."

"Me too." Tightening her grip around him, she kissed the top of his head and began singing the song to him again. Josiah, Michael, Naomi, and Hope piled into the closet with her, snuggling into a huddle of Keim legs and arms as they held each other.

Van came to the door and peered inside.

Jolene swallowed hard. "I can't let them be scattered to the wind."

Hurt etched itself deep in his face as he nodded. Was that a look of compassion for her and her siblings or heartbreak for himself?

Maybe he already knew what she was just beginning to see. The life they'd wanted was already gone, whether they housed the children or not. They could never be the couple he'd been dreaming of because she was no longer the girl he'd fallen in love with. But she would be. Someday. And she longed to ask, Will you wait for me? Wait for me to raise my siblings? Wait for me to heal and become me again?

But that was too much to ask of anyone. All she could do was hope he'd remain her friend until he fell in love with the person she was becoming.

3

Ten years later

Andy put fresh straw in the horses' empty stalls before filling the feed and water troughs. A refreshing May breeze flowed through the open barn doors, bringing with it the aroma of an earth coming alive after a long winter. Once the chores were done, he moved to the corridor between the stalls on each side of the barn and began coiling the hose. Amigo stuck his head out of his stall, bobbing it and making low rumbling sounds. He should be eating his oats, but instead the horse was talking to him — in his own way of course.

Andy hung the hose on its wall rack and walked over to him. "What's going on with you today, Amigo?" The horse lowered his head, trying to reach Andy, and Andy moved in closer. Amigo rested his head against Andy's chest. "*Ya*, I hear you." Andy patted the horse's forehead with one hand

and rubbed his cheek with the other.

Sometimes the thoroughbred was aloof and self-assured; at other times he was as needy as a lonely lap dog. Andy assumed it was the ruckus from the newly delivered group of horses corralled in the round pen that had Amigo needing assurance. "It's okay, ol' boy. It's just new thoroughbreds — stallions and mares — stomping around in the pen. They'll settle down in a day or two." The Fishers regularly brought in plenty of new horses to train, but this was a particularly large and aggressive group.

Andy picked up a brush and went into Amigo's stall. He talked to the horse while he brushed him. Years ago Amigo had thrown his brother, Levi, fracturing his neck and breaking his leg, but Amigo would never be sold. He was trustworthy ninety-something percent of the time. That was good for an animal. Even humans weren't on their best behavior more than that. As horse trainers, he and Levi had learned to develop a gut feeling about a horse and stick with it.

"Daed." Tobias took long strides toward his dad, stretching his nine-year-old legs as far and fast as he could without running, because rowdiness was forbidden in the barn unless it was done intentionally to help train the horses. "You've got to see what I discovered. Uncle Levi didn't see it until I pointed it out."

Andy smiled. What could possibly be in that group of horses that he hadn't seen a hundred times over?

"Tomorrow will be your last day of school for the year."

Tobias grinned. "It's the Friday I've been looking forward to for months. But no changing the subject. Kumm. You've got to see it to believe it."

Andy hoped his son never lost his excitement over God's creatures. If a person bonded with a dutiful creature that has no voice, it meant his heart was capable of deep tenderness and compassion for people. It weighed on Andy that Tobias wouldn't have many more years before his open heart would be tested to its breaking point. One day his son would understand that his mother had abandoned him when he was three years old and that she had not called or sent a letter since. When the full weight of her rejection hit, Tobias would need all the capacity for love and understanding a man could muster.

"Kumm." Tobias motioned for him. Andy patted Amigo before leaving the stall. He put the brush away, grabbed a few rope harnesses, and walked toward the round pen, eyeing the twenty new horses. Even with Levi in the pen feeding and petting a mare, the other horses whinnied, snorted, and herded to the far end.

Sadie's eyes were fixed on Levi, which Andy found amusing. No doubt his brother and sister-in-law were in love — but not some ego-boosting, delicate kind of love. What they had was strong and real, and Andy was grateful. After Andy's wife, Eva, left, Levi wouldn't let his guard down long enough to give dating — much less love — a chance. But about two years ago, late on the Fourth of July, Levi was riding across a dark field when fireworks startled Amigo, and the horse threw him. Thankfully, Sadie, a visitor from a district more than a hundred and fifty miles away, was riding horseback through that field. What began as Levi needing Sadie's help eased into a reluctant friendship between them. Each had been wounded — Sadie by a deceptive, cheating fiancé and Levi by Eva, whom he had loved like a sister. He had believed that she loved Andy and Tobias . . . and then she left.

"Daed, look." Tobias pointed to the horse that was eating out of Levi's hand. "She's the most gentle one in the herd."

Sadie folded her arms across the top of

39

the split rail. "That may not be saying much in this group."

Tobias frowned. "Sadie, you're not helping."

She smiled. "Maybe I am and you just don't know it yet."

Andy moved beside his sister-in-law and propped a foot on the lowest fence rail. "What does Levi think?"

She chuckled. "He's as excited as Tobias was on Christmas morning."

"Gut." They had their work cut out for them with this herd, but he and his brother enjoyed running the horse farm.

Tobias climbed the split-rail fence and sat on the top rail. "Levi, can you bring her over here?"

Levi glanced at Andy, probably wanting to know whether they were going to tamp down Tobias's excitement or address it head-on. Andy nodded, and Levi led the horse to them. For two years Tobias had constantly asked his Daed to give him one of the horses.

"Look, Daed. She's solid black except for the half pastern on her legs and the markings on her face." He pointed at her face. "I've never seen anything like those markings. Have you?"

Sadie leaned in. "Is that what you call an

irregular star?"

"A star?" Tobias shook his head. "Women."

Andy was confident that one day Tobias would see Sadie's entry into their lives for what it was — the best gift a motherless boy could have. But since Tobias had no memory of a woman living under their roof, right now Sadie seemed a little too girlish for his liking. To him, a world of menfolk and manly thinking was all life needed.

"Hey." Andy nudged his son's arm. "She doesn't have to know horses like we do."

"I don't see why not. She makes me study math, reading, and writing so I can know them like she does."

Sadie pursed her lips, clearly trying not to laugh. "He does have a point."

"Maybe." Andy studied his son. He appreciated Sadie's sense of humor, which seemed endless. But was he letting Tobias get away with being disrespectful, or was he giving him room to figure out some stuff on his own?

"So" — Sadie angled her head — "what is that shape on her face called?"

"It's unusual. I'll give you that much." Tobias straddled the fence. "I say it's an irregular, thin blaze shaped like a T."

"Ah, for *Tobias*." Sadie winked at Levi.

41

Andy hadn't picked up on what Tobias was thinking as Sadie had.

Tobias straightened his straw hat. "Ya, that's right."

A look of amusement passed between Sadie and Levi at Tobias's hint that he wanted the horse.

Andy shook his head. "You're not ready for a horse of your own yet."

"But, Daed," — Tobias jumped off the fence — "all the boys my age got their own horse, and lots of boys younger than me too, and none of 'em have a dad who owns a horse farm!"

Was Andy too strict about this? In his dream vacation he'd have a week off from second-guessing himself when it came to single parenting. "I don't blame you for wanting one. They're magnificent creatures, but you're not ready yet." Despite its stature and strength, a horse had emotional needs, lots of them, and none were easily conveyed. Most boys rode horses for themselves, for their own joy and pride, but Andy needed more from Tobias than that. And changing people's mind-sets *after* they had what they wanted was tough. He should know. He dealt with people and how they treated their horses all the time.

Tobias yanked off his hat and threw it to

the ground. "Man! That's not fair."

Andy wanted to give the boy his own horse, had wanted to for a couple of years now. It should be one of the natural perks of being Amish and living on a horse farm, but he had to trust his gut, and his gut said Tobias didn't respect the animals enough.

Not yet. He was doing better. Less than two years ago, he would sit on the fence and complain to his uncle for being too patient while training them. Tobias had wanted to use unnecessary force to make the horses comply. He didn't feel that way anymore, which was good, but it wasn't enough.

Levi released the horse's harness, and she trotted off. "You're not helping your case by acting like that."

Tobias folded his arms, staring at his hat.

Sadie pursed her lips and gazed heavenward, looking determined to control her response, but Andy wasn't sure whether it was to keep from teasing Tobias or laughing out loud.

He was grateful that Levi had found Sadie and that she had wanted to move into Andy's home rather than getting a place of their own. The four of them — Andy, Levi, Sadie, and Tobias — made for an unusual family, but the oddity also helped dilute Tobias's reality. As the son of a grass widower, Tobias lived with the constant reminder that, unlike other boys his age, he didn't have a mother.

As for himself, Andy no longer carried the weight of what others thought. He'd dealt with all that years ago, but the frustration of the situation got to him at times. She had all the power — the power to leave or return, the power to have a life he knew nothing about. But there wasn't anything he could do about that. He couldn't even divorce her. It wasn't permitted. Well, there were a few exceptions. If the spouse who left demanded a divorce and a judge agreed, the Amish had to comply, or if the spouse who left threatened to fight for custody unless divorce was granted, the church leaders would grant the divorce to protect the child or children. In all his days Andy had heard of only one Amish person getting a divorce. But the dream of divorcing her lived on, because it would give him some semblance of power and a voice in what she'd done to him and Tobias.

Sadie nodded toward the driveway. "FedEx is here."

The truck pulled to a quick stop, and a man in a navy-and-purple uniform went between the two front seats and into the back of his truck.

Almost every item that had arrived via FedEx the past few years came from the Pennsylvania Humane Society. Andy and Levi housed and retrained the occasional abused or neglected horses the society needed help with. After months of working with the horses, Andy would let the Humane Society know they were ready to be adopted. Andy and Levi had strong convictions about their volunteer service. But the Humane Society always talked to Andy or Levi before sending the written information, which usually arrived a day or two ahead of the horses.

Andy turned to Levi. "We haven't received a call from the Humane Society, have we?"

Levi shook his head, glancing at his wife to confirm.

Sadie held up her hands, grinning as she tossed an innocent look Levi's way. "*I* post every message on the refrigerator." A look of amusement passed between the two, obviously an inside joke.

The courier hopped out of his truck. "I need a signature." He held up a large white envelope in one hand and a metal clipboard in the other.

Andy signed for the item and opened it as the courier pulled out of the driveway. "It's from the Humane Society."

Levi left the round pen and fastened the gate. He moved to his wife's side, and they began talking about the horses.

Andy pulled a newspaper clipping out of the envelope and read the headline: "Thirty-Two Horses Seized from Pennsylvania Hellhole." A large yellow note was attached: "We need your help, please. We removed the horses two days ago, but the temporary holding place is unacceptable. If you could take at least half of these horses, I may be able to find a place for the other half. Renee"

He'd worked with Renee for a decade, and she wouldn't ask for this kind of help unless her back was against a wall. But since they had received twenty rowdy horses earlier today, they could take only a couple more.

He removed the note and grimaced as he read the details in the newspaper article. The rescue team had removed thirty-two Morgan horses from a dilapidated farm near Hershey before sickness and starvation killed them. It had taken the fifteen-person team all day to round up the feral horses from filthy pastures knee-deep in mud and with manure piles almost four feet high. After making an initial visit because of an anonymous tip, the director of the Humane Society had obtained a search warrant, and she and the team of rescuers had returned to the farm. Clearly, the horses had received no veterinary or blacksmith care. Very young horses, pregnant mares, and stallions were all roaming together in the same pasture, and a nine-month-old horse was locked in a dark, crumbling barn.

Andy's reservations melted. He had to find a way to help as many horses as possible. But how?

He passed the article to Levi and waited as he read it. Levi shook his head. "What kind of people treat animals like this?" He handed it to Sadie.

Andy shoved his hands into his pockets. "Maybe people who are hoarders by nature and they're hoarding animals. I recently read an article about people who did that with cats and dogs. Whatever their reason, the owners of those horses are looking at some stiff jail time, but that won't help the horses. Renee is looking for places to board them and for people who can help acclimate them to human handlers, getting them used to halters so they can be examined by a vet."

"I get how you feel, and I feel the same way, but our hands are tied, aren't they?"

"Maybe." Andy pondered the issue, and an idea came to him. "Do you think Uncle Lester would let us use his corrals and barns for this?" Their great-uncle used to train horses too, so he had the facilities.

"Even if he would, his place is three hours from here by car, and those horses could need boarding for months." Levi pointed to a line in the article. "It says the horses might not be eligible for adoption until after the trial."

"We can't think about all that right now. The Humane Society has an immediate goal: to calm the horses where they'll let a vet and blacksmith tend to them. That's where we come in. Then after the initial health care, we begin taming them."

"Which could easily take three to four months," Levi said.

"Ya, it could."

Tobias took the article from Sadie, running his finger under the headline as he read it. "What happens to them if no one steps up?"

Levi's shoulders slumped. Apparently the reality Andy saw was just now dawning on his younger brother. "They'll try rescue organizations first, but the resources are always stretched for those groups. They'll be left resorting to questionable places, causing the horses to become more traumatized. The weakest and most temperamental — often the ones who were the most abused

48

— will probably be euthanized."

"Daed, we can't allow that."

"I agree," Levi said. "It would be hard to live with ourselves if we don't respond to this plea for help."

Sadie returned the article to its envelope. "Call your uncle and see if he's willing to board them for free and if he knows anyone who could help you tend to them. Levi and I will ask your Daed to help us run the farm for the summer. Surely you could have most of them ready to be adopted in three to four months."

It was a huge sacrifice of time and money, but how could they make a living from buying, training, and selling horses and not give back when the need arose?

4

The aroma of the pastries Jolene was baking wafted through the air as she grabbed a clean, wet shirt from the laundry basket. When she snapped it sharply in the wind, a faint spray of water danced from the shirt and into the crystal-clear air. Sunlight played with the miniscule dots of water, causing the colors of the rainbow to speckle the air for a brief moment before disappearing. Desire to capture the moment in paint swept over her. If time allowed late this afternoon, she'd unlock her hiding place, climb the stairs, and paint.

She pinned the shirt to the clothesline, breathing in the warm spring air. It was such a gorgeous day here on earth. How much more so was it for her Mamm and Daed?

After attaching the last article of clothing to the line, she picked up the basket. While heading for the house, she saw remnants of the Mother's Day festivities in the side yard and walked that way. For the last five years, her siblings had honored her on Mother's Day. Even now the joy of yesterday made her grin. She walked to the hammock her siblings had given her, gave it a gentle push, and laughed.

Her three brothers — Josiah, Michael, and Ray — had hung it for her between two old maple trees. But when she'd tried to lie in it, she'd fallen out. Numerous times. With their help she'd finally gotten the hang of using it. She had lounged there while the family sat in chairs around her, sharing warm and funny memories from both before and after their parents died. Josiah's two-year-old son had climbed into her arms and snuggled with her until he was fast asleep.

It was days like yesterday that refreshed her and reminded her what a blessed life she had. She couldn't imagine being any more content than she was — even if Van had chosen to marry her and help her raise her siblings.

But he hadn't.

To his credit, when he realized they wouldn't marry, he didn't simply break up with her and walk off. He'd remained by her side, giving her someone she could confide in as she carried the grief of such loss. Someone she could turn to when she didn't know how to write checks or balance a checkbook, or where to order propane for the tank out back, or how to pay the water bill. He helped her with those things for six months. Then he gently said he couldn't do it anymore. Apparently she and her siblings were an obstacle to his desire to move on with his life. According to Van, that was especially true of Ray, who was struggling with the loss of their parents and exhibiting it through impulsive and often violent outbursts. After telling her that, Van left the Keim property, shoving her back into that thick, unbearable grief once again. About two weeks later Jolene saw him in town with Donna Glick on his arm, a girl who'd been trying to outdo Jolene since they'd attended school together.

It had crushed her all over again. When she had healed enough that she could take full breaths, her hurt turned to anger, and she wrestled with herself until she found peace with losing Van and watching him fall in love, marry, and welcome children. Or maybe she'd just found resignation. She only knew that what bothered her wasn't so much that he'd left her and married someone else but how he'd done it. That used to keep her up at night, but she had finally submitted to it and decided it was best to refuse to think about it. But the *how* had ruined every bit of friendship that could've been salvaged.

Was anything on this earth more ugly or difficult to bear than true love turning into bitter disillusion?

She studied the old clapboard house where she'd been born. Across the yards — the front, sides, and back — were six dogwood trees, one for each of Benny and Rosanna Keim's children. Jolene had carefully nurtured each from a cutting of the original tree her Daed had given to her Mamm as a wedding gift. The original tree had died within a year of her parents' passing.

Thanks to Lester Fisher lowering the rent in exchange for Naomi and her cleaning his home, doing laundry, and cooking a few meals each week, they'd been able to stay in this house. At first Lester was gruff and difficult, but as time passed, they became good friends, and he'd made some really generous offers to help her and her family. As they grew closer, she began to confide in him. When she told him about her desire to paint and about the last gift her Daed had given her, Lester did something she never would have imagined possible. He gave her a way to free a piece of her soul. Although they didn't live in the same church district, they did have the same bishop, and despite artwork being against the bishop's edicts, Lester set up an art studio for her in his attic. At times that haven had seemed essential for her sanity. He'd put a padlock on the door to his attic, and he'd installed a warning bell that rang in the attic so that if she was up there painting when a visitor came by, she had time to scurry from the attic before anyone entered the house. It was a good system, because all these years later no one else knew their secret. This exacting, difficult man had a soft spot for her.

She studied the house again. She'd been painting it when time allowed, but for the most part that only made it look worse — new rows of paint against weathered, peeling rows for months at a time. The home sat within easy walking distance of downtown Maple Shade, a small, now-thriving historic town at the heart of Winter Valley that had a clinic and a doctor. Wouldn't her Mamm have loved to live long enough to see that?

In addition to the pleasure of the Mother's Day celebration, Jolene had much to be grateful for. One of the biggest blessings was that whenever challenges had arisen — lack, frustrations, arguments, and everything else — she and her siblings had faced them together. Of her five little chicks, as they called themselves, only two remained in the nest — eighteen-year-old Ray and fourteen-year-old Hope.

Josiah, now twenty-six, Michael, now twenty-four, and Naomi, now twenty-two, were married. Michael had married last fall, and Naomi had married five months ago in December. Both had moved out, but they hadn't gone far. Jolene still found it surprising how quiet the house seemed after two siblings moved out mere months apart.

How different would her life look in another decade? She was twenty-nine now, only ten years younger than her mama was when she died.

"Jolene?" The familiar voice washed over her, and she turned to see her oldest brother riding bareback toward her. What was he doing here this time of day on a Monday? He held up an index card. "Ruth wrote out the recipe last night for the carrot bread she brought over yesterday."

"Gut. I'm going to make it and see if the bakery would like to carry it as a regular item. It was *that* good." Jolene made pastries from home for the bakeshop four days a week, and she worked behind the counter about twenty hours a week in addition to cleaning a few houses. She baked at home to avoid being gone too much, because Ray still had some impulsivity issues from time to time. She didn't know whether it was the lingering effects of having been struck by lightning as a child or simply a lack of maturity. Whatever the cause, she and Ray would get through this.

Josiah studied the upstairs windows and then looked at the small barn. It was more of a shed really, but it served as a barn for their horse.

She followed his gaze. "Something on your mind?"

"Oh, uh, no. Not really."

She laughed. "You're a really bad liar. The recipe was an excuse, wasn't it?"

"I intended to bring it by this evening on my way home from work." He shrugged. "But, ya, it was my excuse."

"Why fib?"

"Trying to protect you from too much worry." His lopsided grin let her know *that* was the truth.

Ah, so now they were getting down to the real issue. The way he was studying the house and barn, she wondered if someone from the town council had come to him with another request that they complete the painting of their home.

They would finish, but it was a huge task to paint a clapboard house. She'd discovered that the hard way. Preacher Glen had offered to get a group of barn raisers together this summer to help Josiah, Michael, and Ray finish the job. But she hadn't accepted, assuring him other Amish families had far more needs than her family did. The Amish didn't accept government assistance of any kind, didn't have standard insurance to cover health or property, and didn't limit the number of children a couple had, so there was no shortage of Amish families in need.

She appreciated Glen's offer. She'd known him all her life, she supposed, although her first real memory of him was attending his wedding when she was ten. She was also present six years later when he was chosen to be a preacher. He and his wife helped her navigate through the nightmare of losing her parents and Van.

In turn, Jolene was there for them when, a little more than two years ago, his wife's body succumbed to what had begun as breast cancer. By the time his wife was diagnosed, the cancer had spread to the lymph nodes and bones. Within a few months she yielded to death, leaving him brokenhearted and with five of the cutest little boys Jolene had ever seen. Jolene was one of many women who'd cooked meals and helped take care of his children.

But one thing bothered her a little. Had Glen offered to get a work party together to paint her house because he wanted to spend time around her? She hoped not. As far as being well suited, they were capable of being good friends, but husband and wife? She couldn't see that ever happening.

Before she could ask Josiah again what was on his mind, a horse trotted onto the driveway, pulling a wagon driven by Naomi. "Hey!" She was breathless and clearly in a hurry, so Jolene and Josiah strode to her.

Naomi gulped in air. "Lester's in a tizzy. Apparently he called my phone shanty four days ago and left me a message to come cook and clean. Something about his great-nephew from Apple Ridge and volunteers from the Humane Society coming . . . or are there now. He'd wanted breakfast, lunch, and dinner too, but I didn't get the phone message. He sent his grandson David to my place to see why I wasn't at his house. David said Lester is upset because men have been there since daylight, working. They're already hungry, and I don't have any food for them."

Jolene held up a hand. "Naomi, breathe."

Some of this panic could be considered Jolene's fault. She and Naomi had worked for Lester for the last ten years, but Jolene didn't have a phone. She felt that it, like a lot of things, was an expense they could live without. But that wasn't the real reason she got rid of it. She'd had it removed because she couldn't bear people calling here looking for her Mamm or Daed, especially newly pregnant women hoping Jolene's Mamm would be their midwife. So they made do without a phone. Naomi and she had set days when they cleaned people's homes, and if people needed to change the schedule, they would inform her or Naomi well in advance.

Since getting married, Naomi had access to a phone that she shared with several of her in-laws. The problem with multiple families in the vicinity sharing a phone was that messages didn't always reach the intended party.

"I have dozens of fresh-baked pastries for this afternoon's delivery to the bakery. We'll use those and lots of coffee to take the edge off their hunger. Then we'll make sandwiches and soup for lunch while we put roasts on for tonight. When we get through

59

with all that, we'll make plans for tomorrow. I can drop everything and go right now. You?"

"Ya, but it's ten o'clock, and he expects clean sheets on the beds and the floors done, and there could be twenty people to feed."

"Goodness, girl." Jolene winked. Most who knew Lester Fisher were afraid of him, but Jolene had grown to love the old man. He was often prickly with those he didn't like, but to her, he was a secret keeper and a good friend. "We can slay this dragon and have time left over to prop up our feet." Big exaggeration, but Naomi's taut shoulders relaxed.

Jolene turned to Josiah. What had been on his mind when he arrived? "Hope is helping Mrs. Pinson clean windows this morning. You know where Mrs. Pinson lives, right?"

"The small brick home on the corner of Walnut and Chestnut."

"That's right. On your way back to the cabinet shop, would you stop by there and tell Hope we need her to join us at Lester's house as soon as possible?"

"Sure thing."

"And it'd be best if Ray stayed at the shop all day today and went home with you after work."

Josiah's face formed lines of concern, but he nodded. "Sure."

Was Josiah here because of something with Ray and work? If so, they would need to discuss it later. Not only did Lester need them, but Jolene had left the key to his attic hanging on the nail near the attic door. What had she been thinking? Surely no one would need to unlock it and go up there.

Surely.

Jolene turned to Naomi. "Let's get the pastries and go slay this dragon."

Ray hid inside the dilapidated building, wishing it would fall on him and end everybody's misery. He kicked a support beam, causing dust and debris to rain down. So what if he'd messed up at the cabinet shop and drilled the holes for the hardware in the wrong place! Old Man Yoder didn't have to yell at him in front of everybody. He hated that kind of work. Hated that Josiah still treated him like a ten-year-old little brother.

Life stunk! He shoved the support beam, and it creaked and moaned while shifting a fraction. A board on the other side of the room fell, causing dust to fly. Ray wiped tears from his eyes. He was too old to be a crybaby.

The sound of horse hoofs against pavement drew his attention, and he stepped out of the dark building. Trees surrounded him on all sides, so despite hearing a rig on the road, he couldn't see it. Not yet anyway. Not until it rounded dead man's curve. He looked at his watch and realized he'd been gone from the shop quite a while. He started for the road.

Josiah hadn't been at the shop when Ray messed up and Yoder yelled at him. If his brother was back, it'd take him about two seconds to realize Ray wasn't there, and he'd go searching for him. And he'd start by going to the house.

Dead leaves crunched under his heavy boots as he walked toward the road. Ray's thoughts reached into the past, going back thirteen years. He couldn't remember being struck by lightning, but he remembered having sausage at breakfast just a few hours before it happened. Would life be different for him if he hadn't been struck? Would he be better? Better at math or blueprints like his brothers? Would his mother have loved him more? He'd never told anyone, not even Jolene, but Ray had overheard his mother talking to his aunt one night. Just above a whisper she said that he was worse than useless, that he was a burden to everyone around him. His mother's haunting words continued to ring in his ears. He could barely tolerate the thought that Jolene might feel the way their mother had, but these days as they argued more and more, he wondered.

He just wasn't good at anything . . . except worrying Jolene.

"Hello!" The elongated word from a male voice caused Ray to look up and realize he'd walked half a mile down the paved road while lost in his thoughts.

The three guys in a buggy — Alvin, Urie, and James — were a few years older than he was. Alvin had the reins. Ray ignored them and kept on walking.

"Where you headed, Ray?"

Ray shrugged, ignoring Alvin.

"Maybe he don't know," Urie piped in.

"I know," Ray hollered over his shoulder.

"You want a ride?" James asked.

Ray stopped. James was one of Van's younger brothers, and unlike the others James had never been mean to him. Then again, Ray and James never attended school together. James had moved to Winter Valley a few years after he'd graduated, coming here to apprentice under Van. Besides, Ray didn't have a problem with James. Only Van. Not many months after his parents died,

Ray needed to ask Jolene something, so he went looking for her. She was near the barn, and he overheard her and Van talking. He didn't know what Van had said, but she was crying. Ray had wanted to punch him, but he was afraid Jolene would be upset that he'd been eavesdropping, so he remained hidden. Van never came back after that. But from that day to this, Ray had refused to talk to anyone in the Beiler family unless forced to.

"Kumm on." Alvin grinned and nodded. "We're all friends."

Ray glanced at Alvin and Urie. "I've got blisters on my feet that are better friends than you two."

Alvin laughed. "You're all right, you know that?" He motioned for him. "Can't blame a man for calling it as he sees it. We haven't been friends, and we shoulda been nicer in school. It's way past time we started fresh. Okay?"

Ray's leeriness eased when James smiled and nodded, and he didn't see any harm in hitching a ride. He did need to get back quicker than he could by foot. "All right."

Alvin shoved Urie's shoulder. "Get in the back and let the man have your seat."

Ray got in. It felt sort of good to hang out with these guys. All the girls wanted to go out with them.

"Where to, Ray?" James asked.

He slumped. "The cabinet shop."

Alvin clicked his tongue, and the horse started down the road again. "You say that like it's no fun at all."

"It's not." Ray propped his arm on the open window.

Urie leaned across the back of the seat. "We're on our way back to work too. Mondays are the worst. Thank God for weekends, though. You do anything special on the weekends?"

He shook his head. "Just rest and do chores."

Alvin's eyes lit up. "You could go with us. We don't do much, but we'll help you have a little fun. Sometimes we meet up with a few girls."

"Can't." Although he wasn't sure why. He was eighteen. His siblings had gone out with friends on the weekends when they were his age. He turned around, catching James's eye. "Should I?"

James shrugged and Alvin elbowed him. When James didn't say anything else, Ray faced the front again.

"Well" — Alvin turned and looked at James — "I think he should consider going. Don't you, James?"

"Ya, sure."

Alvin came to a stop in front of the cabinetry shop. "We could meet you right here Friday night, say, around eight o'clock."

He sort of wanted to, but it didn't feel like a good idea, and Jolene said he should trust his gut in such matters. Sometimes it seemed as if Jolene was his mama, and he needed to cut the apron strings. But he shook his head. *"Nee."*

"Having fun on the weekends makes the workweek more tolerable."

"At eight?" Why had Ray asked?

"Ya."

Hmm. That would give him time to get his chores done, but would Jolene mind? He was old enough to decide on his own. Besides, Jolene might be glad to have a few hours outside of work when Ray wasn't underfoot.

"I'll think about it."

5

"It's okay." Andy gently eased toward the horse, hoping to encourage her to back out of the trailer and down the ramp. He'd arrived at Lester's farm at dawn in the cab of the truck pulling the first trailer of horses. Five hours later he was unloading the last of the twenty-three horses, and she was every bit as skittish and difficult to handle as the first one had been. He could hear the other horses in the corral, whinnying and stomping against the fence to see if they could get free.

After letting the horse sniff him, he patted her and inched forward, trying to get her to back up. She reared and whinnied. Andy flung himself back to avoid a direct kick. There wasn't a spot on his body that didn't hurt, either from the days of hard work or from bruises inflicted by feral horses. "You're doing great," he murmured gently even as his heart feared taking another hit.

Despite wearing protective gear, he was banged up.

He eased forward and stroked her neck. "Let's just keep backing up." He continued to crowd her by stepping closer to her face as she remained inside the horsebox with its narrow sides. She whinnied and stomped in protest. "I know," he cooed, "but you've got to be unloaded." She took a few steps back. "That's a girl." She reluctantly walked backward down the trailer ramp. When her back hoofs stumbled off the ledge where the ramp met the dirt, she reared, knocking Andy down, and bolted into the corral.

Some of the volunteers who were watching him clapped as the last horse entered the corral. Andy just sat on the ramp and gathered his wits, grateful to finally have these horses where they needed to be. After FedEx had dropped off the information, he'd called Uncle Lester, who agreed to the plan. Andy had then called Renee, the executive director of the Humane Society. As she explained the situation, it became clear to him that the Humane Society needed as many skilled volunteers as possible. Within two hours he was on his way to the makeshift triage center in central Pennsylvania. He'd left home Thursday night. Today was Monday, and he'd slept little in between.

He stood and removed his helmet. At home he and Levi never used protective gear when training horses, but it was a government regulation when he helped the Humane Society, and wisely so. He and Levi had worked with some high-strung, abused, and traumatized horses but never feral ones.

His uncle Lester ambled toward him, cane in hand as he limped across the patchy grass. "I didn't doubt for a minute that you could handle those horses."

Andy walked off the ramp. "You should have. I sure did."

"The Keim girls arrived. There was a mix-up concerning the message I left. That's why there wasn't any breakfast ready when you and the team arrived, but they have some pastries, fruit, and coffee set up on tables under a shade tree at the side of the house. They'll have lunch ready in less than two hours."

He didn't know who the Keim girls were, but his uncle seemed to put a lot of stock in them. "Denki. I'll get something to eat in a bit. I want to check the fences first." Hunger rumbled through his stomach as the aroma of coffee rode on the air.

When volunteers removed the trailer

ramp, Andy closed the gate and began walking the perimeter of the corral, shaking each fence post and rattling the railing. This particular pen covered an acre. As he continued to work his way around it, he saw a few Amish and Englisch men and women in the yard with plates of food and coffee, eating and chatting. The backdrop for the tables and meandering people was pastures and tame horses with one sprawling white dogwood in full bloom. He remembered the fields and fences well from a few childhood visits, but had that dogwood always been there?

An Amish woman walked toward him, toting a tray. When she got close enough, she held it up. "Lester asked me to bring you coffee and Danish."

Andy looked at his filthy hands. He couldn't eat, but surely he could at least gulp down a little coffee. He wasn't a fan of Danish pastries, but he'd surely like something in his stomach.

Once she was near him, she moved the edge of the tray to her hip and balanced it with one hand before picking up a pint-size, clear container. "Hand sanitizer will fix that, at least until you can wash up with soap and water. Hold out your hands." She waggled the container over the grass, away from the tray of food.

He did as she said, but he'd been working around the clock for days without the benefit of a bath. "This kind of dirt needs lye soap and scalding water."

"Maybe." She poured gobs of the clear liquid into his hands. "But this will do. Just rub your hands together as if it's soap and water."

The smell of alcohol overpowered the aroma of the coffee. The sanitizer landed on his hands as a clear liquid, but it dripped from them as if it were muddy water. She squirted more into his hands, and he rubbed it on his arms. She then passed him a wet, white hand towel. Before he used it on his hands and arms, he scrubbed his face with it. When he saw the grime on the white towel, he tensed. "Sorry." With the damage already done to the towel, he went ahead and wiped his hands and arms.

Her expression didn't change, but he was sure he detected some humor in her eyes as she took the towel from him. "It's my fault for bringing you a white one." With the towel dangling from her fingertips, she held out the tray.

He took the cup of coffee and Danish. "Denki."

She nodded and backed up several feet. A

71

good Amish woman kept a physical distance from any man she wasn't related to. He ate a bite of the blueberry Danish. "Wow," he mumbled, looking at it, "maybe it's because I'm so hungry, but that's better than I expected."

"Good." She dropped the towel onto the tray. "Lunch will be ready in ninety minutes, and we're getting your room set up now. Lester said your bedroom is to be the one on the second story. At the top of the stairs, turn left, and it's the door facing you at the end of the hall. It has its own bathroom and a view of the corral and barns. Do you have luggage of some sort we can put in there for you?"

"Just a backpack I shoved clothes into days ago. What little is in it is now dirty."

"We can take care of that too. Just put whatever you want washed in a pile outside your bedroom." She studied him from his feet up, but he kept his attention on the horses, pretending not to notice. "I have a brother about your size. I'll get you some of his clean clothes until we get your stuff washed and dried."

"I appreciate it." He was sure he smelled like dirty horses, and he probably looked more unkempt than the feral horses since he hadn't shaved his upper cheeks or mustache in four mornings. He had a lot to do today, but he sure would like to shower, shave, and change before he crawled into bed tonight.

"Just set the mug on a fence post when you're finished, and I'll get it later." She started toward the house.

But Andy remembered several other things he needed. "Excuse me."

She turned. Her coolness wasn't surprising. This was typical of nonrelated, adult Amish with the opposite gender — polite, stoic, and minimal.

"My brother and my son, Tobias, are arriving later today." With the help of a driver, Levi would bring Tobias and maybe stay for the afternoon to help Andy. "With these horses as out of sorts as they are right now, I'll need to find someone to watch Tobias when I can't."

An almost-imperceptible wrinkling of her brow crossed her otherwise-blank expression. Had Lester not told her he had a son who would join him? "How old is your son?"

"Nine."

"That's a pretty easy age to keep up with. We can watch him for you."

"We?"

"My sisters, Naomi and Hope, and me. I'm Jolene Keim."

"Ah, the Keim girls my great-uncle is so fond of."

She smiled, and he realized how attractive she was — rosy lips, white teeth, and auburn hair framing sun-kissed skin. And sapphire-blue eyes. He wouldn't know what color to call her eyes if it weren't for Tobias's collection of marbles and Sadie's pleasure in giving a name to every color and shade.

"I'm the oldest of the sisters, and, as we're doing now, I would appreciate any requests going through me first."

Andy guessed she was in her midtwenties and probably wasn't a Keim any longer. But once the females in a family got a nickname, they kept it even after they married. "Andy Fisher."

She shifted the tray, clasping it with both hands. "What you're doing here with these poor animals is good of you, and we want to help in any way we can."

He'd have to take her up on that offer more than he was willing to admit to her right now. He wasn't leaving Tobias elsewhere for the summer while he was here. "I asked Lester to contact a local blacksmith. Do you know if he did?"

Her lips pursed ever so slightly, and he got the feeling he'd touched on a less-than-favorable topic. "I'm sure he didn't. He would leave that to you."

"I don't know anything about smithies in this area."

"There's only one. Beiler's Blacksmith Shop. I can write the number for you on the pad in Lester's phone shanty."

"They make house calls, right?"

"Ya. The business has a wagon and one worker who travels as needed —Van Beiler."

"Is he good at his trade?"

"Very."

"Is Van Beiler the kind of man who might dicker on prices?"

"My understanding is he doesn't barter or dicker. Cash only. In advance."

"Well, I'm not sure that will work in this situation." Andy rubbed the back of his neck. "I could do the shoeing myself, but I don't have the equipment with me. Lester probably has some old shoeing equipment around here somewhere, but these horses will need a blacksmith *and* a handler to get through the process without hurting someone or themselves."

Andy was sure he noticed a faint sigh before she nibbled on one side of her lower lip, studying the horses. "If I made the call personally, he would give the best price possible." Her raised eyebrow and slight shake of her head said she wasn't fond of the idea.

Sometimes his life would be easier if he didn't pick up on body language, but the more time he spent trying to understand horses, the better he could read people too. Well, honest people. If she was aware of her body language and trying to conceal it, he doubted he could pick up on any of her feelings.

"Okay. I'll call him." She sighed. "If you and Lester can make the sacrifice to oversee the well-being of the horses, I can swallow my pride for a few minutes and ask Van for a favor." Her eyes met his. "Apparently I can't do it without venting."

Andy chuckled at her honest review of herself.

She shook her head. "Van Beiler." A hint of a friendly smile crossed her lips. "You couldn't need a simple favor like asking for my firstborn."

6

The screen door creaked and the wooden porch moaned as Jolene tiptoed out of her house, carrying baking supplies to the carriage. She would fix breakfast for Lester and his two remaining guests, but she also had to make her pastries for the bakeshop while at Lester's this morning.

Crickets chirped softly, and silvery moonlight sliced through the darkness. The early morning air smelled of honeysuckle, and she paused for a moment to thank God for another day of life.

May I use it well, Father.

After retrieving the key to Lester's attic and putting it safely in her pocket, she'd spent the rest of yesterday quite focused. She wouldn't be able to escape to the attic to paint while Lester had houseguests. But she consoled herself with the truth that if not for Lester, she wouldn't have had the freedom and the privilege of being allowed to paint. So she would have to get by without sneaking to the attic to paint until the houseguests were gone.

How would her parents feel about her secret? They'd had an open-mindedness that wasn't typical. The older Jolene became, the more she saw who her parents had really been. They were quite liberal thinkers by Amish standards, but they'd chosen to tuck themselves under the authority of the Amish church. They didn't feel as the bishop did about art. He stood on the scripture "thou shalt not make unto thee any graven image." Her parents felt that the verses referred to worshiping the image as if it could save them, and that's not what art was about. But they submitted to his authority, not allowing her to paint or draw because the bishop was their authority. If her Daed had known she wouldn't move to a district with a bishop who allowed artwork, he wouldn't have given her the paintbrushes. Would he disagree with her decision to paint anyway?

One time when her Mamm was responding to a question from an Englisch neighbor about the Amish way of life, Mamm had said, "I can tell you how the Old Order Amish view each topic, and then I can tell you how we view them." Mamm was one of a handful of educated Old Order Amish people. She had only an associate's degree in nursing, but she had that because the bishop had come to her, asking that she earn a GED and then attend nursing school. The mortality rate for women giving birth and their newborns was too high, and the families needed some type of nurse to answer their abundance of health-related questions. So the bishop felt that God wouldn't mind if she increased her learning as long as she used it to serve the Amish community.

Would her parents understand her need to skirt the bishop's authority, or would they be disappointed in her? She used to ask herself that question all the time, but as the years passed and her contentment grew, it didn't come up anymore . . . until she feared being found out because Lester had a houseful of guests.

Her privacy aside, she felt that yesterday had been well spent despite having to call the blacksmith shop and leave a message for Van. His uncle said he'd gone to visit his parents in Ohio, of course taking his wife and children, so he might not be able to help after all. She guessed that depended on how long he intended to visit. When his Daed needed his help, Van and his family sometimes went there for a full month or more. Anger rumbled deep within her. If he liked it there, and apparently he did, why had he stayed in Winter Valley after marrying Donna? It only made Jolene's life harder. She rebuked herself and tamped down her frustrations. It was his life, and it wasn't hers to question.

His uncle had said he'd get the message to Van. The idea of having to ask a favor of him made her shudder. When she'd made the decision to keep her siblings together, she'd feared he would never marry her. But she hadn't expected to lose his friendship within six months or to see him marry someone else within a year of her parents' death. Or . . .

Her hands began to tremble, and she clasped them together, refusing to give in to the anger that tried to surface. *Stop, Jolene.* It did no good to rehash things that had taken place many years ago. Van had needed to pull away from her and find another.

She understood. Truly. But when he left that night, she wiped the tears from her face and decided never to call him again. If the hens stopped laying eggs, the cow stopped giving milk, or the horse ran off or became lame — all of which had happened over the last ten years, plus much more — she would figure it out or do without, refusing to call Van. And she'd stuck to that decision.

Until yesterday.

But she wouldn't let Lester down. He'd been too good to them over the years, and since he wasn't a relative, he'd been giving for no reason other than the love in his heart. So she would do her best to help Andy Fisher in any way he needed, including actually working with the wild horses.

Going back to get the last items for today, she went up the porch stairs, and Hope stumbled out the front door. Jolene steadied her and waited a moment. "You got your footing?"

Hope blinked, patted Jolene's hand affectionately, and silently gestured toward the buggy. Jolene released her, suppressing a chuckle. Hope wasn't a morning person. Besides, what teen was ready to get up before daylight? But it couldn't be helped.

After grabbing the blueberries and some whipping cream from the gas-powered refrigerator, she climbed into the rig and drove toward Lester's. It took nearly forty-five minutes to get there, and she wondered if she and Hope should plan to sleep there on the really long days.

Hope slid across the seat toward her and propped her head on Jolene's shoulder, ready to doze off. "Having to start this time of day is cruel. Lester knows that, right?"

Jolene chuckled. Since the Englisch volunteers and Humane Society people had left last night a few hours after dinner, Jolene was certainly capable of fixing breakfast for those at the farm — Lester, Andy, and Tobias. Even Andy's brother, Levi, had a driver pick him up around ten last night. He didn't want his wife and Daed to have the full brunt of the morning's responsibilities on the horse farm with a group of new and rowdy horses. Andy seemed to fully agree with him. None of the volunteers could help today. They had regular jobs to return to. Most had used vacation days to help with the horses thus far. And those within the Humane Society had two issues keeping them away. Some were due in court today to testify in a case concerning animal abuse, and the others had to return to their regular duties, which included dealing with a pack of possibly rabid dogs that had been abandoned in an old apartment.

The realization of such cruelty to animals turned Jolene's stomach. Didn't life dish out enough pain without people turning on each other and helpless animals? The busy schedule of the Humane Society meant those people could provide no service to

Andy for at least a few days. Unfortunately, last night Lester kept assuring Andy that whatever he needed, Jo could help. Andy didn't complain about the idea. Actually, he seemed grateful.

But what was Lester thinking? She appreciated the confidence he put in her, but it was misplaced. Her knowledge of horses was limited to knowing they needed oats, hay, and water. Oh, and she was quite skilled at knowing when a horse stall needed cleaning and telling her brothers to see that it got done.

After all, in her estimation it was man's work, best left to those who could lift a bale of hay and roll a wheelbarrow full of manure out of the barn without whining about it, which she couldn't do. In her defense, her brothers couldn't tote a basket of wet laundry to the line or wash dishes without whining about that.

So fair was fair.

Realizing she needed to find a man to help Andy, last night after she'd finished washing the dinner dishes and getting Lester's kitchen in order for today, she had gone by her brothers' places — first Josiah's and then Michael's — asking if they could help Andy Fisher. They couldn't. Once she was home, she'd asked Ray. He'd seemed tired and sad and had told her he couldn't do it either. If Lester weren't so hard on his many male relatives, Andy could find the needed help.

So she searched through her books and found one on training horses, which recommended several things. One suggestion caused her to gather her work clothes for today and put them in a horse's stall last night. Since the rogue horses didn't like humans, it made sense that it might help if she didn't smell so strongly of lavender soap and Downy fabric softener. When she went back inside, she read the book until she fell asleep. Now both her clothes and the book were tucked under the driver's seat of her carriage.

But her heart was with Ray.

His sullen, sad mood of late nagged at her. What was going on?

She pulled into Lester's driveway. "Hope," she whispered, patting her sister on the cheek.

She stirred. "Wake me at noon, please."

"Sure no problem." Jolene opened the door to the rig. "But first help me tote the boxes of stuff inside . . . and help make breakfast, bake pastries for the shop, and do laundry."

"Very funny." Hope was the only girl

Jolene knew who could frown while laughing.

"I was quite sure you'd like it." They grabbed their stuff and tiptoed inside. Lester never locked a door. The smell of the old house and the way the moonlight fell across the rugs and floors reminded her of *Mammi* and *Daadi*'s house when she was growing up. Poor Hope never had a chance to get to know her grandparents, and her memories of their parents were a couple of granules. Was Jolene doing a decent job of parenting Hope? Was it Jolene's fault that Ray seemed unhappy?

They set their boxes on the kitchen table. Jolene opened a drawer and fumbled around, trying to locate the matches in the dark. This was their assigned spot, and she'd put them in this drawer before leaving last night. Where were they?

Hmm. Giving up, she moved to the drawer where Lester tossed the occasional loose, unused match. Soon she felt the thin, rough edges of one. That would get her started. She continued searching the drawer until she touched the smooth, waxy roundness of a candle. After using the lone match to light the gas stove, she held the wick to the flame. Once the candle was lit, she used it to light several kerosene lanterns.

She and Hope moved around as quietly as possible while setting the table, brewing the coffee, frying bacon, and making pastries and blueberry biscuits. Pancakes needed to come hot off the griddle, and since no one was up yet, they decided to make biscuits. Those could be eaten cold and still be good.

While cracking a dozen eggs into a bowl, she looked out an open window. Dark had given way to the gray light of day. Fog rolled across the lower valley, and the sounds of nature — birds, horses, and cows — grew louder as the dawn grew brighter.

Hope came up behind her, placed her hands on Jolene's shoulders, and rubbed them. "You have to be a little weary this morning. Naomi and I left hours before you did last night."

Naomi had a husband to prepare supper for. Jolene couldn't allow Lester or the needs of feral horses to come ahead of that. And Hope was worn-out by the time they had fed dinner to sixteen people. Growing bodies of teens needed more rest than adult bodies, so Jolene had asked Naomi to drop off Hope at home.

"Today will be *a lot* easier than yesterday as far as meals go." She cracked the last of the eggs and began beating them with a whisk. "I'm glad of that. Still, you'll be busy.

Your main task is to stick with Tobias."

"Ah, I'm the baby-sitter, but he's not to know it. I can do that."

"Exactly." Although Hope was the youngest, she seemed to be a natural mother hen. "You'll also need to help keep the kitchen clean and laundry done." Jolene glanced at the clock and went to the oven to check the puff pastries. The biscuits needed more time, but the pastries were done.

Hope moved to the island across from her and sat on it. "Did you reach Van?"

She shook her head. "I left a message. He and his family are out of town." Jolene set the baking sheet on the oven. "Naomi needs to take these to the bakeshop as soon as she arrives, so we have to fill these with cream as soon as they're cool."

"Does it bother you?"

Jolene moved the pastries to a cooling rack. "What? Baking pastries every morning?"

"Van."

Jolene turned, studying her sister. Hope had been only four when Jolene and Van broke up. Did she have any memories of that time or just broken pieces of understanding from what others had told her?

Loud, quick thuds came from the stairs that led to the kitchen, and something rattled like a child's toy.

Tobias bounded into the room, shaking the missing box of matches. "Something smells good!"

"There is much to choose from," — Jolene gestured across the island and counters loaded with baked goods — "and if it's okay with your Daed, you're welcome to pick whatever suits you, but there is a price to pay."

Tobias moved closer to the counters, looking over the various pastries. "If it costs money, my Daed will pay it. He's always got lots of cash in his billfold."

Andy eased into the room from the same back stairway. He favored his left knee, and his movements were stiff, probably from days of minor injuries, but he was clean-shaven, and he didn't seem as weary today. He looked as interested in the percolator of coffee on the stove as his son was in the pastries. "He's right." Andy got his billfold from his pants pocket. "I have *lots* of cash." He pulled out all the money — four one-dollar bills.

"You do." Hope laughed. "That looks like what I have in my savings account."

Tobias's face went blank. "It's not enough?"

"Sorry." Jolene shook her head. "The cost

is one missing box of matches."

Tobias thrust them toward her. "It's Daed's fault."

Jolene took the matches, choking back laughter. When she glanced at Andy, he was looking at the floor, shaking his head. His facial features, sandy-brown hair and beard, and his thin, muscular build made him really attractive. But the idea caught her by surprise. When was the last time she'd thought that about a man?

The sound of a cane against a floor echoed, and Tobias's eyes got big. "I hear Uncle Lester coming down the steps."

"He's using the main staircase." Jolene knew, because unlike the back stairs that entered the kitchen, the main staircase had wide treads and a really strong banister.

Tobias held up one finger. "I'll be right back."

He took off, and Jolene caught Hope's eye. "From a child's or teen's perspective, parents have unlimited money. We are expected to pay for everything, and whatever can be blamed on us will be." She put the matches in their drawer and got a mug from the cupboard.

Hope gave a nod toward Andy. "Did it hurt when your son threw you under the wagon?"

Andy seemed a little amused and perhaps a little unsure of their crassness. But maybe that was just his way — a sort of quiet thoughtfulness.

"Sorry if we're too vocal." Jolene poured coffee into the mug. They had cups and coffee on the kitchen table, but he was here and clearly interested in coffee. She set it on the island in front of him. "In our household we're very outspoken against childlike behavior — even when the behavior is coming from the oldest adult in the room."

Andy picked up his mug. "Levi says I should vent more."

Jolene lit a fire under the awaiting skillet. Once hot, it would take only a few minutes to cook the eggs she'd already whisked. She then put the biscuits on a plate. "I think it's a good idea to let out your pent-up thoughts and feelings" — she set the plate on the island — "just as soon as you return home."

Hope giggled and hopped off the counter. "If you need an honest opinion, ask my sister. For every year she ages, she becomes a decade-worth of opinionated."

Jolene winked at Hope. "That I do." She shooed her. "Now get the biscuits, bacon, fruit, and cheese on the table, please."

Hope disappeared into the dining room.

Jolene poured the eggs into the skillet, making it sizzle.

"Denki for all of this." Andy held up his mug and motioned toward the breakfast items.

"You're quite welcome, although Naomi will take most of the pastries to the bakeshop when she arrives." She turned off the oven and stirred the eggs with a wooden spoon. "Do you mind if Tobias chooses which pastry he wants?"

"Not at all. I remember being his age, and you're reminding me of my grandmother. Her breakfasts looked and smelled delicious like this. I'm glad he'll have this memory."

Jolene continued to stir the eggs, but she raised one eyebrow at Andy. "I remind you of your Mammi?"

His blue eyes grew large. "Not that you actually look anything like her."

In an effort not to come across as flirting, she resisted teasing him. "Perhaps you should join Uncle Lester before you have shoe for breakfast while the rest of us eat a feast."

"Good thinking," he said as he left.

When the eggs were almost done, she turned off the fire and covered the skillet with a plate. While Hope finished getting the needed items on the table, Jolene prepared a platter of pastries for Tobias to choose from. "Tobias," she called.

He ran back into the room.

"If you want a filling added to the cream horns, you have three choices. You can have vanilla," — she lifted the appropriate pastry bag that held the filling — "custard, or chocolate."

"I'm supposed to choose just one?"

She laughed. "If you like all three flavors, I could make one with a hefty glob of each. My mama used to do that for me when I was about your age, and I've done it for my siblings when they asked."

"I like that plan. Your mama must've been nice. Sadie's nice like that."

Just Sadie? What about his Mamm? It seemed odd that after nearly twenty-four hours of knowing the Fishers, not one of them had mentioned Tobias's mom. Jolene put the tip of the pastry bag into the flaky, golden-brown cream horn. "Sadie is your uncle Levi's wife, right?"

"Yep. I like her. They ain't been married long, but before her, my Mammi used to cook for us some, not breakfast though. Mostly casseroles for dinner, and she only made cakes and puddings for desserts."

His grandmother did the cooking before Sadie? Was Andy a widower? It would make several things add up, like Andy's desire to keep Tobias with him this summer and Andy's need for a sitter. She'd assumed his wife was at home with a brood of children, perhaps too far along in pregnancy to travel. Jolene's Daed and lots of others she knew tended to keep their sons close to them during the summer months — for bonding or apprenticeship reasons and for occupying high-energy boys when the Mamm was busy with younger ones.

But as the new possibility dawned on her, the hair on her arms and neck stood on end, and her heart rate increased as her curiosity rose. Her internal reaction surprised her. She'd had several widower suitors over the last ten years, mostly older men who were willing to help her raise her siblings if she would marry them and help raise their children. One man came from Indiana to get to know her, in hopes of finding a wife. But after spending a little time with each one, she had zero interest in being courted by them, let alone marrying them.

Jolene put down the bag of vanilla filling and picked up the one filled with chocolate. "Cakes and puddings are good too."

"Ya. Mammi doesn't cook much for us anymore. Does your mama ever cook for you?"

"No." Jolene held the tip of the pastry bag out to Tobias, and without needing instructions he put his index finger directly under it. She squirted some onto his finger. "She's gone."

He licked his finger. "My Mamm's gone too."

Jolene's heart quickened its pace. Her interest in Andy, however fragile, wasn't at all like her, and it seemed really inappropriate. His heart could be broken, and here she was mentally eyeing the man and thinking of only herself. She hated when widowers did that to her — disregarded her heart as if she were no more than a workhorse or milk cow on an auctioning block.

Lester came to the kitchen door with a mug of coffee in hand. "It looks as if we're ready to eat, right?"

"Oh." Jolene would prefer a few more answers from Tobias first, but she knew Lester well. His polite question was actually a gentle command, and he gave only one gentle command before he started barking orders. "Ya." She squirted the custard into the pastry and gave it to Tobias. "Take that to your plate." She hurriedly filled a few more pastries.

Lester strode over and grabbed one. He popped the whole thing in his mouth and mumbled something — perhaps "that's amazing."

She dumped the skillet of scrambled eggs into a huge bowl. "Lester, is Andy a widower?"

He nodded and mumbled a couple of words that ended with *widower* — maybe *trace widower.* Her Mamm had used that term, but Jolene hadn't heard it since then. It meant Andy had a deep mark from the loss. Lester licked his fingers and took a few drinks of his coffee. "A very sad and difficult situation for Andy, but Tobias was a toddler, so he has no recollection of her at all. Kumm. Let's eat."

Jolene entered the dining room, carrying a platter of pastries and a bowl of eggs, but she hadn't felt this self-conscious since the day she had to attend Van's wedding. With everything on the table — breads, meats, eggs, cheese, and fruit — she and Hope took a seat, and all of them bowed their heads during the silent prayer.

While heads were bowed, Jolene did something she hadn't done in a decade. She opened her eyes to catch a glimpse of the man across from her. There was something compelling about him — something she'd noticed since they met. It wasn't just his looks. He seemed to have a gentle, strong demeanor.

She closed her eyes, embarrassed by her thoughts. He could be seeing someone. Or maybe he would never be interested in her. Or perhaps he didn't intend to marry again.

Actually, she knew almost nothing about him, but for the first time in her life, she liked the idea of getting to know a widower.

7

Andy took the last bite of cantaloupe and perched his fork and knife on the edge of his plate. The food was great, but what he really wanted was to know if Jolene had reached the traveling blacksmith. He'd hoped she would volunteer the information since it was clear she hadn't wanted to call him. He'd rather not have to ask if she'd followed through. Seems as if she had, she would've said so.

Still, he had to admit that this meal was like a Thanksgiving feast, only for breakfast. He'd eaten his eggs, meat, and fruit, so he picked up a cream-filled pastry and alternated between it and his coffee. Delicious. Too much so. Surely the Keim girls wouldn't cook all summer the way they had yesterday and today. If so, he'd have to ration himself. Sadie was a good cook, and she fixed a lot better meals than he or Levi. But her goals were more like his and Levi's:

make it healthy, get it done, and move on with the day.

Uncle Lester pushed his plate back. "So what's the first thing to do today?"

Andy wiped powdered sugar off his lips. "Calm a few of the horses enough that they'll let us bathe them. Most are matted with mud and manure. No matter what task we undertake, I'd prefer that you and Tobias stay away from the barn and corral at least until the horses settle."

Lester nodded. "I broke my hip messing with a high-strung horse a few years back, and I can't afford to do that again. But Jo will be here to help."

Andy nodded. That was good news. When he'd called to ask his uncle about using his facilities, Lester was on board. He'd assured Andy he could get him some skilled help, so apparently Joe was that help. But what time would Joe arrive?

"Daed said they'll likely break free and bolt." Tobias ran his finger across his empty plate, scooping up some spilled filling. "They'll need shoeing too."

Uncle Lester frowned at Andy. "You're bringing in a smithy, right?"

"I haven't made plans for that, no."

"You need to. I was sure you knew some other smithy than Van Beiler . . . since you

98

work with horses."

So Lester wasn't a fan of Beiler's either. What had the man done? Andy tucked his napkin next to his plate. "You want me to try to bring one here from Apple Ridge?"

Jolene shook her head. "No, he doesn't."

"Yes, I do." Lester propped one leg on the other. "I won't pay money to support any man who has no business living in Winter Valley."

Andy knew Lester could be as difficult as the day was long once he was set against someone. He was known in the family for being that way. Thankfully, his great-uncle didn't have anything against him.

So what did he do when his horses needed to be shod? Whatever it was, it must not be a current option.

Jolene intertwined her fingers and leaned in. "Lester, I appreciate your sentiments, but Van is a good man. I keep telling you that." She angled her head, her eyes narrowing at the elderly man. "And Andy needs his help. End of discussion, please."

Uncle Lester tossed his napkin onto the plate. "A good man," he mumbled.

"Ya." Jolene nodded. "He is. Do you want us to argue about it in front of my little sister, Andy's son, and a man who's nearly a stranger to me?"

Lester grimaced. "Sorry. I didn't think about that." He pushed back from the table and grabbed his cane. "Unless I can round up some volunteers, you'll have to make do with Van's and Jo's help."

"Actually," — Jolene shrugged — "Van is currently out of town. I left a message at the shop for him to call me. We haven't spoken more than a passing *hello* in years, but I'm assuming if he gets the message, he'll return the call."

"Of course he will." Hope stood and began gathering plates. "Whenever I see him around town, he's quick to do anything he can to help out us Keims. My horse threw a shoe a year ago, and I walked him to Smithy Beiler's place. The fires were cold, and Van was locking up. But he unlocked the place, fired up the furnace, and put all new shoes on my horse. We talked about gardening and my family and stuff the whole time."

Lester didn't look impressed, but when he opened his mouth, Jolene arched an eyebrow at him, a clear warning that Hope didn't see.

Andy thought it best to change the subject. "So what time can I expect this Joe fellow to get here?"

Jolene raised her hand. "Present."

"You?" Andy jolted, knocking the flatware

off his plate and onto the floor. "I . . . I'm sorry, Jolene." He turned to Lester. "But that won't do."

Jolene and Hope gathered several items and went into the kitchen.

Lester scratched a scraggly eyebrow with one shaky, weathered hand. "Jo is the available help, and it'll have to do. You've given your word to the Humane Society."

"And when we talked last week, you said there would be skilled men to help. This change means we don't have the needed manpower."

"You have womanpower. Make it work."

"I know you like and believe in Jolene. That's obvious. But we're talking feral horses. I need someone with experience, someone who can watch my back as much as I'm watching his — emphasis on the word *his.* Horses are stout, massive creatures, Lester. You know that. One unexpected kick, especially to the head, and she could be seriously injured." He picked up his flatware and put it on his plate. "I mean no disrespect, Uncle Lester, but what are you thinking?"

"You trained Levi to help you back when he was no bigger and had no more muscle than she does. Am I right?"

"I was young and careless about a lot of

things back then." Including his confidence that he could marry a young woman with a few emotional issues and help her get stronger. "Since Levi was thrown from a horse and fractured his neck a couple of years ago, I'm far more cautious."

"You aren't trying to ride these horses. You just want them to get used to being near humans and touched by them so you can wash the horses."

"I'm not teaming up with an inexperienced woman."

"I tell you what. Why don't you walk into the kitchen and be a horse's rump to her about it? Would that satisfy you?"

While Andy was growing up, his cousins had told many tales of wanting to avoid Uncle Lester, and Andy was beginning to see why. Since he rarely was around the old man, he'd not seen this side of him.

"Uncle Lester, has it dawned on you that maybe I'm not the problem here?" Sometimes old men who had lived by themselves for years were just ornery. They had spent too much time without anyone challenging their perception of situations.

"Look" — Lester placed the flat of his hand on the table and tapped it — "we've signed papers, agreeing to what we would do with these horses. We will calm them, then wash and shoe them as quickly as possible. The only other people available on short notice are Tobias, Hope, me, Naomi, and Jolene."

Tobias swiped the back of his hand across his mouth. "Sadie helps Levi, and they have fun."

"That's different. Levi doesn't work with rogue horses." Some were high-strung and traumatized, but Levi would never put Sadie in a small space with an animal that could suddenly get out of control, and that's where he and Jolene would need to be — in a small space with a terrified animal. Hope returned and began gathering butter and jellies and whatever was left.

Andy picked up his plate and Tobias's and started toward the kitchen.

"Andy."

He paused.

"Be nice to her."

Andy nodded and went into the kitchen. Jolene had her back to him, washing dishes. He couldn't recall the last time he'd needed to tiptoe around a woman's feelings — six years ago maybe. Eva's response to all stress was to crawl into bed sobbing, and it was his job to calm her and cajole her out of it. "I . . . I hope you understand why I feel the way I do. It's not you. I'm sure

103

you're quite capable in the right circumstances."

Jolene turned, lips pursed, eyes fiery with displeasure, but there were no tears, and she certainly didn't give off a hint of a vibe that she might crumble. "I agree with you, and I told Lester that." She scraped bits of food into the trash. "But with no other alternative available, let's figure it out."

"Do you know anyone else who could lend a hand?"

"No, Lester and I put some effort into it, but no one could miss time from work to help. I'm all that's available right now."

"Surely you have a Daed or husband or boyfriend who would object to Lester's plan of putting you in this kind of dangerous situation if he knew about it."

Hurt reflected in her eyes. "I have none of the above. Thanks for reminding me."

Jolene went to the hutch where there was a stack of white flat cardboard. She grabbed one piece and unfolded it while returning to the island. The container reminded him of an oversize pizza box, and she began putting pastries in it.

He hadn't meant to hit a sore spot. Who would've dreamed that a woman her age would already be without her Daed? Or that one so beautiful and skilled at running a home wouldn't at least have a boyfriend? But despite feeling like the horse's rump Lester had mentioned, he wasn't wrong to try to protect her. Actually, her lack of someone to stand up for her made him more right.

"I . . . I didn't mean . . ."

"Look, you need the help, and I'm all you've got." She stopped filling the box and focused on him.

Was she waiting for him to respond?

He found himself staring into the sapphire eyes of an auburn-haired beauty who was studying him.

His heart lurched, and he walked out of the kitchen.

8

The cab of the delivery truck smelled of stale tuna fish and decades-old cigarette smoke. Ray's stomach churned a bit as the big vehicle lumbered toward their destination — Coldwell mansion.

The driver leaned forward, rummaging through old invoices and trash between the dashboard and the window. "Stop squirming, Ray."

How could he? It stunk in here, and even if it smelled like fresh air, he wanted out. Out of the cabinetry business. Out of being the little brother Jolene and Josiah kept an eye on. Out of being hounded by his Mamm's whispers.

Josiah pulled his attention from the scenery. "Maybe he'd stop squirming, Chad, if you'd quit leaning across him."

Chad sighed and sat back, evidently giving up on whatever he'd been searching for.

Josiah nudged Ray's arm. "You okay?"

He shrugged. "Feeling sort of nauseated." Probably because he made himself sick.

Josiah nodded. "Sorry about that. Did you eat?"

"Jolene was gone, and I slept through the alarm."

"You know she left you a plate of food in the oven or fridge. Did you look for it?"

"I sort of thought of it, but then I forgot when you arrived, rushing me to hurry up."

Josiah shook his head, chuckling. "Well, that means I win, right?"

It was a running joke. Josiah often pulled some sort of trick or made a wordplay and then said, "I win." And the other person would say, "Ya think?" It was a game Jolene approved of, one intended to make Ray think of ways to get back at Josiah. Ray won at times, and that was particularly fun. The game also made him better at understanding horseplay between others when he saw it, which was good, because a couple of times when Ray was younger, he didn't realize what was going on between two people, and he'd thrown a few punches, angry at one person for picking on another.

Josiah fiddled with the knob to the window. "We will get you something as soon as we can. This delivery could be interesting.

I've heard about the Coldwell place for years."

Nothing here would interest him, and he longed to do some kind of job he was good at, but what? At least he wouldn't be around for Old Man Yoder to scream at him. On those days Ray hated himself the most, and then his thoughts became a garbled mass of pain and confusion. It was as if being yelled at in front of people made him step back in time, to the months following his accident, when his sentences were choppy and childish.

Last night his sister had suggested he help a man named Andy Fisher with some rogue horses. Yeah, right, as if somehow dealing with the unpredictable behavior and manure of wild horses would be any different than his current job.

Chad started fumbling through the stuff on the dashboard again. Josiah dug under two smashed Coke cans and several stained papers and found a pack of cigarettes. He tossed them onto Chad's lap. Chad mumbled something as he pulled a cigarette out of its package. Had the man changed out of the filthy dark-blue pants once in the last month?

Three men were often needed for this kind of delivery — one Englisch driver and two

Amish workers. Ray was supposed to stick with Josiah. He got into less trouble that way. The only reason Old Man Yoder screamed at him the other day was because Josiah wasn't there. But when delivering cabinets, Ray always got sandwiched between the other two men. Always.

Uncle Calvin had other drivers, ones who weren't miserable with life in general. Is that what Ray would be like in thirty years — too disinterested in life to bathe or put on fresh clothes? Would he only find comfort in a few bad habits that grated on others' nerves and end up smelling of smoke and stale beer?

Surely not. He didn't drink or smoke. Maybe he should start. It might help. He doubted that it could hurt.

Chad pulled onto a gated driveway. He reached through the open window and pushed a button on a keypad.

"Yes?" A young woman's voice came through the speaker.

"Delivery from Keim Cabinets."

The woman didn't say anything else, but the double-wide iron gates slowly began to open. Josiah smiled. "I'd like automated doors on the barn in winter."

Ray nodded. Josiah lived in a small house on his in-laws' property along with several other families related to his wife, and besides other jobs, all the men also helped tend the milk cows. The barn doors were on rollers, and they froze open or shut during the winter, especially when the air leaked in around them.

"Look at this place." Ray couldn't imagine the work that was involved in the manicured yard and flowery gardens, and the house was as big as several large barns. How many children did these people have?

A young Amish woman came out the front door, waving a dish-towel. No doubt the help. There was no way she or any of her relatives lived here. Any Amish who had this kind of money, and there were some, would never live in this manner. She pointed to a side door and headed that way. Then she paused, squinted at him or Josiah, and waved.

Josiah waved back, a halfhearted, embarrassed wave. "You know her?"

She looked a tad familiar. "Maybe."

"Interesting." Josiah elbowed him. "Very interesting."

"Don't be ridiculous."

Chad maneuvered the huge vehicle, aiming to get the back of it as close to the right entryway as possible.

"What?" Josiah propped his elbow on the

open window. "You expect to live at home and remain single forever because you think differently than some of us? No one believes that, Ray."

"No one" meant his siblings, but if any of them could see the fractured, reckless, and rash thoughts inside his head, they wouldn't be so naive. Some he battled against. Some he ignored.

Once parked, they got out, and Ray waited as Josiah opened the back of the trailer. Ray felt more awkward than usual as the girl moved to the top of the brick steps and stood there watching him. He and Josiah carried the first piece down the ramp.

As he drew closer, she whispered a one-syllable word. Had she said his name? He was unsure, so he said nothing. She grinned. "It's so good to see you, Ray."

In the length of time it took her to say his name, his insides became as frozen as the pond he played on each winter, only this was missing all sense of adventure. No one beamed at him like this girl was, except maybe Jolene at times, but that didn't count. Anyway, if he'd met this girl, and apparently he had, where had it been? When he said nothing, she turned and led the way.

"Ray," Josiah whispered while walking backward as he held his end of the four-foot-long cabinet, "you're supposed to speak when someone talks to you."

Ray shrugged. All his thoughts had collided at once when she spoke to him, and responding hadn't entered his mind. He studied the house as they walked through it. He'd never seen anything this grand — perfectly glossy floors, stately mirrors framed in silver, and inset lights in every ceiling. Clearly the owners liked dark wood and brushed silver. It was similar to other new houses with its sleek, clean lines and open spaces. But if the walls were papered with money, Ray figured it couldn't scream wealth any louder.

After walking for entirely too long, they entered a kitchen. When they set down the piece, the girl stepped forward. "I've laid burgundy runners here and there to mark your way. If the cabinets get heavy as you unload them and you need to set them down, please rest them only on the rugs provided until you enter the kitchen area."

Josiah peered back at the way they'd come in, probably taking note of the rugs. He nodded. "Not a problem. I'm Josiah Keim."

She wrung the dishrag in her hand, glancing at the clock before looking out a large bay window into a garden in the backyard. A woman in jeans held a basketful of flowers as she cut a purple one. The Amish girl returned her attention to Josiah. "Teena Miller."

Ray choked, coughing loudly. *Teena?* Memories flooded him. "Good grief. What happened to your hair?"

Josiah made a face, shaking his head at him in a way he probably hadn't intended Teena to see. Was Ray's response wrong? Somehow impulsive? He didn't think so. Wasn't he just being honest?

"My hair?" Confusion flickered through her eyes for a moment, and she touched her well-groomed hair that was parted down the middle and pulled back. "Oh. I stopped bleaching it."

"I guess you did." He hadn't realized her white-blond hair had come from a bottle.

It'd been two years since he had to attend the Old Order Amish regional conference with Jolene. Three days of Bible and prayer meetings, ceremonies, and traditions. Thankfully, the youth were mostly required to keep the younger ones entertained and out of danger. He'd been sixteen at the time. Teena had been seventeen, and she'd been as broken outwardly as he was inwardly. So while all the others acted like life was a fun game, Teena and Ray hung out, talking about real things.

"Ray," Josiah mumbled under his breath, pushing the cabinet against him.

"What?" Ray glanced at his brother before turning back to Teena. "It's a lot darker."

She nodded, and unlike Josiah she seemed unperturbed by his awkwardness. Teena glanced at Josiah and then smiled at Ray. "He wants you to say that my hair looks nice, whether you mean it or not."

He never understood that. Why was lying discouraged with threats of hellfire on one hand and completely encouraged on the other? And people considered him the odd one for not understanding things like that.

But this was one of the things he remembered about her. She wasn't like the other girls — no double-talk or hesitancy to say what she was thinking. At the same time she didn't baby him.

As memories of their time together began to form more clearly, he felt something he hadn't experienced in a long time — a moment of being comfortable inside his own skin. "Is that what you think I should say?"

"I'm just glad you remember me. I'd forgotten I was a blonde the last time we saw each other, and I have only sketchy memories of parts of that weekend but very vivid ones of you."

It felt good to think he'd gotten at least

one thing right in his life — giving her somebody to talk to when she needed it.

As Josiah was leaving, he gestured toward the entry to the kitchen. "I'll use a set of dollies to bring in some of the smaller cabinets."

Teena chuckled. "Is he a sunshine boy?"

Ray had forgotten about that term she'd introduced him to. "Pretty much, ya." Sunshine people saw life differently than Teena or Ray. When heavy rains stopped, they basked in the beauty of the rainbow and ignored the destruction and death the flooding had caused.

Why did Josiah leave him here? He constantly nagged Ray to stay with him and stay busy. Should Ray volunteer to go after him, or did Josiah need a few minutes on his own? Jolene would know. She understood people and what she called "subtleties and decorum." Ray was only familiar with the wad of anxiety in his gut and the roar of conflicting voices in his head, all telling him too much info at once. Jolene said people had numerous voices inside them at once and the trick was figuring out which thought held the wisdom for that particular moment and then following it.

Teena got a glass from the cabinet and pushed it against a dispenser on the refrigerator, and ice came out. With the touch of a button, she got water. She held it out to him. "You kept our secret."

He took it. "Said I would."

"Lots of people say that. Few do it. My life is in a much better place these days."

He didn't need anyone telling him what to say this time. He just had to say what he felt stirring inside him. "That's good."

"How about yours?"

"Still working at the shop, so everything is the same." He couldn't even say he was better at the job now than when he was sixteen.

"Not completely the same." She held out her palm and raised it up a foot, and then she held her hands apart, like measuring a fish, but he knew she meant his shoulders. "You've been growing."

He straightened a bit. "Over a foot taller."

"You look good."

"You too."

Her eyes grew wider. "Denki. You're better at picking out one thought inside your head and voicing it."

"A little. Jolene never quits working with me."

Teena put a coaster on the island and tapped it, letting him know to set the drink there when he was done. "After making the delivery today, will you be coming back here?"

"Don't know. Nobody's said." He didn't think to ask. It never mattered.

"I work for Mrs. Coldwell five days a week, and she said there will be at least a week of tearing out old cabinets and installing the new ones."

He nodded. There were a lot of cabinets in this oversize kitchen. Plus they were replacing the cabinets in all five of the bathrooms. "Uncle Calvin said it would take two weeks."

She glanced at the clock again and patted her hidden pocket, making it rattle like a child's toy. "I need to take something to Terri . . . Mrs. Coldwell." She pulled a small bottle of juice from the refrigerator. "When it's time, would you like to take your lunch break with me in the garden? There's a wrought-iron table and chairs toward the back of the property."

He shrugged. It was nice she still appreciated the time they'd had two years ago, but he had nothing to offer. It'd been a fluke that he'd made a difference in her life, and it wasn't one he could duplicate.

She opened the back door near the bay window. "Bye."

"Hey, Teena?" She closed the door and

waited. She hadn't seemed surprised Ray was here, and wasn't it strange that Mrs. Coldwell chose their cabinetry shop, ninety minutes away by motorized vehicle, when other Amish cabinetry shops were closer? A person didn't have to be good at math or at reading people to add up those things. "Did you have something to do with us getting this job?"

She nodded. "Mrs. Coldwell began talking about wanting new cabinets maybe eighteen months ago, so anytime the subject came up, I suggested the shop you work for."

"Why?"

"I wanted to say hello in person."

"That was a lot to do just to say hello."

"That's a figure of speech. We've already said far more than that today, and I knew we would." She moved in closer. "I needed you to look in my eyes and see that I know what you did for me, Ray."

He didn't know what to say, but memories of that night came rushing back in. Darkness had surrounded them as they walked for miles and then sat on a curb. He continued to listen while she talked of the unbearable pain inside her. Then she took off running as if she could outrun the memories. When he tried to follow her, he tripped on his shoelaces and fell on his face. He jumped up, but after that, no matter how hard he tried, he couldn't catch up to her. One after another, street signs reflected car lights. Then tires squealed. Her body thudded against the shell of a car. She crumpled. And silence — utter, ugly silence — followed. He knelt, wanting to scream at God for how unfair life was. Instead, he bent and breathed life back into her as the driver phoned for an ambulance. No one Amish came to the scene, so no one recognized him. When the ambulance arrived, he gave the police the information to reach Teena's parents, and then he disappeared into the crowd and slid back into being nobody again.

Too confused to explain to Jolene what had taken place and too afraid of getting Teena in trouble, he'd never said a word to anyone about what had happened.

Who would believe he was capable of doing something so right it was almost heroic? At least to Teena.

She opened the small juice bottle. "I went from one hospital to another, spending months of time as I went through rehab. When I finally got out, I wasn't in a place to contact you, not until now."

She went outside, and he watched as she

took the drink to Mrs. Coldwell.

Josiah came into the room and eased the dolly to an upright position. "She seems nice."

Nice wasn't the right word. She was real. She'd once told him she was lost inside herself — the kind of thing that happens when a girl loses her twin.

Had she found herself? If so, how?

9

Jolene slid two more boxes of baked goods onto the shelf in the pastry buggy. Naomi had arrived about fifteen minutes ago, driving the rig Jolene used to deliver pastries to the bakeshop. It was designed to keep the items from breaking or being exposed to dirt, insects, and flying horsehair. But the stationary cases were shelved to carry pastry boxes, and that had made it impossible to use this rig to carry all the items and ingredients she'd needed to bring here before dawn.

Why was she trying this hard to help a man who clearly didn't want her here?

Lester's voice rumbled from the porch swing, where he sat talking with Hope and Tobias, and Jolene remembered why. She would do anything Lester needed. He'd been too good to her over the years, making it possible for her to stay in her home and giving her a room for painting. Oh, how she'd love to climb those steps and paint right now. Her skin still prickled with heat as she remembered Andy's abrupt departure from the kitchen more than an hour ago. He hadn't said a word after she told him that he needed help and she was all he had.

A longing to prove to him that she could be the help he needed had latched on to her heart as surely as the desire to paint. She wasn't backing down, and he could just deal with it.

Naomi swooshed open the screen door as she hurried from Lester's house, carrying more boxes of pastries. "Sorry I got here so late."

"It's not a problem." She and her sisters were doing all they could, and she refused to feel overly responsible for things that weren't in her power to fix. "Just let them know at the bakery that unless they send a driver for the pastries, they can expect to have them mid-morning for the next week or two." If she had to hire a driver, she would pay more than she made baking for the shop. The owners had cars, so they would need to step up and get the pastries to the store or accept that they would arrive late.

That wasn't a very gracious attitude. She hadn't told them of the situation with

Lester, and she should've done that yesterday. Truth was, at the moment she was simply in a foul mood.

Why did Andy have to scrub off all her hints of feeling smitten before she got a chance to enjoy the notion for a few days? He seemed completely determined to frustrate her. Couldn't he allow her to revive her waning hope that there might be a man out there somewhere she could fall for . . . eventually? It wasn't as if she was in a hurry, although she couldn't deny that the idea of finding love while she was still young enough to have at least one child did weigh on her. It wasn't a heavy weight. Actually, it'd only been a notion a couple of years ago, just a little thought that passed through her mind here and there. She imagined the once-flighty thought would come home to roost about the time she turned thirty-six or thirty-seven.

"Hey, Jo?" Naomi parked her feet on the gravel drive mere inches from Jolene's. "If it's okay that I'm running late, what's got you so agitated?"

Jolene glanced at the porch swing, noting how well Hope, Tobias, and Lester were getting along. Hope's mothering nature seemed in full force where Tobias was concerned. Jolene looped her arm through Naomi's, and they walked a few feet away from the others. Jolene was rarely sure where the line should be drawn between sister as parent and sister as friend. As a parent of sorts, she held back much of who she was from her siblings. Despite being only seven years younger, Naomi wasn't even a teen when their parents passed, and Jolene had needed to parent her through those difficult years. That mission had left little room for Jolene to share any secrets, but it seemed that today Naomi could read her too well and too easily. "I'm a little annoyed with Lester's houseguest." She patted Naomi's arm. "I imagine he's feeling the same toward me. But if nothing else, this will be an interesting summer."

Naomi squared her shoulders, ready to argue with Andy on Jolene's behalf. "What did he do?"

Jolene sighed. "Nothing, really. But I'm not caving, and I'm pretty sure we aren't going to make a very good team."

"Some men," Naomi huffed. But then her countenance changed, and joy reflected on her face. "Well, at least others of them totally make up for it."

Jolene's eyes met Naomi's, and they shared a silent moment as Jolene searched for and found assurance that Naomi's husband was every bit as good to her in the privacy of their home as he appeared to be when in public, and Jolene's frustrations melted.

God had given Jolene the privilege of helping raise her siblings, and He'd given the married ones excellent spouses. All her siblings were quite healthy and had jobs. Added to that, Jolene had more love in her heart for them than there were hours in a day to share it. Did she really want to mourn what she might never have when she'd already been given far, far more than she deserved?

"I'm afraid I'm just irritable." Jolene released her sister's arm, and they returned to the rig. "I can feel it in my emotions and hear it in my thoughts. When I finally got home last night, I should've gone to sleep rather than stay up reading." However, she had something to prove to Andy . . . if she could prove it.

"You gave up sleep to read?" Naomi raised her voice as she went to the front of the rig. "That just can't be true!"

Jolene chuckled. Maybe something she'd read would be useful today. She secured the latches on the stationary wooden container that held the pastry racks. "You are now ready to go."

Instead of climbing into the rig, Naomi returned to the back of it with Jolene. She held out a small pair of muck boots. "They're just hand-me-downs, and they're for boys, but they'll fit, and they have steel toes in case a horse stomps on your foot."

Where had her sister gotten these, and how much trouble had it been to get hold of them? She wouldn't ask. It would be like asking how much money someone spent on a gift. "Denki. They'll keep my feet dry and warm as we spend days washing horses."

"I'll be back in a couple of hours."

"Be sure to ask if they can pick up the pastries here for the rest of this week and maybe next week too. Surely we can find someone to work beside Andy by then."

"I will, and I'll ask around town if any teens want a summer job. Bye."

Naomi was too optimistic if she thought she could find an Amish boy sixteen or seventeen years old who didn't already have a job. It wasn't as if they had just gotten out of school for the summer. They had graduated a couple of years ago, and they had full-time jobs.

Anyone younger than that wouldn't be helpful in this situation, because Andy was correct about the dangers. Jolene had to concede that. As Naomi drove the rig onto the road, Jolene scurried up the porch stairs. She changed into the clothes that had shared an aromatic evening with a smelly horse. Ugh. Her dress and apron smelled more of hay and leather than of sweat from a horse. Would a wild horse appreciate a human that smelled like harnesses and saddles? Or like hay for that matter? It wasn't as if they could eat the clothes . . . she hoped.

Taking her horse-training book with her, she walked out on the porch and gave Hope and Tobias a dozen instructions and then hurried toward the corral. Andy had maneuvered three horses into three small round pens, and he seemed to be in the process of separating one more horse from the herd, probably to get it into the fourth and last small pen.

Andy glanced at her as if an insect had caught his attention for a moment. He then returned to his task as if she didn't exist.

Great. So maybe it wasn't going to be an interesting summer after all. She stayed back from the fences, watching. Her goal was to help, and since he'd realized she was here, it was up to him to say what he wanted her to do.

In Lester's younger days he trained horses, but after he broke his hip, he sold all but a few horses and never bought any more. Until right now she'd never given much thought to how well his place was set up for dealing with horses.

About a year after her folks died, he'd made a reluctant but generous offer to let the Keims live with him, but she'd declined. He'd been too unsure of his offer, and that alone was reason enough to turn him down. But also, by that point she was certain that she wanted to surround her siblings with as much of her folks' parenting influence as she could. Even though Lester had a good and giving nature and encouraged her at times like her own Daed had, Lester was a strong-willed man with opinions and ideals that would have prevented Jolene from creating the home she wanted for her siblings. She reached into the hidden pocket of her apron and felt the padlock key to the attic. Whatever else he was, Lester was definitely a good encourager and an excellent keeper of secrets.

After getting a beauty of a stallion extracted from the herd and in a pen, Andy moved to the center, coiled rope in one hand, and stood his ground. The horse charged toward him, threatening to run over him.

She felt the coarse, dark-green cover of

the book in her hand. Her heart had raced with anxiety last night while simply reading about the taming of wild horses. Right now her head spun as nervousness pulsed through her. She squeezed the book, wishing she could close her eyes tight and not watch this event. But Andy might look her way, and she refused to be seen with her eyes shut.

As the horse came at Andy, seemingly trying to get the man to yield his tiny bit of ground, Andy raised the coiled rope, keeping it looped tightly, and flung it toward the horse while he yelled several short-syllabled sounds. The horse ran the other way. Andy then put his arms by his side and waited. Was he humming?

The steed ran at him again, and he slapped the rope against the chaps that were over his pant leg. Then he hollered and flailed the rope against the horse's face and neck. But Andy didn't allow his feet to budge from his spot of ground. Andy and the horse were in a battle to see which one would rule the other.

The horse took off running to the other side of the pen, and Andy lowered his arms and waited. This time it was clear. He was humming. Her heart pounded. Would she have to enter the pen with Andy? Or worse, enter one by herself? Sweat beaded across her upper lip and trickled down her neck and chest on this cool May morning. How could he calmly stand there as a thousand-pound creature thundered toward him, wanting to knock him down and stomp him?

After a few more deliberate runs to try to knock Andy down, the horse ran toward him again, but this time Andy didn't raise his arms to defend himself. The horse stopped just short of knocking into him and retreated. How had Andy known the horse would stop short this time?

She understood what he was doing because she'd read a little about this method in her book. She opened it, looking for answers, hoping it would say a woman shouldn't take on such a task. Instead she found a page that said the size of the adult trainer made no difference. Whether a trainer weighed three hundred pounds or one hundred, he or she was no match for the power and strength of a horse. It was patience, knowledge, and agility that made the difference.

Hmm. Was that true? Patience wasn't an issue, and she was trying to gain knowledge as quickly as possible. But how agile was she? Her racing heart said she needed years of experience to enter a pen with a wild animal. The dance between man and horse continued for half an hour while she watched them and read more of the horse-training book. Finally its charges toward Andy weren't as fierce, and its retreats weren't lightning fast. His approach made sense. Apparently his first goal was to calm the horses, probably followed by getting the animals comfortable with his touch. They certainly couldn't bathe a horse that was completely terrified of touch. But since Andy was a trainer, she'd hoped he had some magic trick to calming and bathing them that wasn't listed in the book. His way was not magic. It was terrifying.

He'd singled out four horses. Could she make herself get in the center of one pen and let a horse stampede toward her in order to win its trust? Unlike the horse Andy was working with, a much smaller, white filly was in one of the pens. Determined to be of help, she squeezed the old book into her hidden pocket, went to the barn to get rope and a helmet, and returned. She put the helmet on over her prayer *Kapp* and wiggled her bun to a lower position so she could fasten the helmet in place.

Drawing a deep breath, she opened the gate where the filly was.

Andy gave two short, rather-soft whistles.

The filly picked up its frantic pacing. Jolene turned to see why Andy was whistling, and he shook his head at her and pointed for her to move away from the fence. Andy's horse raised its head and stomped its hoofs, seemingly protesting Andy's whistle. What would the horse have done had he yelled?

Did Andy think he could treat her like a child? Ignoring him, she eased into the ring and was thankful the filly ran the other way. Jolene closed the gate, her fingers trembling against the warm metal as she secured the latch.

10

The blue digital numbers on Mrs. Coldwell's stainless steel stove said it was 12:16. Teena had provided plenty of drinks along with trays of crackers, cheese, vegetables, and dip on the patio a couple of hours ago, so Ray wasn't hungry. Not for food anyway. But as the morning hours drained into the afternoon, he longed to talk to someone his age who didn't confuse him or make fun of him, someone who cared but wasn't obligated to, like Jolene and Josiah were.

Until today he had thought Teena might be mad about what he did after she was hit by the car. Thought she might resent him for breathing air into her lungs and telling the police how to reach her parents. He'd never considered she might be grateful for his help.

He often felt stupid, but maybe he wasn't as dumb as he felt. That was a thought he'd like to hold on to for more than a few fleeting moments.

"Pizza." Teena walked into the construction zone, held up five boxes, and retreated outside.

Josiah removed his tool belt, and they went into the workers' assigned bathroom. "I don't know about you, but I think this is bound to be better than another sack lunch."

It did sound good. "We don't eat sack lunches."

Josiah shrugged and washed his hands.

Ray stepped up to the sink next. "We do eat sack lunches, don't we? We just happen to carry them in a lunch pail."

"Exactly." Josiah finished drying his hands and passed the towel to Ray.

"Josiah," — Ray kept running the towel over his hands even though they were already dry — "do you ever want to talk to somebody at the same time you want to avoid them?"

"Ya. In all sorts of situations. When I first met Ruth, I wanted to spend every minute with her, but I was so nervous I dreaded it as much as I looked forward to it. Then there are times when I'm angry with someone I love, and I want to clear the air, yet I don't want to talk about it." Josiah put his hand on Ray's shoulder. "Trust me. If I had done as my nerves wanted, I wouldn't have pushed through and talked to Ruth." Josiah squeezed Ray's shoulder. "And look how well that turned out."

"Ya." Ray laughed. "Until she figures out you're a bozo."

"Don't go telling my wife my secrets." Josiah brushed dust off his shirt. "And if I buried my anger rather than talked to the one I'm upset with, I'd begin to love others and life less." Josiah smiled. "And, ya, I said some really stupid stuff to Ruth when I was nervous. She probably did too, but I was too nervous to notice. I don't think humans have found a way to avoid talking nonsense when they're anxious, but it's worth it."

Ray twisted the towel, considering his words.

Josiah tucked in his shirt a little better. Suspenders kept the pants up, but the waist was loose, and shirts regularly needed tucking again. "Are you going to keep torturing the towel, or are you going to talk to Teena?"

Ray wasn't sure. The towel was a known object, and he could predict exactly what it would do in various situations. People not so much. He put the towel on its peg and left the bathroom.

"Hey, Ray." Josiah fell into step with him. "If you're worried she might bite, don't be.

I know right where to take you to get a shot for rabies."

Ray focused on his brother's joke, aiming to form a clear response. "It's gut you know that. Because if she shows any signs of biting, I'll sic her on you."

Josiah roared with laughter. "Keep it up, and I'll tell her that you intend to sic her on me, and I won't mention my part of the conversation." Josiah stepped in front of Ray and faced him, balled his fist, and punched at Ray's stomach, stopping just short of hitting him. At the same time Josiah slapped his other hand against his chest, making a popping sound.

Ray doubled over as if he'd been punched. Teena walked in just in time to see Josiah "hit" Ray. She looked annoyed as she glanced from one brother to the other.

A sheepish look covered Josiah's face. "We were just playing. I didn't really hit him."

Teena looked doubtful.

"Tell her, Ray."

Ray gave a pained look while rubbing his belly. "I'll be okay. I'm used to it."

"Kumm." Teena motioned toward the door. "We'll eat at a table by ourselves." She went outside.

Ray grinned. "I win." And it just might be his best win ever.

Josiah laughed. "Ray, you have to tell her."

"Ya think?"

It'd been a lot of years since Ray had felt this good, had been this clearheaded. Was it because Teena reached out for friendship? If so, then maybe he should go out with Alvin, Urie, and James this Friday. Maybe that's what friends did — lift the heart and clear the mind.

He didn't know, because his only friends were his siblings, and that was good, but after today he wasn't sure it was enough.

Andy's heart thudded as fear and anger pulsed through him. "Jolene." He kept his tone soft while motioning for her to leave the pen.

Holding on to the gate, she barely glanced his way, pursed her lips, and stayed put.

Her behavior was so typical of a novice horseman, which was actually a contradiction of terms. She wasn't a horseman, and beginners tended to be overconfident. At least she was showing some caution by wearing a helmet and staying near the gate.

Keeping his voice calm and his eye on the horse he shared a pen with, he eased toward the fence that separated his pen from hers. "With your attention on the horse, open the gate and get out of there. Now, please, before the filly gets over being leery of you and charges."

Jolene looked his way, her eyes filled with emotion. He couldn't be sure whether it was anger or resolve, but it was clear she wasn't responding to his entreaties.

She released the gate. "Lester used to run a horse farm, and he thinks I can do it. I'm not letting him down." She took a few steps away from the fence.

The filly pranced back and forth at the far end of the pen. The horse's next move would be to charge. "Jolene." Andy rattled the fence, trying to get her attention. "Remove yourself. Now!" He gritted his teeth as he whispered as loud as he could. She eased to the middle of the ring and stood still, watching the filly and waiting.

His mouth was dry, and visions of climbing the fence and forcefully removing her flashed through his mind. Within the hour the horse would win the battle of wills with Jolene. He was sure of that. What could he do so that Jolene's loss didn't result in more than minor injuries to her?

He had no choice but to remain close to the fence that separated him from Jolene, ready to scale the railing and charge at her horse when the time came. With her head protected by the helmet, she should be safe from head trauma, and any gashes, bruises, or broken bones she sustained would heal . . . eventually.

Apparently Jolene was going to prove challenging at every turn. He found her beauty disarming, her responses to his disagreement with Lester refreshing, and her stubbornness terrifying.

The minutes ticked into an hour without her getting hurt, and Andy's heart rate slowed a bit. As the next hour waned, Andy moved away from the fence and to the center of the pen. He couldn't believe it when both of their horses were calm enough for them to begin working with the next two. When he moved pens, Jolene did too.

He refused to talk to her. If she was going to put herself in a high-risk position, he wouldn't encourage her. While working with the last two horses he'd corralled that morning, his stomach growled fiercely, reminding him it was well past lunchtime and they'd yet to take a break.

Six hours passed, and Jolene had yet to get hurt. He wasn't sure if he was more impressed or annoyed.

Despite being fiercely hungry and weary, he hesitated to leave, afraid to lose the momentum. The horses had begun to trust and bond with them. He didn't like thinking of the term *with them,* but as the hours ticked by, he'd had to accept Jolene was here to stay — at least for today.

The animals' positive responses to him and Jo were as fragile as her pastries, but it was a good start. Maybe he . . . *they* could get at least two horses washed today, all four if things went really well.

The process of building trust would take weeks for some, months for others. Some might not get past being flighty. But the first days with any traumatized horse were the most intense. The horses were having a new imprint branded into their psyches, and he didn't want to interrupt the work to eat.

He had started out glancing Jo's way every few seconds to make sure she was safe. But as his fears and frustrations eased, looking her way caused him to notice too many things about her — the way she faced her fears, the way she sang to the horses, the way her openhearted, responsive touch seemed to meet a skittish horse's need when it finally warmed up to her. She was intuitive about what to do for them and how; otherwise, the horses wouldn't be responding to her as well as they were. He also noticed that those boots threw her off balance, but she managed to stand her ground anyway. Those were the upsides, which were no upside at all, really — not if he intended to ignore the very things that appealed to him.

Maybe he needed to focus on her faults. Isn't that what people did when they didn't like someone? One fault was quite clear. And annoying. She kept glancing at that infernal book while working. It reminded him of people who texted while driving. If she kept studying it in the pens, she'd get plowed under and trampled. She had opened it and read little bits for hours, but he couldn't see the title. What was on those pages that meant so much during a time like this? Was it a romance novel where men acted as women wanted them to? If he had a novel in which women behaved as he wanted, the woman wouldn't ignore his telling her not to enter that round pen.

On the other hand, he was impressed by how successfully she had mirrored his efforts without getting hurt. He'd given her a few instructions, and she'd nodded. He wasn't sure who started out more nervous — her or the horses.

Good job, Andy. You managed to find one flaw before you caved.

The horse in the pen with her was at the moment reasonably calm and at her side, sniffing her and fleeing at the least little

141

thing. When he backed away, Jo flipped open her book and then walked toward the fence between her and Andy. It was her first time to approach him since he'd walked out of the kitchen that morning. "Andy, do you think . . ."

As if he were stuck in slow motion, he knew what was about to happen but couldn't get the words out fast enough. Did she have him tongue-tied? The horse crowded in behind her and lowered his head. "Jo, behind you."

But before his words registered with her, the horse butted her back, sending her sprawling across the dirt. He debated whether to rescue her or to stay put.

She was clueless about what she had just let happen. By allowing the horse to take her ground, she now had to prove herself to the animal. Again. The coiled rope she'd been holding had fallen out of her hand, but she continued to hold tightly to the book.

He sighed. A horseman would've kept the rope and released the book!

Andy eyed his horse, making sure it wasn't sneaking up behind him. If he rescued her, the only lesson the horse would take from today is that he could bully Jolene, and perhaps he'd think he could do the same to all humans of smaller stature with higher-pitched voices — meaning most women and all children. "Jo, get up. Now!" He waited a few seconds, but she didn't budge. "And do it while flailing your arms and yelling. You've got to make the horse back away from you."

Jolene shot him a look that said she didn't like the way he was talking to her, but she jumped up, blood and dirt on her forearms and the palms of her hands. She barely swung the book toward the horse, and she gave a pitiful yelp.

"Jolene Keim." Andy gritted his teeth, restraining himself from climbing into the pen and rescuing her. "You just let him bully you. Now you've got to regain your authority. Immediately. Go on the offensive and make him back down."

Pity for the animal was evident in her eyes as she glanced at Andy. "It's my fault."

"I fully agree, but that's not the point. Take back your domain before you do the animal more harm than good."

She glanced at the book clutched in her hand, threw it to the ground, and flailed her arms into the air, yelling. The horse stood its ground.

"Here." Andy tossed his coiled rope at her feet.

She picked it up, snapped it against her

leg, which had to hurt since she didn't have on chaps. She yelled, and the horse laid his ears back.

"Again, Jolene."

She did as he said but this time with real determination in her voice. The creature hesitated. Then twenty seconds later it took the first step back.

"Now move in until his body language says he yields to you, even if that means you make him flee."

Jolene did so, and when the horse moved to the far end of the pen, Andy took a deep breath, relieved. Jolene returned to the center of the pen and waited for the horse to approach again. Wild, penned horses want to be loved, but that is buried under their instinct to dominate.

The phone rang for the fourth time today, and for the fourth time Hope scurried across the yard to the phone shanty.

Andy climbed one rung of the fence that separated the two rings. If Jo was going to work beside him, she had to think about animals and the hierarchy of authority . . . *before* she got hurt. "You never turn your back on a wild horse. Maybe if you'd stop trying to read while working . . ."

Anger radiated from her as she glanced at the horse at the far end of the small pen.

She then turned to Andy, flailed her arms, and yelled, telling him in no uncertain terms to back off. It might be funny if he didn't fear for her safety and if she wasn't so furious with him.

He didn't have trouble getting along with people — men, women, and children of all ages. What was his problem with Jolene? He knew part of it. He was used to focusing on the horses, not worrying about the person in the pen next to him. Her inexperience in a pen with a wild horse had him jittery, and the horses he'd worked with today seemed to pick up on it, making his task of calming them harder. How was he supposed to focus on his work when he was worried about her safety?

However, for the first day as a volunteer on a job, she'd done really well. So why hadn't he been able to simply talk to her and share a few encouraging words?

She went to her book, picked it up, and brushed off the dust. "Are you okay, Jolene?" she asked herself. "I'm scraped and bruised, but I'll be fine. Denki," she answered. "I appreciate your efforts today," she mocked. "Denki," she said. "I hoped you would, because like it or not, we're stuck in this situation for a while."

That was the problem. They were trapped

in a situation that had him every bit as skittish and overwrought as the horses. "You shouldn't be out here. You can't read a book while in the pen with a wild horse."

The fire in her eyes equaled that of the angriest horses he'd worked with, only there was no fear lurking behind her fury. But she said nothing.

"Jolene!" Hope called. "Van's on the phone."

Her shoulders slumped slightly, and her face showed a different kind of dread now than when she'd entered the pen with a wild horse this morning. Since it was apparent she didn't want to talk to the blacksmith, should he offer to do it for her? He knew the answer. Definitely not. Any woman this determined to handle tough situations wouldn't appreciate being treated as if she needed to be rescued from a phone call.

"Be right there." She thrust the book toward him. "Maybe if you'd talked to me about what I needed to do, I wouldn't stand in a pen with a wild horse while reading!"

When he took the book from her, she walked off. It didn't have a title on the outside, but when he opened the thin, hardback book, he read the title page and realized what it was.

"Great," he mumbled as his face flushed

with guilt and embarrassment. The one flaw he'd found in her wasn't a flaw after all.

11

As Jolene walked toward the phone shanty, the blue sky and green grass seemed to fade into each other like watercolors on canvas. Her hands trembled, and her knees threatened to give way. Was it from the hurt Andy had inflicted or from a day of too much stress and too little food and water? She removed the helmet, causing her now-smashed prayer Kapp to almost come off too. Shoving the head covering back in place, she sat in the folding chair near the homemade desk in the shanty and took a shaky breath. The receiver of the black rotary phone lay on the desk, its short line leading to the old cradle. She put the helmet on the desk and picked up the phone but didn't speak. What should she say? "Hello"? "This is Jolene"? "Hi, Van"?

She cleared her throat. "Denki for returning my call."

"Sure, Jo. Anytime. You know that. Is there

something I can do for you?"

His kindness hit hard, and tears welled as the toll of the last two days threatened to pull her under. Who would've thought the most encouraging voice she'd come in contact with this week would belong to Van Beiler?

Of course he'd never been unkind, at least not in words or tone. About nine years ago she'd read a book called *The Five Love Languages,* and she'd found the love language for each of her siblings, as well as her own. She hungered for kind words and an encouraging tenor in someone's voice. Keep the gifts, hoard your time, don't be of any help, and withhold all hugs, but when you speak, do so with kind, reassuring words. Of all that had been taken from her when she lost her parents, she missed their spoken affirmations the most.

Her hands and arms were covered in dirt, bloody, and scratched up. But more than the physical discomfort, her feelings were hurt, and now she felt like the awkward, lonely girl she'd been after her parents died.

"Jo? You there?"

All she could manage was a nod, hoping the words would follow.

Andy came to the door of the phone shanty, and the pooled tears in her eyes spilled down her cheeks. Ignoring him, she took a deep breath. "Ya, I'm here." Her voice trembled, and she wanted to smack Andy for it.

"You okay?" The concern in Van's voice was frustrating. She had gone all this time standing on her own, and now she sounded like a weepy, brokenhearted girl again, just as she had the day he said his final good-bye.

Why had Andy come to the phone shanty? Whatever his reasons, he'd caught her as she fell apart, and he seemed as tied in place as a horse to a hitching post.

She covered the mouthpiece with her palm, wiped her cheeks with the back of her wrist, and drew several deep breaths before removing her hand. "I'm fine, Van. And you?" But her voice broke again, and she had to cover the mouthpiece and gasp for air. She had to face facts. She simply wasn't up to talking right now. "Actually . . . could I call you back in about fifteen minutes?"

"Sure. I'll wait right here for your call. You name what you need and when, and I'll do it, okay?"

No, it wasn't okay. Why did she have to be in this position of needing to ask him for a favor? "Denki." She hung up the phone and stared at it, trying to bite back more tears.

She refused to look at Andy. "What?" She sounded every bit as exasperated with him as she felt.

He set the book on the desk in front of her and brushed more dirt off of it. "I'm sorry."

His words made another wave of sappy emotions crash over her, but she kept herself in check, not so much as flinching.

He grabbed a folded chair that was leaning against the far wall, opened it, and sat. "You're untrained and working with rogue horses, and it scares me, but more than that, I've apparently become a crotchety old horse's rump."

Her throat seemed to close, and fresh tears threatened. "You really hurt my feelings."

"And there was no call for that and no excuse."

She finally looked at him. His tanned face had smudges of dirt, making him look rugged and handsome, but far more important, she saw sincere repentance in his eyes. She didn't want to imagine how ridiculous she looked with grimy clothes, a flat head covering, boy's boots, half-fallen hair, and dirt-stained cheeks smeared with tears. "Girls get their feelings hurt. Have you and Tobias been on your own so long you've forgotten?"

"No." His lone word was barely audible. He sighed, shaking his head. "I didn't forget. It seems as if I've just grown callous."

Fighting back more tears, she nodded and left the phone shanty. She went to the cast-iron water pump, removed the hand towel from it, and pulled and pushed the handle a few times until the water poured. She cupped her hands under it, pocketing water to wash her face. When the water stopped, Andy stepped forward and pumped it for her. She buried her face in a handful of water, grateful for a bit of reprieve from the emotional overload. Gaining a bit of composure once again, she scrubbed dirt and blood from her hands and arms with the hand towel, and then she walked to the shade of an oak and sat in a metal chair. Like Lester's phone, the lawn furniture was probably from the mid-1950s. How many lunches had she shared out here with the old man over the last several years? The view of the surrounding pastures with tame horses grazing was picturesque as the orange sphere eased toward the horizon. It made her wish she was free to go to the attic and pick up a paintbrush. She would start with the thickest one her Daed had given her, with its wooden handle covered

in beautiful, vibrant stains. Reaching deep into her hidden pocket, she touched the key, and a moment of feeling free to be herself brought a bit of peace.

Andy walked to where she sat, his face and arms dripping water. She dangled the towel on two fingers.

He took it and scrubbed his face. "Do you want time alone, or do you want to vent?"

"It's not just the yelling at me. Why did you stop talking and simply walk out on me this morning? Why not one kind or encouraging word while we worked?"

He shifted, staring into the distance. Was he at war with himself to answer her? "I stand by my assessment that the job is too dangerous for a novice. Why would I say anything that might encourage you to stay inside the ring?"

His demands for her to leave the ring were consistent with the following hours of hi silence. Could she fault a man for being tru to his beliefs? She took a shaky breath ar leaned back in the chair. "My meltdov wasn't all you. I arrived this morning w my emotions pushing and shoving r Sometimes all the little feelings and stre pile up until it's a mountain crashing dov

"Ya. It is, isn't it?" He sat beside he Lester's usual chair.

"I'm not leaving you to do this job by yourself."

He tapped the ends of his fingers together, looking heavenward and shaking his head. "Ya, that's pretty clear at this point."

"Can we do this?" She nodded toward the corrals to their far right.

"It'll be weeks of harder work than today, because we'll have to juggle taming with washing and shoeing, but I think we've already proved we can do it. The first horses should be ready to be washed late this afternoon. The question is, can we do it without you getting hurt?"

"You can teach me the safest ways to do the job, but" — she gestured toward the tame horse just on the other side of the fence — "pain and life go together like pastures and horses. Still, you could try to keep yourself from being the source of it."

"You don't pull any punches when it comes to saying what you're thinking or feeling, do you?"

In a lot of ways, she stayed quite hidden; she kept far more to herself than she spoke aloud. But with Andy it was different somehow. Since he was neither sibling nor church-district member, she found that surprisingly liberating. "If that's a problem, I can work on keeping more to myself."

He propped his forearms on his legs and stared at the ground between his feet. "It's unnerving." He shook his head, seeming as confused by his behavior today as she was. "But I like it . . . I think."

She chuckled. "Ya, that's how I feel too."

"Have you always been so direct?"

"Honestly, I'm not sure why I'm being so straight with you. I tend to keep a lot to myself. I have since I was nineteen and lost my parents. They were two of the most open people you could meet." Why had she begun this conversation?

He angled his head, and his brows furrowed as he looked up at her. "Jo . . . both parents?" The disbelief in his whisper sent chills over her. He sat upright, the ground no longer holding his interest. "I'd like to hear more."

"Our last moments together had been amazing — direct, open, and filled with such love and joy that I still call on those memories for strength and peace. If my life hadn't been redirected that day, maybe I would be more like they were. At least it seemed I was headed that way." She was supposed to have moved to a district that would allow her the freedom to pursue becoming an artist. Yet here she was, a woman who painted in an attic as if it were

155

a sin and doled out parental advice to younger siblings as if she had the benefits that came with age. "But it's good to know I'm capable of being open with you. Maybe that's because your uncle pushes me to be my real self whenever I'm here. So . . . can we manage to get along, or do you have a problem working with a woman?"

He looked unsure. "Lester told you of my . . . marital situation, right?"

"He didn't volunteer it, but I asked him about it this morning before breakfast."

He studied her. "It's not a problem?"

"Should it be?"

He shrugged. "I guess not." He leaned in. "Who raised Hope?"

"As the oldest with five younger siblings, I guess the answer is me. But I couldn't have done it without the help of the district. If it hadn't been for your uncle Lester, I'm not sure we would've managed to stay together. Three of my siblings are married now. I can't imagine what my life will be like when the other two marry, but I'm sure it will look to most as if I'm too heartbroken over Van to —"

"Van? You and he . . ."

"Ya. We were engaged when my parents died. The breakup wasn't his fault any more than it was mine. He wanted . . . *we* wanted to marry, but it was too much stress and responsibility. My heart and all my under-pinnings and perspectives were shattered, so I wasn't the same person he thought he was going to marry. Can't fault a guy for that. It was years before I could find one familiar piece of myself again."

"Hey." Hope's voice caused Jolene to turn. She and Tobias were coming across the yard, each holding a tray. "Lester said it was time to make you two eat."

Jolene's heart jumped. She'd forgotten that Van was waiting on her to call back. She stood. "What day and time do you want Van to be here?"

He looked up at her. "We can find another blacksmith, Jo."

"No need. Van is the answer we need, and I'm fine with it."

Andy remained in place, studying her. His blue eyes seemed to look beyond her disheveled outer and inner selves and see straight into the heart of who she was. And it dawned on her just how many years she'd missed the camaraderie that came with talking to a man who was about her age.

Losing the two men closest to her within the same year had left a hole inside her. Now she dared to hope Andy was the kind of man who could give her a long summer of good conversations that had nothing to do with bickering.

Her heart thundered much like the hoofs of a charging horse. Could they be on the brink of more than a good summer and a budding friendship?

12

It seemed odd for Jolene to be gone so much this week. Ray had eaten dinner with Josiah every evening since Monday. Yesterday when Ray told her he was going out with friends tonight, she'd asked who he'd be with, where he was going, and what time he expected to be home.

He'd told her two of the names, leaving out Van's brother. Then he told her that they were meeting at the cabinetry shop and would just ride around and hang out. He'd expected a lecture on how to behave, but she smiled, looking pleased. She'd said, "You'll follow your conscience and not your emotions, right?" He'd nodded, deciding not to tell her that when his emotions were riled, his conscience became stony silent.

As he walked toward town, he noted that Friday evenings had a different feel than any other night of the week. Sunday nights through Thursday nights, he dreaded going to work the next day. Every other Saturday night was okay because the next day wasn't a church meeting. But Friday nights? Those were his favorite, especially this one as he ambled toward the cabinetry shop to meet up with some guys. It felt so . . . cool.

First he'd reconnected with Teena and had even eaten lunch with her every day this week. Mrs. Coldwell had ordered expensive cabinets for her garage, so one day next week he'd get to see Teena again, which sounded like lots of fun.

Now he was going out with three people who weren't his siblings. Of course he'd feel a lot different if this was a setup and they were planning to make fun of him. But maybe it wasn't. He wasn't nearly as slow or awkward as he used to be. He'd made lots of progress, even in the last year — unless he got rattled. Then his thoughts became jumbled like piles of broken old cabinets during a demolition.

He saw a carriage waiting outside the cabinetry shop, and as he drew closer, he could see James in the driver's seat and Alvin next to him. Ray relaxed a bit, reminding himself that Van's brother was always nice to him. If James was in charge tonight, and usually the one driving the rig was the leader for the evening, then Ray didn't need to worry how the night would go.

Alvin got out of the carriage. "Hey, you're right on time."

If Ray was good at anything, he knew when to leave his house to reach the shop on time. Alvin stepped to the side, and Ray climbed into the backseat with Urie. Alvin had just gotten in and closed the door when Ray spotted a small cooler between Urie's feet.

Ray gestured toward it. "You forgot to take your lunchpail home."

Urie grinned. "No." He opened it. "I brought a few cold beers."

But Urie didn't bother to get any out. James talked about his workweek at the blacksmith shop, saying he wished he hadn't moved here to apprentice under Van. All he wanted to do was go home.

James drove out of town, and soon the horse was lumbering up a deserted dirt road. Urie passed James and Alvin each a beer. He then held out a beer to Ray.

Unease clutched Ray's gut. "Nee."

"Why not?" Urie thrust it toward him.

"I'm three years younger than you guys, so it's not legal for me."

Urie looked at the beer and then at Ray. "Legal age or not, and being in our *rumschpringe* aside, if our parents knew, we would

161

be in just as much trouble as you, ya know?"

James pulled off the dirt road and drove up a path, then brought the rig to a stop. "Leave him be."

Alvin stretched, taking a long sip of his beer. "We just drink one or two, no big deal. But if you don't want to, tell Urie to go drown in a river."

Visions of his parents drowning hit hard. James shoved Alvin's shoulder and shook his head at him.

"Oh." Alvin turned. "Sorry, Ray. I wasn't thinking."

Maybe James was a good influence on Urie and Alvin. Those two and others at school used to think that upsetting Ray was fun, and they were good at it. That was for sure. Then he'd bust one of them in the jaw or trip them or throw whatever was closest at their heads and get in trouble with the teacher and bishop. Jolene didn't like it when he acted out, but she stayed calm and aimed to help him figure out other ways to cope with the bullying. Maybe if James had gone to school with him instead of being in Ohio, Ray wouldn't have had such a tough time.

"Kumm on." James opened the door and grabbed his backpack. "Let's go."

Alvin got out.

"Is this it?" Ray followed Alvin, hearing dogs barking in the distance. "You guys drink some beer and wander through the woods."

Alvin stretched again. "Looks that way, don't it?" He took another sip of beer.

Urie brought the cooler with him, and they set off. Wherever the dogs were, they were barking furiously now, but they didn't seem to be coming after them.

They came to a campsite of some sort. There wasn't much here — some well-placed logs for sitting, a spot where they built fires, and a tarp covering, but he couldn't tell what was under it. James straddled a fallen log. Alvin sat on a stump and put the cooler on the ground beside him. Urie grabbed some fire-starter logs from under the tarp and tossed them onto a heap of old ashes. He struck a match and held it to the paper covering the starter log. Once it caught fire, he sat on the ground and finished his beer.

James pulled a brown bag out of his backpack and unloaded crackers, chips, candy, and a pack of cigarettes. "Help yourself." He took a deep breath. "It may not look like much, Ray, but it's our way of blowing off steam when we don't really have anywhere to go."

Ray eyed the beer before walking over and getting one. He twisted off the top, took a sip, and quickly spit it out. "Yuck."

The guys laughed.

Alvin lit a cigarette. "That was my reaction when I had my first beer. It might grow on you."

Ray held on to it and took a seat. The fire grew, sending sparks heavenward, as the dogs continued to bark. The guys talked about their workweek — what went wrong and who was to blame. They laughed about some of the things their bosses did, which in each of their cases was their uncle. James moaned about having to live in the carriage apartment on his brother's property. "Donna's such a pain sometimes, telling me what to do, and if I'm anywhere near, she's got a long list of stuff I need to get done. I have no idea how my brother stands it, but that's why I come out here." He gestured toward the fire.

Alvin tossed his cigarette onto the ground and stomped it. "Maybe he shoulda married Jolene instead."

James shook his head. "Van seems to love Donna. I just don't see why."

Urie had a stick in hand now, digging in the dirt. "Maybe sisters-in-law are a lot like sisters in that it's hard to imagine someone falling for them, only with sisters-in-law you don't have the bond you do with your sisters."

"Maybe." James nodded.

Ray had drunk about half a beer. He rubbed his head, feeling a little feather-brained. "My head is swimming."

The guys laughed. "After one beer?" Alvin asked.

Ray picked up the bottle and sloshed it about, peering through the dark-brown glass. "After half of one, I think."

"I guess it could do that if you're hungry or dehydrated."

Ray dumped out the rest and stood. "Where's that barking coming from?"

"Old Man Yoder's place." Alvin pointed. "It's about a fourth of a mile straight through the woods. He's got nobody but himself, and yet he keeps those poor dogs tied at the back of his yard year round — rain, snow, whatever. I've heard they're skin and bones."

"If he's as mean to those dogs as he is to people, maybe we should cut 'em loose. You know, set them free." Urie stood, peering in the direction of the dogs.

"Why?" James tossed a stick onto the fire. "So they can run off and starve or maybe get caught by the pound and put to sleep?"

"Well" — Urie shrugged — "then maybe we should rescue them."

Even with Ray's fuzziness, he thought Urie's idea sounded like a win-win situation. Ray hadn't ever owned a dog, and he could do for them what no one did for him — free them of Old Man Yoder's meanness. Ray pointed. "Straight that way?"

Alvin came to him and turned Ray's shoulders several notches to the right. "See that hint of yellow flickering. That's coming from the lanterns in his house."

Ray squinted. "Oh, ya." He could catch a glimpse of them when the branches swayed in the breeze.

"Ray, sit." James motioned to the log. "You can't steal the man's dogs."

"Maybe *you* can't."

The other two guys hissed and laughed at James for being a wimp.

Ray started toward the lantern light.

"Ray, wait." James joined him. "Don't do it, man. It's not worth it."

"Mistreating animals is against the law, ain't it?" He looked from one boy to another. "I work with the man. If he's that mean when other people are looking, just imagine what he's like to those poor dogs." He waited, and one by one the guys nodded.

166

James grabbed a package of cookies and held it out. "You'll need to make friends with them first. If they've been chained their whole lives, they're likely to be mean." He motioned. "Kumm on. We'll help you."

Ray grinned. These guys hadn't tricked him. Tonight *was* fun.

Urie led the way. "What'll you tell Jolene?"

Ray hadn't thought about that part.

"You can tell her that the dogs needed adopting and no one but you is willing to do it, which is true, isn't it?" James asked.

"Ya." That was good thinking.

Alvin followed closely behind. "Just convince her that it will be good for you to learn to take responsibility for them. She'll go for it. Mamms like that kind of thinking."

"You'll have to keep them sort of hidden somehow."

"I'll let them stay inside. Think they're housebroken?"

"No idea. But you'll know soon enough."

Despite feeling a little woozy, Ray was excited. Not just about the dogs, but also because he'd finally made some friends.

13

With a lead line in hand, Andy tromped through the woods, following the others as the black stallion he'd been working with walked beside him. He'd protested this picnic outing. All he'd wanted to do was give two of the horses they'd been working with a walk through pastures and woods, but he'd been overruled. Even Lester, who'd stayed at home, had sided with Jolene, Hope, and Tobias. They trod in silence, leaves and twigs crunching under their feet, rays of light streaming through the freshly sprouted spring leaves. Birds flitted and sang loudly, but the goal of the humans was to avoid spooking the formerly wild horses. Tobias and Hope were riding Lester's personal horses bareback, enjoying being included in this mission. Jo was directly ahead of him, leading the white filly she first worked with eight days ago.

Had he known her only nine days?

The fight between Jolene and Andy on Tuesday of last week had cleared the air and changed everything between them. Some of it was for the better. Some was for the worse.

The better part was that they got along. He had dropped his armor, or maybe she'd ripped it from him. He wasn't quite clear which had happened. In trying to be so guarded, he'd only managed to be difficult and rude to Jolene . . . until she came unglued with him. And she'd been right to do so, but it had made him go from a horse's rump to an unarmed, vulnerable human in less than a day.

She had unique qualities, like her quiet power over her will — from unselfishly choosing to raise her family to befriending Lester, a person no one found easy to care for. But based on his limited knowledge, she seemed to have areas where the ground had been stolen out from under her, and she hadn't taken it back. If he could do one thing for her this summer, he'd like to help her regain every inch of ground possible. Taking back the ground stolen during a battle or tragedy strengthened and encouraged the person. It made people ready to step into new territory in the future and claim that too. In his opinion if anyone

169

deserved to regain what had been stolen, it was Jolene.

They entered the clearing Hope had talked about over breakfast. Lester had cleared this area more than a decade ago, and he paid someone to take a swing blade to it at least once every spring. It had some outdoor furniture — an old side table and several chairs covered in pollen. Around the outer edge were a few half-filled bird feeders, and in the center was a small firepit. The cleared ground led to the banks of a creek. One of the huge oaks had a limb overhanging the water with a tire swing attached to it by a rope. The elderly man had some strange ways about him, but this picnic area might be the weirdest thing Andy had discovered yet.

"Daed, look." Tobias pointed at a fallen tree that lay across the water, bridging the two banks of the creek. "Can me and Hope eat our lunch there?" He kept his voice soft around the skittish horses.

"Ya, can we?" Hope's eyes were filled with almost as much excitement as when she talked about the dogs Ray had brought home and Jolene had agreed to keep.

Jolene turned to Andy, distress burning in her sapphire eyes. "We don't go near the creek. The dry land on the bluff over the creek is a haven for wildlife, and we'll see a lot while here. Even deer come to get a drink, but . . ."

Had neither she nor her siblings gone into a creek since her folks died?

"It's called adventurous eating." Andy wasn't giving in to her fears that easily. "Can you handle it?"

She stared at the creek. It had a lazy current and was only a few feet deep, but what did she see — her parents drowning? He waited. He would give her whatever time she needed to work past her anxieties, but for her sake he wasn't yielding to them unless necessary.

Since their argument, he'd pitched in whenever he could. As determined as she was to help Lester, it meant she currently had a full-time job to add to her other responsibilities. So they had spent dark, cool mornings unloading her wagon, and then he helped her and Hope in the kitchen. He was, after all, one of the handiest of men in the kitchen. If he hadn't become a decent cook, Tobias would've gone hungry too many times, even with Andy's mother bringing dishes a few times a week.

He and Jolene spent long, sunny days training and washing the horses. After sunset, when dinner and the dishes were done and they were too weary to work anymore, they spent breezy evenings with Lester, Hope, and Tobias. They'd sit in lawn chairs near the corral as Jolene read aloud by lantern light, entertaining the listeners and helping the horses continue to get comfortable with humans. All the while Andy and Jolene were getting to know each other.

Those things led straight to the worst part of their getting along — they were too good at it. But he had little choice. There was no hiding from the likes of Jo, and she seemed to need him to talk to — a man she hadn't helped raise and didn't feel responsible for molding his character or preparing him for the world ahead. Perhaps she needed to talk to someone who knew a similar heartache to the kind she'd had with Van. They'd both been left behind while their loved one moved on. He wasn't sure about that part because they hadn't discussed it. But most of all, she seemed to want someone she could be herself with — not the guarded, parental Jolene or the breadwinning, I-can-do-it Jolene but the one who'd given up marriage to a man she loved in order to hold a family together. And now her siblings were leaving, two in the last eight months, to begin lives of their own.

Jo told him she'd walked the floors for years, praying each one would grow up whole enough to be happy and independent and whole enough to be a strength to a spouse for the rest of their days. Still, their leaving brought up thoughts and emotions that needed to go somewhere.

Wisdom said he shouldn't allow himself to be that place, so he aimed to guard his heart and hers while being a friend. She finally pulled her eyes from the silky current and rubbed her palms together. "I can hardly breathe. Why can't coming to enjoy the wildlife be enough?"

"It's not that deep. If they fall, they just need to stand up."

She eased a few steps toward the bank, studying the water, but she didn't seem convinced. Her breathing was in short spurts now.

"Jo, I can rescue them if need be."

"Both simultaneously?"

"Absolutely. I promise."

Her sapphire eyes locked on his, searching him and herself to know if she trusted him that much. She gave a reluctant nod, and Hope squealed, apparently aware of the conversation she couldn't overhear.

Andy motioned toward a small tree. "Be sure to secure your horses. And let Tobias test the fallen tree first so he can warn you which direction it will wobble as you walk it and where it's slick, okay?"

"Sure." Hope laughed. "This *is* adventurous eating."

Tobias and Hope tied their horses, and Andy knew Jolene wasn't going to budge until the two explorers reached their designated spots and were sitting.

"You know" — Andy studied the hoofs of the horse Hope had ridden — "I think Lester may need his horse shod too."

Van had arrived at Lester's last Friday, giving Jolene and Andy whatever they needed of his time. Andy asked for a couple of hours each day, because they couldn't shoe horses that weren't calm, and he and Jolene couldn't calm horses without spending most of each day working with them individually.

"You should mention it to him. He'll take them into Scarsboro."

"That's ridiculous, especially with Van coming to the farm daily right now."

That familiar resignation entered her eyes when speaking of Van, but she didn't take her focus off Hope as her little sister tried to find her balance on the fallen tree. "You can talk to Lester about it if you want."

When he and Van worked as a team to

shoe the horses, Jolene disappeared. Van was deeply respectful of Jolene, but she didn't seem to notice. Around Van, she was quiet, speaking only when spoken to. It was as if she became someone else. "Have you and Van talked since the breakup?"

Andy wanted to understand her, what made her tick . . . and what caused her to skip a beat. Van definitely caused her to skip a beat.

"Sure." She tensed, watching Hope. Jolene angled her head and fisted her hands as if helping Hope keep her balance. "When necessary."

"That's all?"

"We're in the same church district and attend the same meetings, so I have to interact with him and his wife, and I'm very careful to be kind. When I have to work beside his wife serving meals or what have you, I'm always polite. What else do I need to do?"

"Not for them. For you. It's been a decade, Jolene, and yet you still aren't able to be yourself when he's around."

"I'm not around him much, so it doesn't matter."

"I would agree except you disappear as often as possible when he's around. When he speaks to you, even just to say hello, your shoulders stiffen, and your hands draw into fists — every time."

She shrugged, still focusing on Hope. "I hadn't noticed."

"Are you afraid of him?"

"Van? No way. He just . . ." She shrugged again. "It doesn't matter."

Maybe it didn't. He had no interest in making a mountain out of a molehill, but the more they talked, the more clearly he saw a pattern — avoidance. A phone call drew her parents away from home that night, so she didn't own a phone. A raging creek stole her parents, so she viewed it only from afar. He didn't know exactly what Van had done, but the issue went deeper than just the breakup, because that was her decision . . . sort of. Something about Van caused her to fist her hands before going into hiding whenever he was near.

If Andy could, he would leave at the end of summer having given her the gift of freedom — freedom to wade in creeks, own a phone again, and hold a conversation with Van without needing to flee.

"I'm glad you like Van." She tilted her head, watching Hope's steps. "It doesn't surprise me that you do, but the relationship works fine as is."

What? "This has nothing to do with whether I like him or not. How do you feel about him?"

Disgust flickered through her eyes. "I'm not in love with him if that's what you mean."

"Okay." He didn't think she was. "That should make dealing with whatever is bothering you easier to figure out and fix."

She raised an eyebrow, stone faced. "Nothing needs to be fixed."

"If you say so . . ." Without releasing the lead line, Andy walked to a chair, removed his backpack, and set it in the seat.

Hope paused in her walk toward the center of the log, turned, and waved at Jolene. Jo waved back. "Let's make the topic of Van off-limits, please."

Andy guessed that was fair. He certainly didn't want to talk about Eva.

Jolene took a deep breath when Hope and Tobias finally sat on the log. The children put their backpacks beside them and began getting out their food.

With Hope and Tobias settled, Andy eyed the hitching post on the far side of the clearing. Two weathered round posts held up a third horizontal one. He went to it and shook it. He'd seen better. It was plenty steady for tame horses. Of course a stick on the ground would work for a trained horse. But if his and Jolene's horses were startled, would the animals bolt with the hitching post in tow?

Jolene tied her lead. "You're okay with children perched on a log over rushing water, but you're worried about horses tied to a hitching post?"

He smacked the side of his neck, ridding it of a mosquito. "The log-and-creek situation is predictable. The horses aren't."

"Ah. Well, just so you know, if a fish flops, making an unexpected splash, I won't respond in a predictable manner." The lilt in her voice indicated her amusement.

"Has anyone ever told you that you're a little annoying?" He couldn't keep from smiling as he teased her. There was no way of knowing what she'd say back to him.

"Nope. Not one person has used the word *little* with the phrase *you're annoying.*"

He suppressed his laughter while tying his horse next to hers. "Imagine that." But from his ten days in Winter Valley, he'd come to realize that Jolene was greatly esteemed. Lester said that even those who'd disagreed with a girl being the head of a household respected her nerve and sacrifice. So Andy doubted anyone had told her she was annoying.

She pulled a handful of baby carrots out of her backpack to reward the horses.

He swiped leaves off a chair and sat.

The one exception to their work routine had been Sunday. The Keims weren't in the same church district as Lester, and Jolene's district had a church meeting. Late that evening Jolene, her family, and Preacher Glen had come to Lester's, prepared a meal, and stayed until bedtime. It'd been enjoyable to watch Jolene interact with her siblings, their spouses, and her two-year-old nephew.

But Andy knew only one reason why the widower preacher would come with them. He was interested in Jolene. It seemed to Andy that Glen could be a good match for her, but Jo's body language didn't indicate any interest in him. Lester said the man was only doing his duty as a preacher by coming for a visit with her and her family, making sure everything with Andy and the horses was above reproach. Andy appreciated any checks on appropriateness. He didn't want to do something that might lead to rumors about Jolene and him.

Jolene returned to her backpack, scrubbed her hands with disinfectant, and pulled out a gold hand towel. She brushed the towel across the back of the chair, working her way toward the seat.

He interlaced his fingers and put them

behind his neck. "If you had washed the horses like that, the first one would still be filthy. Besides, waving that towel as if it were a wand, you look like one of those fairies in that book you were reading to Tobias and Hope the other evening."

She dangled it against his face. He sputtered and pulled it from her hand.

"Hey." She tugged on it. "Let go. I wasn't finished. My chair is still covered in debris."

He leaned forward and made one swipe across the seat. "There. Now sit."

She sat and pulled a sandwich out of her backpack. "Here, put a sandwich in it."

He took it. "I think I will. Denki."

A sense of something unfamiliar tugged at him. Was it an awareness that they were becoming a little too comfortable around each other?

As a grass widower, he'd wrangled with wayward desires. Who wouldn't when left with such loneliness? Women were attractive and interesting, but he hadn't been drawn to anyone in particular. And he had no interest in that changing. He might not look it or feel it, but he was married, and right now Jolene was like nectar to a bee. The pull scared him.

He knew what he needed to do. He needed to begin praying for Jolene, asking God to bring her a man she could fall in love with and have the family she'd told him she longed for.

She pulled another sandwich from her backpack.

Andy noticed a bright-red male cardinal on the bird feeder and a female sitting on the limb above it. The male was taking food to the female, one seed at a time. This must be the mating ritual Jolene had told him about. He pointed to the birds.

She watched them, smiling. "They pair for life, and he feeds her seeds every spring before they mate. He'll bring the supplies for the nest, and she'll build it while he watches. Some books state that when they have young, he'll feed her or sit on the nest while she eats."

Jo obviously liked the idea of romance, and seeing the cardinals like this, he understood why. Lifetime mates, one feeding the other every spring as they built a new nest together. And each year they raised a brood together until one mate died. It was impressive.

She stood, catching a better view of the children. "What are they doing?"

Andy glanced. "Feeding the bread from their sandwiches to the fish."

"Oh." She sat. "Did I tell you that Ray

plans on going out with his friends again this Friday?"

"You didn't, but he must've had a good time last weekend."

"Clearly. I told him he cannot return with any more stray animals. But why doesn't he want to talk about who he's been with?"

"He's eighteen and probably looking for a little independence. Did you tell your folks the name of everyone you spent time with?"

"Absolutely. I had nothing to hide." She sighed. "Maybe if I'd been a little more defiant, losing them wouldn't have been like losing myself."

"I doubt anything would've eased that time. My guess is even those who are estranged from their parents grieve deeply when they die, only for different reasons than you grieved." Did Eva miss Tobias? When she died and Tobias was informed of it, whether his son was a young man with children or a grandfather, would he grieve for her, for all they never had?

"After all this time, I'm not sure how much of myself I've gotten back."

"It's understandable, Jo. You lost a lot in less than a year, and few people could've done half as well as you have. Most would be a wreck." This was a perfect opening. Should he take it or not? "But you did lose some ground, and you, of all the people I know, deserve to regain it."

She leaned in, smiling. "I like the way you see me." Looking pleased and beautiful, she sat back. "So what is missing from my life that bothers you?"

"Enjoyment of simple things, starting with the creek." He motioned from the chairs to the creek, indicating the distance from one to the other. "You and Lester come here, but you've never gone down the bank or sat on the log?"

"I can't swim."

"You could at least wade in it or sit on the log and feed the fish or put a chair on the bank and read a book while letting the water rush over your feet."

She watched the creek. "You honestly think something like that matters?"

"I do. None of us can get back every piece that's been stolen from us, but we should retrieve as much as possible. Get a phone. Play in the creek. Clear the air with Van."

"You seem to have me pegged." She pulled an apple from her backpack and held it out to him.

"Am I out of line?" He reached for it.

She pulled it back, just out of his reach. "No. Not as long as I get an invitation to spend ten days at your place and discover all your weaknesses."

It was an invitation he could never give. Surely she knew that and was just teasing. "I'm sure I have plenty of weak areas I'm not aware of." He hoped the young woman sitting next to him wouldn't become one of them.

"Jolene," Hope whispered loudly, grinning. "Look." She pointed down the path that led to the clearing and waved.

They couldn't see through the underbrush of the woods, so Jo got up and walked to the start of the path. She put her finger over her lips, telling whoever it was not to yell, and then she waved before returning to her chair. "It's Glen."

Glen? Immediately he felt concerned for Jolene. He shouldn't have caved and agreed to this picnic. Working beside Jolene at the farm was already pushing the boundaries, but for a married man to go for a picnic beside a creek with a single woman was careless on his part.

Jolene pulled a water bottle from her backpack and opened it. "I had no idea he was off work today."

"What does he do?"

"Renovations of old but fine hotels. He came to this spot a few Saturdays last fall with his boys, but it seems strange he'd come here on a workday, doesn't it?"

"Not strange at all." Andy figured the man had numerous stakes in this situation, starting with his job as a preacher to protect Jolene's reputation. Most of all, he apparently desired to protect his interest in Jo. Had the two gone out already? She hadn't mentioned it.

The crunching of leaves grew louder until Glen came into view and stopped at the edge of the clearing. A little boy about five was holding his hand, and another boy about four sat on his shoulders. Both were jabbering to Jolene and waving. Glen's straw hat was in his free hand. Andy knew from the years of Tobias riding on his shoulders that a man could not wear a broadbrim with a little one on his shoulders. Glen was lanky with a little gray edging in his black hair and beard. The other thing Andy had noticed was that he had kind eyes, especially when talking to Jolene.

Jo smiled and went to Glen, speaking in Pennsylvania Dutch to the little ones. "This is a surprise."

"Ya." Glen glanced to Andy. "I was going by Lester's and decided to drop in to see if I could lend a hand. He said you were out here." He removed his son from his shoulders. Both boys headed straight for the old firepit. They started gathering sticks and stones and tossing them into the pit.

"I have graham crackers and water if they're hungry," Jolene offered Glen.

"They would like that, Jolene. Denki."

While she grabbed the crackers from her backpack and returned to the children, Glen meandered to the chair next to Andy. The boys asked to feed the fish, but Jolene talked them into crumbling the crackers and spreading them on the ground for the birds.

Glen leaned back. "I didn't know who you were when you arrived, but I do now."

Andy nodded. Maybe Glen had asked Lester, or maybe he'd called Andy's bishop to talk, one minister to another. That was common, but however he'd learned about Andy, he now had something pressing on his mind.

"I need to ask you something, Andy." Glen propped an ankle on his knee. "It's not an easy thing to ask, but it'd be much worse to have to approach Jolene."

Andy figured he was here for a specific purpose. "Sure. Ask anything." It was the preacher's job to look out for those in his flock.

Glen watched Jolene with his sons. "She's a remarkable young woman. Smart. Gutsy. And sweet." He shifted. "It seems to me that she's incredibly innocent about certain things. Would you say that's right?"

Glen had known Jolene her whole life, so he should know the answer to his question. "That's my impression, ya."

He pursed his lips, nodding. "Since we never shave our beards once we're married, and grass widowers are such a rarity, I was wondering if it's clear to her that you're married."

"Ya, of course it is. I asked her about it."

Relief seemed to ease through Glen. "That's good. She wouldn't spend this kind of time around a married man she was attracted to. Your bishop assured me that up to this point you've been a man above reproach, so I trust you will continue in that same manner."

"I'm trusting that I will, ya." Andy could control his actions, but where Jolene was concerned, he sensed that his emotions wanted to branch out further than a married man could allow.

14

Ray helped move cabinets onto the truck while Chad sat in the driver's seat, waiting to take him and Josiah to Mrs. Coldwell's place. All the work was done at the Coldwell place except for installing the cabinets in the garage, which wouldn't take more than a day, so this would be Ray's last chance to see Teena for a while. "Josiah?" They edged the tall cabinet into the truck and set it upright.

"Ya?" Josiah was a little out of breath.

"You sure I have enough money to hire a driver to take me to visit Teena?"

Josiah dusted his hands together. "You need to think about that question for a bit." He headed to the loading dock to get more cabinets.

Ray followed. Did he have enough money saved to hire a driver? More than half of everything he earned, which according to Old Man Yoder wasn't much, went to help

Jolene pay bills. But for the last two years, he'd saved the rest, almost every penny.

After their folks died, Jolene and Josiah worked really hard to keep bills paid, including those for Ray's physical therapy. Plenty of good Amish folks gave money on a regular basis too. Maybe that's why he believed in saving.

But his need to save probably had more to do with a recurring dream in which he desperately needed food but couldn't afford to pay for it, and no one would loan him the money. Each time, terror gripped him as he handed over all the cash he had, and the person behind the cash register said he was two pennies short. In the dream no one was allowed to loan him the money, and he couldn't take a single item off his tray. Either he could afford every item, or he had to do without.

When Ray woke from that dream, he was in a pool of sweat, and his heart pounded like mad. So in the real world, after Ray gave Jolene a portion of his paycheck to help with bills, he put the rest in the bank, hoping if he was ever caught in a similar real-life situation, he would be prepared.

But he could spare enough to hire a driver to visit Teena. What was he thinking? Embarrassment burned inside his chest and climbed up his neck. He was slow and scattered on a bad day or when he was upset, but he wasn't naive. Teena wasn't looking for someone like him to be a boyfriend. It was enough that she wanted to be his friend.

Josiah said they could take an extra-long lunch break today. Today would have to be enough . . . unless Teena asked him to visit her. That would make a huge difference. He smiled to himself. Today was going to be a good —

"Ray!" Old Man Yoder's voice echoed from somewhere inside the shop.

Why did Uncle Calvin rely on someone like Yoder to be his right-hand man? Yoder was a screamer whenever Calvin was out of the shop for the day. Ray rolled his eyes, but Yoder's anger didn't shake him like usual. Ray had helped Josiah do a really good job at Mrs. Coldwell's, and he had Teena, Alvin, Urie, and James as friends now. Oh, and he had the man's dogs. Is that why Yoder's screaming didn't bother Ray today? He stood on the platform of the loading dock. "Out here."

Yoder busted through the swinging doors of the shop, a clipboard in one hand and a small plastic bag in the other. "You put the wrong hardware on the cabinets for the McClains' place, and we're supposed to deliver them this afternoon!"

Josiah stepped forward. "We'll get it straight. It's not that big a deal."

"*He* will get it straight. You're heading to the Coldwell place. Take another worker with you."

Ray jolted. "I need to go to the Coldwell place with Josiah."

"And I needed you to follow a simple set of instructions. All you have to do is read the numbers on the order sheet and compare them to the numbers on the boxes of hardware *before* installing the hardware!"

"I did. I triple-checked the numbers."

"And now you can redo the work because you did it wrong. It'll take all day. Josiah goes. Ray stays." He pointed his finger in Ray's face. "And try not to be useless without your brother here."

Josiah raised his voice and snatched the order sheet from Yoder, saying something to the man, but Ray couldn't catch it. The world became blurry, fragmented moments. This felt worse than his money dreams. It was as if he was a child again, injured from being struck by lightning, lying there afraid and too weak to move while his mother was outside his room whispering mean things about him. The familiar sense of self-hatred and powerlessness returned.

"Ray." Josiah snapped his fingers in front of Ray's face.

Yoder was gone, and other workers were now outside on the platform, staring at him, thinking the same thing Yoder did — that Ray was useless.

Ray shook himself free of his thoughts, but something didn't let him loose. "What?"

"I went inside and checked. Yoder's right about the hardware, so we'll just do as he says, okay?"

Ray fought not to march into the truck and kick in the doors on the cabinets. "Why are you trying to reason with him?"

His brother shrugged. "What do you want me to do? I'm not sure what happened, but a mistake was made. It's not a big deal, but it has to be fixed."

"What about Yoder? I'm supposed to let him treat me like this?"

"We work here because of Uncle Calvin's generosity, Ray."

Ray's anger stopped cold as disbelief took over. *They* didn't work here because of Uncle Calvin's generosity. *Ray* worked here because of that. Josiah was good at the job, and he'd worked here for ten years. Ray wondered why Josiah hadn't been moved up to a supervisor yet.

Yoder usually made Ray feel broken inside, but something in him was different this time. His thoughts weren't scrambled, and he didn't wish the roof would collapse on him. An idea came to him, and he felt calm, methodical. It was time Yoder experienced the feeling of being shattered inside. But he couldn't be impulsive, not this time.

"Okay." Ray lowered his voice, feeling something new — a sense of power. "I'll stay. By the time you're back, I'll have everything fixed."

Josiah's eyes narrowed. "You're okay with this?"

"Ya, I get it."

"You're sure?"

"Ya. I messed this up, and I'll fix it." He'd fix Yoder too but not right this minute. Ray went to the set of cabinets and began removing the hardware. Josiah left, and all the men but one returned to their posts. Wilmer didn't say a word when he entered the small room where hardware was added to the cabinets. He simply started working beside Ray.

Ray's mind never felt so clear, so sure of what had to be done. But he needed to finish this job first. When lunchtime came, Wilmer and all the other men scattered — some to the small kitchen in the shop, some to the bakery or nearby diner. But Ray kept working. He didn't need food. He needed to be done. Wilmer returned, and by three they had all the right hardware in place.

Wilmer stepped to the door of the small hardware room. "Yoder."

The old man entered, clipboard in hand as he began his inspection. "We'll have to discount the cabinets." He ran his hand over the inside of a door. "I can see where the compound was added to fill in the holes."

The holes made for the first set of hardware didn't exactly match the holes needed for the second set. But Ray and Wilmer had added compound, sanded it, and stained it. The spots were hardly noticeable, and the holes for the knobs were exactly the same.

Yoder frowned. "They'll need to stay here to dry, so we can't deliver them on time, and, like I said, we'll have to give the Mc-Clains a discount. If they don't take it, we'll have to build new doors." He sighed. "All of which is coming out of your pay, Ray, not the shop's."

Wilmer shook his head. "His sister needs —"

"I don't care what his sister needs! You stay out of this, Wilmer. Everybody in this shop mollycoddles him, and those days are over!" Yoder turned to Ray. "You're useless, Ray! If I could, I'd get the money from your account. But your uncle will take the hit, which affects my bonuses, and I'm sick of it!" He sighed. "Just absolutely useless."

Ray's heart pounded so hard he thought he might pass out, and why did it seem as if he was looking through a keyhole? He could hear his mother's whispers again: *He's worse than useless; he's a burden.* "So can I go now?" Ray fought to keep his voice low. "My lunch was in the truck with Josiah, and I'd like to go home to eat."

"I guess," Yoder mumbled. "At least that way you can't cause any more damage."

Hatred and anger burned as Ray stormed out the door. His blood pulsed in his ears as he ran down the street, tears blinding him. It wasn't fair! Why did he have to struggle so?

He strode past Beiler's Blacksmith Shop and then by the bakery. James came out of a sandwich shop, carrying something in each hand. "Hey, Ray."

Ray ignored him and kept going.

James hurried after him. "What's going on?"

"Yoder, that's what!"

"Did he find out about his dogs?"

"No. He made me miss seeing Teena on our last day to work there and called me names in front of everyone!"

"So where are you going?"

"To break a few windows. Maybe then he'll know what it feels like for someone to shatter his insides." His thoughts were becoming fractured again. He could hear it in his words. Ray spotted an empty buggy, and an idea popped into his head. "You won't tell, right?"

"I guess not, but, Ray, this is different than taking the man's mistreated dogs."

Ray stepped forward. "Are you my friend or not?"

"Well, ya, I want to be, but . . ."

Ray turned, ran to the buggy, and climbed in. The ride to Yoder's place was a blur, taking forever and yet no time at all. As soon as he reached the man's driveway, he jumped out and began searching for rocks. He found not only rocks but a few bricks lying around. He looked at the house and at the huge plate-glass window, probably the one in his living room. Ray aimed and flung a brick with all his might. It went straight through, making a hole and shattering the glass around it. Relief raced through him. He stood straight, feeling pretty darn good. He grabbed a rock with each hand this time and threw one at a set of windows.

"Ray." A man's gentle voice called to him. "Kumm now. Put the rock down."

Ray turned. Another buggy was parked behind the one he'd taken. Was that James inside it? Van strode toward him, nodding his head and looking friendly. "I get what you're doing, and you have a right to be angry. I'm mad too, but this could land you in jail."

Feeling defiant, Ray picked up another rock.

"Kumm on, Ray. Don't make the situation any worse."

"Well, I've already started. I might as well make it worth it!"

Van put his hand on Ray's shoulder. "Drop the rocks and let's leave now. I'll make it right with Yoder."

"You can't tell him!"

"He's going to know, Ray. How long do you think it'll take the police to put together that you stole his dogs, took someone's rig, and vandalized his home? A day? Maybe two? I bet you have his dogs at your house, don't you?"

Ray nodded.

"You don't want Jolene to get in trouble for that, do you?"

"What? No."

"You took my brother-in-law's rig, so I can make that right with him easily enough. But do you know what it'll do to your sister if she learns the rest of what you've done?"

"I . . . I didn't think . . ." The idea of Jolene being angry or disappointed in him sent a wave of panic through him.

"I understand, and I'm here to help. Just put the rocks down, and let's go to Yoder right now with an offer to set things right before he goes to the police. Maybe we can buy the dogs from him, but if not, you have to give them back."

"He's horrible to them."

"After we get your mess cleaned up, if we can't work out a deal about the dogs, we can go to the bishop or maybe file a report with the Humane Society. But right now, all the blame is on your shoulders, and I want to help you fix that, okay?"

Ray stood there looking at the rocks in his hands and then at Yoder's house. The very actions that had felt so good only moments ago now seemed to be choking him. What had he done?

Ray dropped the rocks. "Do you think Yoder will let us make this right?"

"I do."

"Jolene's gonna get hurt by all this, isn't she?"

"If she finds out, ya." Van thought for a moment, his eyes narrowing. "But . . . if I can get Yoder to be cooperative, she doesn't have to be told. That'll be my goal, because it would actually be better for her if she didn't know."

"Yoder *really* hates me. He has since the day I went to work for my uncle."

"Then we have to offer him something he *really* loves." Van's brows knit. "Kumm. I have an idea."

15

The light from two kerosene lanterns flickered against the gray cement walls of the wash house as Jolene turned off the compressed air–powered washer. She began feeding the drenched, soapy towels through the wringer one by one while she turned the handle. Flattened towels slid from the grip of the rollers into the warm rinse water of the mud sink. Her back had a twinge, so she paused, working on the kinks while looking out the window.

The low-hanging purple clouds slowly peered through the darkness as the sun rose, bringing the light of day and promising that stormy weather was on its way. Winter Valley needed some springtime rain, but she hoped to get all the laundry washed and hung out long enough to dry before the sky opened up. The first load of clothes sat in a basket near the back door, waiting for it to be light enough so she could safely cross the yard and hang them on the line.

After nearly three weeks of going to Lester's almost every day, she was woefully behind. A smile tugged at her lips and filled her heart. She didn't mind how much time she'd spent at Lester's. Actually, she felt just the opposite — because of Andy Fisher. She'd never once expected someone like him to enter her life. Apparently she had come to accept that *if* she found someone, it would be a make-do relationship. Better than none, but far less than her idealistic romantic notions.

She chuckled. Andy could fill every starry-eyed dream she'd ever had. She knew he could, but what was it about him? He had a quiet, gentle air that she saw the clearest when he worked with the horses, and he had a down-to-earth honesty with a dry sense of humor when he talked to her. He seemed quite disinterested in impressing her, so maybe that was why he was comfortable being himself and speaking his mind. Whatever his reason, she liked it. What she loved was the sincerity in his eyes, his warm smile, his broad shoulders, and his deep, calm voice — except when he feared for her safety.

Taking a deep breath, she aimed to slow her mind . . . and her heart. It'd been only three weeks. Well, almost three. Come Monday it would be exactly twenty-one days since they met. But if all the time they spent working together was tallied, she figured it equaled courting about six months.

She laughed. Obviously she wanted to justify to herself how her feelings could be this strong this soon. But he'd yet to ask her to go for a walk or buggy ride. Actually, he hadn't given a hint that he was interested in more than being friends who got along while working together, which was how she treated Glen. That caused her concern.

Was Andy seeing someone in Apple Ridge and didn't want to tell her? That was an awful thought, but surely he would have asked her out by now if he was interested. However, a man like him — so respectful of proper boundaries — would have made it clear if he was seeing someone in Apple Ridge. Every evening as the group sat around the table after dinner, her heart pounded, thinking, *Maybe tonight he'll say, "Jolene, how about a stroll, just the two of us?"*

"Goodness, Jolene, grow some patience, girl."

But she didn't want patience. She wanted a date. She wanted him to trust her enough to tell her about his late wife and his hopes for the future. But he never mentioned her, which probably was a sign that he carried her in his heart, unwilling to share the preciousness of the memories with Jolene. But he was interested in her, wasn't he? It was subtle, but it did seem so at times.

She shoved the towels deeper into the rinse water and pulled them out again, dipping them up and down to free them of the soap. By the time she ran the rinsed towels through the wringer, her fingertips looked like pale prunes. While the first load of laundry had been in the washer, she'd scrubbed a week's worth of Ray's dirty dishes. Today was her day to get caught up. She'd chosen to stay home for two reasons: it was Saturday, so Ray was home, and Van would be at the farm most of the day, shoeing the last of the horses.

After dumping the wrung-out items into a basket, she grabbed a clean, dry dishtowel and blew out the kerosene lanterns before leaving the room. Since her bedroom was now on the main floor, she had yet to go upstairs to gather dirty clothes. Gloomy daylight lit her way as she climbed the steps of the old homestead. Once on the landing, she faced dirty, scattered laundry. When had Ray done that? She'd left a note in his room yesterday telling him to gather his dirty laundry and set it outside his room or she'd have to wake him this morning to get it. But his clothes were strewn as if he'd slung them out of his room.

Open the eyes of his heart, Father. Help him to see You more fully. Unless You build the house, the laborers labor in vain. And I trust that You, who began a good work in Ray, will complete it. The Scripture-based prayers flowed easily, as they did at the beginning and ending of each day.

Was he awake?

She barely tapped on his bedroom door, expecting at least to hear the dogs' feet hit the floor as they jumped off his bed. Their toenails should be tapping against the wooden floor as they waited expectantly to be petted. They were sweet dogs that seemed to love Ray, but she didn't hear them stirring. She eased open the door.

The bed was empty. And made.

He wasn't one to make his bed unless she insisted, and he liked to sleep until at least nine on Saturdays, so what was going on? She looked at the closet, thinking maybe he'd gotten up early. That's when she saw him sitting in a chair on the widow's walk, completely motionless. The dogs hurried her way, wagging their tails as she reached down to pet them.

"Ray?" She crept just past the doorway of his room, unsure whether she was trying to avoid startling him or angering him. He'd been so hostile since coming home late Tuesday night. It had been almost ten when he'd arrived. Occasionally he came home that late from work, but this time he entered the house without talking to her or stopping by the kitchen to eat. That had never happened before. As he'd hurried up the stairs, she'd rushed out of her main-floor bedroom, the dogs on her heels. She had paused at the foot of the steps and asked if he was okay.

"Fine," he'd snapped, but he didn't turn to look at her or reach to pet the dogs that'd been wriggling around him excitedly. "Just don't ask! I'm not a baby, Jolene!"

Despite his words his voice cracked as if he were on the verge of tears. Still, his rudeness had stung. Fresh doubts and questions had assaulted her. Should she charge up the stairs and confront him, quoting Scripture about respect and self-control? Or should she ignore her hurt feelings, reminding herself that love was patient and kind? How many times while raising her siblings had she cried out to God, asking those kinds of questions? Usually her heart seemed to say that she needed to remain gentle and let God do His work. She remembered relying on her fail-safe entry into her three younger brothers' worlds over the years — food. "I made your favorite dinner at Lester's and brought home a small casserole for you. Have you eaten?"

He'd shaken his head, his back still to her. "I'm not hungry."

"You sure? I made it especially for you."

He hadn't responded to her question. Instead, he and the dogs had disappeared into his bedroom. A moment later she heard the lock turn. Since that night he'd left the house before she got up in the morning, and he was in bed asleep, or pretending to be, when she returned from Lester's around eight.

She'd asked Josiah about it, and he'd said it was growing pains that involved reconnecting with that Teena girl he'd met a couple of years ago and having to pay the price for some mistakes at work.

Okay. That was a lot for Ray to process, and she wanted to give him space to do so without her hovering, but was that *all* that was going on? It didn't add up. If those were the issues, why was he particularly determined to shut her out? Is that what he needed to do to become the man God intended?

"Ray?" She went to the widow's walk.

He stared into the distance, not even blinking.

Needing to see his face, she moved to the railing and turned toward him. The redness of his eyes and the circles under them indicated he hadn't gone to bed at all.

She put the dishtowel on her shoulder and leaned back, trying to look relaxed. "I'm off all day today. Would you like to do something? Maybe walk into town and buy ice cream for breakfast or hitch a buggy and search for yard sales?"

He said nothing. His eyes looked so empty. She'd seen every imaginable mood reflected before, but she'd never seen hollowness staring back at her. When angered, he might need a few hours to calm down, but then his thoughts became adultlike again. And since he'd turned sixteen, he'd had times of avoiding her. Severing the apron strings is what she called it. That emotional need also made sense. And she'd seen him in the aftermath of having done something impulsive and unwise, but what had triggered such despair?

Panic started to rise in her. What if she couldn't figure it out and help him? *God, help me draw him out of himself. Show me, please.*

She sat on the weathered old chest he used for a coffee table and waited. Thunder rumbled in the distance, and the wind kicked up, stirring the green leaves and swooshing the fallen dogwood petals across the ground. She waited.

And waited. Praying. Hoping. Feeling desperate. The emotions she felt right now were so familiar. After his accident she'd feared he would die or be crippled physically and mentally. A therapist worked with her so she could work with Ray between visits. But none of the progress had come easily. Then the trauma of their parents' deaths set him back for years, and she'd been warned that he could at some point suffer posttraumatic stress disorder from it. Is that what was going on?

Finally he blinked. "I wish I could fade into nothing."

"I would miss you so much I couldn't breathe if you did that. You just don't know."

He barely shook his head, as if unable to shake free of a reality she knew nothing about. "It's gone."

"Is it?" She didn't know what was missing, but the health-care providers said that when he seemed folded up inside himself, she should use less direct questions, ones that showed interest without pressing for new information. Her goal was to draw out the problem, like drawing water from a well.

He stared at the horizon. "I don't have the two pennies I need. Everything is gone, all but Mamm's whispers. Even after being dead all these years, she won't get out of my head."

Two pennies? What was that about? Jolene wanted to kneel in front of him and engulf him in a hug, but she stayed seated instead, playing the relaxed sister. They were so much more than siblings, and it was hard to pretend she didn't have an overwrought mother's heart toward him. "What does Mamm say?"

He shook his head, tears forming in his eyes. They remained silent.

Had he done something impulsive that he didn't want to tell her about? Two years ago he'd overreacted when Hope returned home from school upset that the teacher had embarrassed her in front of the class. Jolene knew his emotions were raw from his own years of being teased and embarrassed in school. After learning that the teacher had hurt Hope's feelings, Ray had quietly slipped out of the house and on an impulse had vandalized the school, spray-painting a message to the teacher on the blackboards and oversize maps. That was on a Friday, and by Saturday, when he was calm and before anyone knew the damage had been done, he went to the bishop and confessed his actions. He had to use most of his savings to replace the damaged items.

Thunder rumbled quietly, and it began to sprinkle, the tiny raindrops hitting the lush spring leaves of the dogwood and pattering an odd rhythm. The smell of rain surrounded them — not the springtime fresh aroma, but the scent of asphalt and rotten eggs. How could a gentle rain sometimes carry the aroma of flowers and promises and at other times reek of sulfur and decay?

Ray's lips parted, and he whispered. Chills ran over her. He couldn't have said what she thought she heard. Moving from the chest to kneel on the floor in front of him, she looked into his teary eyes. Had he said that Mamm called him useless?

He leaned his head back and closed his eyes. "She's right, and you're the liar. I think I've known that my whole life, but until this week I kept trusting in all the hope talk you do so much of. I wanted to believe you over her."

Dear God, no. Memories rushed back to her. She never dreamed that Ray knew what

Mamm had said the day their aunt was here and Mamm fell apart outside Ray's room. What was Jolene supposed to have done? Ask him if he overheard their Mamm saying she wished he'd died when the lightning struck?

She reached for his hand, but he pulled away.

"No, Jolene. I can't run from the truth anymore, not after Tuesday."

Guilt seemed to be eating at him. "Did something happen this week, Ray?"

He fidgeted with his thumbs, staring at them. "Can't tell you. But it's all gone, and I don't have the two pennies I need."

What two pennies? She clutched his hand in hers. "Mamm didn't mean it, Ray. She wanted you to be free for your sake. She was at her breaking point emotionally, so weary from watching you suffer, so afraid what would happen to you as an adult if the worst of the doctors' reports were true."

He stood, pulling free of her. "You are a liar, Jolene Keim!"

"I'm not lying. I promise. You were barely able to move, and she lost all hope for just one night. That's all. She ran from the house crying, but before dawn she felt God whispered to her soul, assuring her that you were far from useless regardless of whether you ever walked or talked again. She saw you as He did."

"You're just saying that!"

"I'm not. Do you remember being called anything other than Ray?"

He shook his head.

She stood, grabbing his shoulders. "I have something to show you. Will you wait right here?"

He wiped his eyes and gave a half nod. Jolene ran downstairs and pulled out a metal box from under her bed. The dishtowel still hung from her shoulder, and she ignored it while fumbling to find the document. Hugging it to her chest, she ran upstairs. "Look." She unfolded the birth certificate. "Your given name is Roy, but when you were a toddler, Mamm started calling you Ray, her ray of sunshine that was straight from God. I fully agreed, and before long we had everyone calling you Ray. After she spent that night in the field crying out to God, she discovered a new truth: that whether you could walk or talk or attend school or work when you grew up, you" — Jolene patted his chest — "were still a gift of warmth and light. Your spirit was still alive and well. It was hampered by the physical, and she said you were a different kind of ray of sunshine, like one that breaks through the stormy clouds rather than one that sparkles off the morning dew. But God had assured her that you were our Ray."

His eyes softened for a moment before regret and pain registered on his face. He moved to his bed and plunked down.

Again she knelt in front of him, gazing into his eyes. " 'Neither height nor depth, nor anything else in all creation, shall be able to separate you from my love.' That's what Mamm used to say to you every day after that day. Remember?"

When Mamm died, Jolene took up saying it as she tucked him in bed every night.

A couple of years ago he'd insisted she stop saying it, because it made him feel like a little child when he was trying so hard to grow up and be a man.

"I remember you saying it, but I don't recall Mamm saying it."

"She did. Everything I just said is true. I wouldn't lie to you. Can you trust me on that?"

He seemed to mull over her words. Then he went to his dresser and pulled out a small rectangular strip of paper and handed it to her. It looked like a receipt from a bank.

She studied the faint print, unable to

make out the date stamped on it. "What is it?"

"I did something really bad, and I had to empty my savings."

Not again. Her heart seemed to stop, and taking a breath was impossible. No matter how awful his week at work was, the money he was able to save consoled him. And now, for all his days, months, and years of faithful sacrifice, he had no savings? "Why?"

She listened as he poured out his heart, telling her how Old Man Yoder treated him whenever Uncle Calvin wasn't there. He told about stealing the man's dogs and later breaking his windows. Then he explained about the cash he had to give Yoder.

"You had to give him everything you've saved for the past two years?" He earned seventeen thousand dollars a year before taxes were taken out. He gave half of what he brought home to help with the bills, and he saved almost every penny of the other half.

He nodded. "But for that I get to keep the dogs."

As with the schoolhouse incident, Ray needed to pay restitution, and he once again needed to grasp the full weight of the crime. The dogs were old mutts that would live only a few more years. Ray had given Yoder

214

two years of savings — around fifteen thousand dollars? That sounded more like extortion to her. "Those must've been some really expensive windows."

"I guess so because Van had to match the money I gave Yoder."

"What! Van?"

"He showed up and stopped me from breaking any more of the man's windows, and then we went to see Yoder together to make a deal so he wouldn't call the police . . . or you."

Her blood ran hot. She didn't care if Van's motives were good. He had no right to keep Ray's vandalism from her. If she'd known that Ray broke the windows or stole the man's dogs, she would've searched for a solution with consequences that didn't involve paying extortion money to Old Man Yoder. Was there a way to get some of that money back?

"That happened on Tuesday?"

He nodded.

That explained a lot about Ray's recent behavior. "Just you and Van?"

"And his brother James. He's one of guys I've been hanging out with, and he helped me free the dogs."

Why would James, who was a good three years older than Ray, help her brother break

215

the law to acquire two old mutts? Great . . . this was just great. She also didn't like Ray's use of the phrase *free the dogs.* "You mean James helped you steal them, right? Because you took what didn't belong to you."

Ray shrugged, but he seemed to have little remorse concerning the man's dogs. One thing was for sure — he looked miserable with guilt for the rest of what he'd done and its consequences.

Jolene couldn't process her anger at Van right now. She took a breath, trying to focus on the most important thing — her brother. "I don't understand about the two pennies."

Ray stared at the bank receipt while he told her about his recurring dream. His dream made sense to her. He didn't believe he had what it took to meet the demands of life. He came up short, and no one around him could fix it even if they had the resources to do so. "Ray, none of us has all it takes to meet the demands of life. We do our best, and then we borrow pennies and give pennies as needed. Not only is there no rule against it; God asks us to carry one another's burdens."

"I can't do my job, Jolene. I'm horrible at it, and no one can carry my burden enough to make up for that."

Guilt squeezed in on every side. She

should've seen the extent of his hatred for the job and how it made him feel like a complete failure. It'd been easy to brush off how much he struggled to do cabinetry work. During supper he would share interesting aspects of his job. When they rode past houses he'd been in because of the work he did, he'd sounded pleased and talked about how he'd helped. "If you're that unhappy in your job, then we should've begun a search for something else a long time ago."

"That wouldn't help. I'm not good at anything."

"I know you believe that, but I don't."

"You live on hope, Jolene, and you believe that love is enough. But the world doesn't operate like that. Work is based on skills and being smart, and I come up short every day."

"There have to be answers, Ray. We just don't know what they are. But we'll search for them, and even if we have to leave the state to continue that search, we won't stop looking until we find a job that fits who you are."

"You would do that for me?"

"Absolutely. I wish I'd realized much sooner that you needed us to do that." She wished he could see past his debilitating self-hatred. "Besides, I'm not doing it just for you. When you're happy, I'm happy."

He stared at her, and she imagined he was trying to put together what she meant. Slowly, like watching pastries turn a golden brown, she saw his hurt and confusion give way to hope and gratitude. He stood and swooped her into his arms as he sobbed. "I'm sorry, Jolene."

She held him as years of pain and disappointment seemed to spill out in his tears. When his weeping slowed, he sat on the bed, and she handed him the dishtowel from her shoulder. He buried his face in it and wept.

He didn't need to say more than the two words *I'm sorry.* She understood what he meant. He was sorry for all he'd done wrong, sorry for not being whole and for his years of causing her extra work, and sorry he'd hid his wrongdoing from her.

"All is forgiven." She sat beside him and put her arm around his shoulders. "We're in this together for as long as it takes." One thing still pressed in on her. "Old Man Yoder taking that kind of money for the vandalism and your stealing his dogs is just as wrong as what you did. I think we should talk to the bishop —"

"No!" Ray looked panicked.

Drawing a slow breath, she realized there was more to the events than she knew. "Okay. Take it easy. We've uncovered plenty for today."

But come hell or high water — and she'd survived both so far — she *would* pay every penny to Van Beiler just as soon as she could.

If determination gave her insight on how to do it, she would have his money to him by the close of the day.

16

Rain drizzled off the tin roof of the pole barn, creating a row of dozens of quarter-size mud puddles. Andy let the horse nuzzle against his palm as he murmured to him and stroked his neck. Puzzle, as Andy had aptly named him, had been one of the most difficult horses to tame. Now the formerly rogue creature enjoyed the most intimate connection for a horse — having his muzzle buried in a human's hand. It was unusual for an animal like Puzzle to go from unreasonably difficult and dangerous to a big marshmallow.

With tongs in hand, Van pressed a hot horseshoe against Puzzle's hoof, measuring it. The metal arc sizzled and steamed, but the animal felt only a slight tug, much like a human cutting a fingernail. "Got it." Van pulled back the tongs and horseshoe, released the horse's leg, and returned to the anvil. He hammered the horseshoe, flipping it and pounding it again as needed.

"I shoe horses on our farm, and I thought I was decent at it," Andy commented, "but you make it look more like an art form."

"If I could make a living selling ironwork knickknacks, I would. When I visit my parents, I spend most of my time pounding heated metal against an anvil to make all sorts of creative pieces — everything from fancy weather vanes and butterflies with movable wings to small toys — all to sell to the Englisch, mind you."

Andy thought it odd that Van would spend his vacation doing metalwork. "Is going to Ohio your only opportunity to make whatever you want?"

"Ya. Our bishop doesn't allow creating anything that could appear to be an idol. But I couldn't make a living doing that anyway, so I do it as a hobby when I'm visiting my parents, and my Mamm sells the pieces at a local market."

Lester had introduced Andy to the bishop during a church meeting. Later that day Lester had said that he and Jolene had the same bishop and that Andy should never do anything to get crosswise with him. Bishops covered more than one church district, so Andy hadn't been surprised that Jolene and Lester had the same one — apparently a very strict man.

Van shoved a second horseshoe into the forge to heat it and create two matching horseshoes for Puzzle's front hoofs. Then he'd measure the back ones separately. Shoeing once-neglected horses wasn't easy or quick. "So where is everyone today? I haven't seen a soul since arriving two hours ago."

"Lester is running some errands, and then he plans on making sandwiches for us, and the Keims are off." It felt odd to refer to Jolene and Hope as the Keims. Was he trying to make it sound to Van as if there was more emotional distance between Jolene and him than there actually was? If so, he didn't like it, because it smacked of hypocrisy. Or was he trying to keep her at an emotional distance so he would see her merely as someone his uncle had hired?

His heart turned a flip, rebelling against his will. Puzzle took a step back, looked at him, and shook his head. Andy stroked his face. "It is ridiculous, isn't it?" he murmured quietly as Van banged on the horseshoe. Trying to convince himself how to feel was like trying to tame a wild horse blindfolded. So how could he wrestle with his rogue emotions?

He had no idea how he would cope with

leaving at the end of summer, but he'd never regret getting to know her. And his gut said he hardly knew her at all yet.

Andy reassured Puzzle, talking to him as Van approached with a horseshoe.

"I've been wondering" — Van plunged the hot horseshoe into the bucket of water — "did she tell you about us?" The water sizzled as steam rose, and sweat poured off Van's smudged face.

Andy shrugged. "She gave me an overview, enough to know you were once engaged and the relationship didn't work out."

Van put the tongs in the wooden toolbox and got out a hammer and nails. "It was a tough time for everyone. Her parents were pillars in the community, and they were really great people. Losing them was hard, even for those who weren't their children." He aligned the shoe with the horse's hoof and tapped a nail into place.

"I can imagine."

He put in another nail. "Jo and I were too young for the amount of pressure on us."

"I'm sure it was unbearable." But Andy didn't like where this conversation was leading. "You shouldn't feel any obligation to justify yourself to me."

"No?" With the final nail in place, Van put the hammer back in the toolbox and grabbed a file. "Huh. Feels like I need to." He scraped the coarse file against the horseshoe and hoof, smoothing them. "I can all but guarantee she's never said much to folks in these parts. It's not her way. But whenever I arrive, I seem to interrupt a private conversation between you two, so I guess she's told you plenty."

"She hasn't, and you shouldn't either." If Jolene wanted to discuss the breakup, Andy would be honored to listen. But the idea of Van being the one to tell the story was offensive.

"Our wedding was set for a few weeks after her parents died. She wasn't in any shape to get married, and the idea of taking on our grief as well as her siblings and the responsibility of raising them was simply too much."

"I can understand that, but what's baffling is why you feel the need to explain it to anyone, especially to me." Why did Van want to unburden himself on Andy? He had family and friends of his own for that.

Van continued to file the horse's hoof and shoe. "I know how it must look that I married someone else less than a year later."

"Let's not discuss this, Van. I'm neutral in this matter, it's none of my business, and you seem to want to justify your actions.

But you're only digging a hole for yourself."

"She had to tell you something. I was struggling with the loss of her parents too, and —"

"Van." Andy peered around the horse's shoulder. Why was Van pushing ahead anyway? Did he have a guilty conscience that he was looking to cleanse? "I know that period of time was filled with emotional difficulties, but I've made it clear. I don't want to discuss it, and I'd appreciate it if you'd honor that."

Van released the horse's leg again and stepped back. "I don't like how that mess must look to you."

"So deal with it. I'm sure Jolene didn't appreciate how *that mess* looked to people either, and by your own words, she hasn't tried to win the community over to her side."

Van narrowed his eyes. "That is what I'm doing, isn't it — trying to win over your opinion?" He sighed. "Sorry. Even after all these years, I admire her. We just weren't meant to be."

"Then that's all you need to say."

Van stood up straight, working the kinks out of his back. "But what I don't understand is that the night we broke up, she seemed to really understand and respect the need to go our separate ways. I told her to call me if she needed anything, and I meant it. But do you know when I got my first call from her?" He flipped the flat side of the file in the palm of his hand. "A few weeks ago. Other than polite chitchat or congratulations when Donna and I have another child, Jolene's not spoken to me. It's as if I became the enemy, and I don't understand why."

"She has no shyness about sharing her thoughts, and clearly you don't either, so why haven't you talked to her?"

Van shrugged before bending to put pressure on the horse's leg until it was once again in his hands. "Our breakup was scandalous in these parts. Sometimes I think I can still hear people whispering about it. Has your community experienced anything that scandalous?"

"Ya."

Apparently Van didn't know Andy's wife had left him, or he would realize that Andy understood the difficulties and ongoing disrespect around an unfortunate situation. It'd taken him years to get past the rage and find peace. Most people blamed him for Eva's departure, thinking that if he'd been a good husband, she wouldn't have left. Others pitied him, as if his life had no meaning without her. People having compassion for a spell was understandable, but pity meant that they only felt sorry for him, erasing all ability to see him through the filter of respect.

When people asked him how he was doing and he gave the vague answer of "working through it," a lot of folks condemned him, thinking it was sinful to struggle with lingering issues of anger or hurt — as if they could be treated wrong and immediately be at peace with it. How many times had people quoted the scripture "let not the sun go down upon your wrath"?

Andy didn't understand what that verse meant, but he knew what it didn't mean. God created people with a lot of emotions, and throughout the Word He gave room for every emotion. So the verse didn't mean Andy was supposed to respond as if he were dead, and it would have taken someone being dead not to feel more than a day's worth of anger over losing a spouse.

Puzzle jerked his head, whinnying. He shifted his body, and Van stumbled and fell on his backside. Puzzle snorted, stomping his feet.

Andy moved to the far side of him. "Easy boy." The horse was picking up on something that made him nervous.

Movement near the side entry of the pole barn caught Andy's attention.

Jolene.

17

Jolene stood just under the tin roof, drops of cold rain sliding down the back of her dress. Her stomach muscles quaked from the pent-up emotions, and she tightened her grip on the envelope of money in her right hand. Getting a hold of the money hadn't been too hard. She had uncles and two brothers who'd chipped in to loan her the cash, and when they asked what the money was for, they allowed her to keep the reason to herself. But it would take Jolene a tremendous amount of work to pay it back. She spotted Van as he got up from the ground and dusted off his hands and pants.

Jolene strode toward him. "Van."

He turned. The horse near Andy had his side to her, but he edged away as she moved forward.

She stopped a couple of feet from Van and held out a small white envelope. "I'm sure you meant well, but I disagree with what you did."

Disappointment filled his face. "You know." The resignation in his voice seemed tainted with dread.

When he didn't reach for the envelope, she shook it at him. "Take it."

"You can't afford to pay me back."

The idea of him telling her what she could and couldn't do only irked her more. "The money in the envelope is not an illusion, so apparently I can."

"How?"

Just who did he think he was to her and her family anyway? "That's not really your concern. But the next step is to involve the ministers and lay out this whole mess. Yoder should be allowed to keep only enough money to cover damages and some inconvenience."

"You can't do that. Ray, James, and I gave our word that news of the situation wouldn't get out and wouldn't be taken to the church leaders or anyone else."

"What?" Her heart rate increased. When Van stepped in and took action, did he even pause to consider the cost? "Why?"

"It was our bargaining chip."

"All that money wasn't enough?"

"Yoder doesn't want to get caught in his extortion, and we didn't want you to find out what we'd agreed to, so we gave him our word that no one would take the incident to the church officials."

Good grief! She thrust the envelope at him again. "Take it."

Hurt reflected in his eyes. "Why won't you let it go? I took care of it."

Her insides trembled so hard she feared her shoulders and arms would start trembling too, but she managed a controlled shake of her head. There was no point in trying to make Van understand. Was there a more clueless man in Winter Valley? "Most of my siblings are mature adults now and can make their own decisions, but never again go around me or help Ray or Hope behind my back. Will you agree to that?"

"You're being overemotional and silly, Jo."

Her face burned. Just how condescending could he be? *Silly* and *overemotional* were meant to put any woman in her place. What else did a man need to say?

Andy appeared out of nowhere leading a horse. If she'd paused to think, she would have assumed he was close by. Seeing him caused her quaking insides to ease.

He nodded at her while keeping his pace. "I'll let you two talk in private." He paused, his eyes locking with hers. "If he's stolen your ground, Jolene, tell him so."

"You think he'll stay here and listen to me?" She didn't care that she was discussing Van as if he weren't right there. He'd pushed her too far by meddling in Ray's life. "Nothing I say matters. I stopped being able to get through to him ten years ago."

The horse whinnied, laying its ears back as it pranced nervously, trying to back away from her.

"It matters, Jolene." Andy patted the animal's neck reassuringly. "Even the horse can feel the quaking inside you. You say what needs to be said whether anyone else understands what you've done or why."

The horse looked at her walleyed, as if frightened of her. She reached out to let him smell her hand, but he backed up. Andy was right. Even the horse could sense this fault line inside her where Van was concerned, an earthquake waiting to happen. She lowered her hand.

Andy gave a nod toward Van. Had Andy decided to stay to make sure Van didn't walk away before she said her piece?

She turned to Van, and memories of all he'd forced her to live with shook her. "Just taking my ground has never been enough for you, has it?"

"Kumm on, Jo. You have no cause to be this angry."

"Your actions almost pushed Ray over that edge he's been flirting with for at least a year."

"Over the edge?" He pondered, hints of concern flicking across his face before his confident look returned. "How was I supposed to know that?"

"If you were part of the circle of family or friends, you would get it. As it is, it's none of your business. Ray is my responsibility. Would you let your wife's former boyfriend step in, take charge of a family matter, and enter into an agreement with your child — one that involved keeping an important secret from his guardian?"

"It's not the same. I knew Ray for several years before we broke up. We were like family for a while."

She gritted her teeth. "The difficulty of raising Ray was a large part of why you broke up with me. You had no right to interfere where Ray is concerned. If you can't see that after all I've said, I really don't know what else to say."

"I . . . I was trying to protect Ray."

"Ya, me too, but the problem is only one of us knew enough about the situation to do it justice. Why would you dare try, Van? Do you need redemption for prodding me to give up my siblings?"

"Maybe. When I look at my children, I see the bond between them and how vulnerable they are. Two of my children are close to the ages that Ray and Hope were when your parents died, and my words and actions from that time haunt me."

"But you can't meddle in our lives and behave as if you have rights in the Keim family because of some delayed remorse that's nagging you!"

He removed his leather apron and hung it on a stob of a nearby support post. The horse snorted, tugging against the lead in Andy's hand.

"Maybe I wouldn't have lingering guilt if you didn't carry such obvious anger toward me for the breakup."

She fidgeted with the envelope of money he had yet to take from her. "It's not the breakup that built a wall between us, Van. It was everything else you did. Since then I've never been sure if you are mean or just clueless."

"Mean? I've admitted the timing stunk. I should've slowed down, but Donna understood. She eased my pain, and I fell in love."

"And *that* I understood. But you did so much more. Tell me you're aware of it."

"If I've caused such offense, then by all means explain it."

She looked at Andy. He gave a reassuring nod.

Jolene patted the horse, and Puzzle didn't shy away from her this time. She felt the weight of stuffed emotions lifting from her heart. "You knew the church leaders were watching my every move to see if I was worthy of raising my siblings. The court system gave me guardianship, but if any Amish man or woman complained about me, the ministers could've caused trouble for me. They could have stirred enough controversy to prevent me from receiving supplemental support from anyone. They could have even gone so far as to remove my parental rights. You knew all that, but you invited me to your wedding, making sure the church leaders knew. You did that because you were more interested in how you looked to the community than in what it would do to me to attend."

Van drew a deep breath and held it a moment. "Some of the older men murmured against you for trying to fill the position of a man, but the rest of the community had you on a pedestal. They condemned me for walking away from the commitment I'd made with you. What harm was there in you being at the wedding for a few hours? It helped set the tone for the community to accept our breakup and my marriage to Donna."

"The harm is you used me. You didn't have that right when we were in love. You certainly didn't have it once you broke up with me. But if that wasn't bad enough, your wedding was on the third Tuesday of September — one year to the day after my parents died. Not the same date, but the same week and day of the week."

Van's brows knit. "I married on . . ." He grabbed his forehead, looking mortified. "I didn't realize that. I should have, but I was so confused when they died. I barely knew my own name, let alone the week or day. I made sure I didn't choose a wedding date in the same month as ours was supposed to be, and then it got so complicated about when certain relatives could come, and . . ." He closed his eyes.

Had he really been ignorant of the day? She didn't believe him. He'd done too many other thoughtless, mean things. "You had a place to live and a better job in Ohio, so why choose to stay in Winter Valley? And the most absurd of all absurdity, you chose to live in my district. So which is it, Van? Are you that clueless or that mean?"

He stared at her, opening his mouth numerous times before words finally tumbled out. "I . . . I stayed in Winter Valley because I wanted to be here if you needed anything. I knew you wouldn't let me help overtly, but I thought if I could stay close enough, I would hear of the needs and could help behind the scenes."

"You stayed to help me? Are you serious? Not only did I have to continue sitting with the unmarried youth after the time I should've been married, but I had to do so in front of your wife. And not many months later I watched as her belly grew with your child. You want me to believe you put me in that position for my benefit? You and Donna may believe whatever you wish, but the very idea that either of you thought of me is the most ridiculous thing I've heard. If you'd wanted to make any of that easier for me, the least you could have done was move into a home that put you in a different church district."

"You seemed fine, so I . . . I assumed —"

"You assumed wrong! We have church meetings in each other's homes. When we women serve the men meals, there you are, time after time."

"Why didn't you say something?"

"Why, so I could give the church leaders cause to doubt I had the maturity to be the head of my home? Or so Donna would feel complete in having won? If you'd cared, *you* would've thought about something besides what you wanted."

"I did, although I can see that it doesn't look like it. I took the job of being a traveling blacksmith because it pays the best. Surely you know I have the reputation that I don't dicker on prices. I insist on top money, so I have some to give —" He stopped short.

Did he add to the money her uncle gave her? Is that how her uncle had grocery money for her during those first five years when everyone lived at home and feeding them cost more than she could make?

"Jolene, I . . ." He wiped his brow, looking lost and confused. "I should've talked to you and asked what you would have me do. I thought I knew best, and I did use your coming to the wedding to smooth ruffled feathers against me. Maybe guilt is why I gave to your uncle Calvin too. I . . . I don't actually know my motivation now." He picked up a file from the ground. "Tell me what to do to make it right. What do you want?"

She held out the money. "I want you to take this."

He took it, turning it over as he peered

down at the white envelope. "Is that all you want?"

She searched her heart concerning Van. They'd been young and trapped by grief, making mistakes left and right. If she hadn't been so stubborn in her pride never to approach him with any kind of need again or so fearful of the possible backlash from the church leaders, she would've confronted Van about the wedding invitation and not gone, and she would've voiced her displeasure at his plan to live in the same church district.

They'd both been wrong — him in selfish actions, and her in prideful and fearful inactions. She forgave him, and she knew he wouldn't interfere in her life again without asking her permission first. "It is."

She didn't have an answer concerning Ray and his job, but her final words, "it is," seemed to lift untold weight from her, and she felt more free than she could have imagined.

Andy stood there in silent support. His thoughtful demeanor was wrapped in a kind of calm, and it called to her. *He* called to her. Didn't he have feelings for her too? His blue eyes didn't reveal his thoughts, and she longed for them to go for a long walk and talk.

"It's not all I want." She studied Andy. Should she be embarrassed at all he now knew? She wasn't. He could know anything about her life. "I want to get a phone again, and I want to wade in the creek until panicked thoughts float downstream with the water."

Andy's smile warmed her as he nodded. "As good as done."

She stepped toward him, not intending for Van to hear the next part but not caring if he did. "And most of all I want you to ask me out."

What?

Andy couldn't feel his legs. If he budged, he was sure they'd buckle. His mouth went dry as he tried to force words out. *God, don't make me have to tell her.* "Jo." He barely heard the whisper above the pounding of his heart. Had he called her name, or had Van?

Andy glanced at Van. His shoulders slumped, and he seemed as dismayed and hurt for Jolene as Andy was. The man grimaced, a friendly regret of sorts, before he turned off the gas to the forge and walked away, leaving them alone.

Jolene stood there, a beauty of wide-eyed innocence. She wanted them to go out? It

240

was an honor to know she thought so highly of him.

Confusion crept into her eyes. "Was that too bold?"

The world spun, and Andy took several deep breaths. He walked the horse to a post and tethered him. "Jolene." He moved closer. Did she have to find out this way? "I . . . I thought you knew. You said . . ." She'd said that she understood about his marital situation, that she'd asked Lester and he'd explained it. "Jo . . ." There was no easy way to say what had to be said, and he'd never hated the facts of his circumstances more than right now. "I'm married."

Disbelief covered her face. "What?" Her eyes bore into him. "Lester said you're a widower."

His heart broke for her. For them.

"I'm a grass widower."

"A what?"

"A grass widower. It means my wife left me."

She seemed rooted in place as she shook her head.

He wished he could at least take her hand into his as he explained the situation. "She's been gone since Tobias was three years old."

Jolene finally took a breath, and then she fled into the misty rain.

241

He went after her. "Jolene, wait."

But she kept going, hurrying along the fence line and away from the house and barns. Where was she going?

He chased after her. "I'm sorry. If I'd thought for one minute that you were confused about my marriage, I would've told you."

She slowed, and he caught up to her. The rain had drizzled on them until they were drenched. "Married?" She didn't try to hide her disappointment, and he knew he was looking at a woman he could build a rock-solid, happy life with . . . if he wasn't married.

"It was a mistake to marry her. I knew Eva struggled to cope with life, but I believed I could help her. I wanted to rescue her, but all I did by marrying her was give her the ability to drag both of us under."

"But you feel it too — the connection that runs between us?"

He hadn't trusted his gut concerning Jolene. He had believed every feeling that crossed the line of appropriateness was his to contend with — not theirs. Glen had said she wouldn't allow herself to be around a married man she was attracted to, and Andy had thought she knew he was married. In hindsight, he realized they both felt a growing bond between them. "Yes."

"It's not because we're lonely. I've thought about it, and I know that's not the reason."

"I agree." He wanted to wipe droplets of rain from her face and feel the warmth of her skin.

"I wish I didn't know about her." Tears filled her eyes. "Now . . ."

He knew the rest. *Now* they had to put distance between them. He could already feel her slipping away from him and closing the doors behind her. What could he say? Eva rarely felt real to him anymore, but whether he ever saw his wife again or not, he was a married man.

What had he done so wrong that he was required to pay with a lifetime of being chained to an empty marriage?

In a blur of movement, Jolene wrapped her arms around him, resting her head on his chest. He could feel her hands tighten into fists, clutching the back of his shirt. He held her, tears stinging his eyes because he knew this was good-bye. No amount of arguing or clearing the air could change their situation.

18

Shivering, Jolene drove past her home and toward the bridge where her parents' rig had been washed into the swollen waters. Rain spattered against her windshield as the horse's hoofs beat a steady rhythm against the pavement. She rarely came this way, and when she did need to cross this bridge, she never slowed or looked. Instead, she cringed and kept her eyes straight ahead, rushing the horse and carriage across the bridge as if she could outrun the memory — or the aftermath — of the loss.

But this time she pulled onto the shoulder of the road and got out.

Trace widower. Was that a real term or only something her Mamm said? Mamm named most things, even if she had to come up with the word herself. Why hadn't that dawned on Jolene before now?

Wrapping her arms around herself, she crossed the road. What was she doing? She was soaked and cold and upset. But she couldn't make herself turn around and go home.

Green grass and shrubs led to the river, and she eased toward the bank, stopping several feet back. Thunder rumbled in the distance as gray clouds ambled across the vast sky. Muddy water swirled and tumbled as it went by. Some of it pooled in little recesses before breaking free to race down-river.

The muscles along her ribs shook like a dog caught outside in midwinter. It hurt for her insides to quake like this.

Some winters this river froze solid, and brave folks ice-skated on it. During droughts it became little more than a babbling brook, and treasure hunters would walk along the dry bed searching for Indian artifacts or more modern items the river had stolen. Even when there was barely a trickle of water, the river still sustained all sorts of wild creatures and somewhere along its journey maybe cattle too. When hard rains came, it flooded its banks, sweeping away anything in its path. From season to season it could change drastically. It could steal, give, play, or fight — all the while never pausing to observe the havoc or joy it caused.

Was much of life like this river, a slave to its environment? Was life sweeping her along as the river had swept away her parents?

Longing to understand churned inside her. Of all the men she'd come in contact with — men offering marriage proposals, singles looking for wives — why did Andy have to be the only one since Van who'd actually mattered?

Something possessed her to move in closer, perhaps the need to feel anew what it meant to lose a part of one's self. If she grew any closer to Andy, she would indeed lose a part of herself. But what would she lose if she stayed away?

As she skirted shrubs and brambles, her dress caught on briars. Pulling free, she ripped the cloth. She wanted to move close enough to the bank that the toes of her shoes would be just shy of the edge, but she couldn't make herself get within a yard of where the bluff was cut as if a child had taken a spoon to the rim of a three-layer cake.

Jolene's breathing came in short spurts, and her legs shook like a newborn foal.

Andy's words ran through her mind. *It was a mistake to marry her.*

How many times would she be left with the ramshackle pieces of simple miscalculations? Her parents had misjudged the weather, leaving her to raise her siblings. Andy had misjudged Eva, and now he was imprisoned. She'd misjudged Van's motives and spent years wrangling with anger. She lifted her face toward heaven, feeling the pinpricks of the cold rain. "Since I was a teen, I've tried to do what I thought was right. Look in my heart, and if I've failed to try, if my soul deceives me, tell me."

But she heard nothing save the imagined screams of her mother before she drowned. Or was Jolene hearing her own screams as she sensed she was drowning? Her prayer brought no warmth of encouragement this time, only the ache of hopes dashed. "He's married?" That same question kept rising within her even as the answer pounded loudly. Andy was bound by God's law.

Was that really what God meant when he said he hated divorce? Was it a decree to bind a man and woman together no matter what one of them did? Didn't God have compassion on Adam and say it wasn't good for him to be alone? Wasn't Andy alone?

Was all of life as fluid and changeable as the river — parents died, fiancés married someone else, children went from normal to challenged, finances became difficult, bodies changed from fertile to infertile in the blink of an eye — but God remained unyielding?

Didn't men of old have many wives and concubines? It proved to be unwise, hardening their hearts in their quest to walk with God, but did that mean all of mankind could have only one spouse until death, no exceptions? She lifted her eyes to heaven again. "Where is Your mercy or grace in that, Father?" Jolene's insides only shook harder as she questioned the very things about God and marriage that she'd once believed with all her heart.

"Jolene!" Naomi ran toward her, holding a blanket over her head. Without pausing, she pushed past the briars, grabbed Jolene's hand, and pulled her farther from the river. Did Naomi struggle with a fear of this river too? "What are you doing?" Naomi wrapped the blanket around Jolene's shoulders and engulfed her in a hug. "We had gone into the next valley for a bit and were on our way to your house when we saw your rig by the bridge." She held her tightly. "When we saw it was empty and couldn't spot you . . ." Naomi backed up enough to see her face. "You frightened us!" She turned toward the road. "Willis! Michael! Anna! Over here!"

Obviously *we* included their brother Michael, his wife, and Naomi's husband.

Naomi squeezed her shoulders. "After you came by asking about money, we were a bit worried. Now you're walking along the riverbank. This isn't at all like you. What's going on?"

Jolene shrugged and turned to face the water. All of her pain and questions seemed to swirl and churn inside her like the river, threatening to sweep away a part of her. She longed to break down the walls that kept her from sharing her heart not only about Andy but also about her love of artwork and paintings — from the great artists to her own amateur work. Wasn't opening up and being real what love was all about? Didn't people search for someone who would include and accept them no matter what?

But she couldn't make herself share her disappointment about Andy, let alone anything else. As she stood in the rain staring at the river, Jolene realized how little of herself she shared with loved ones. She'd closed up when the need to be a pillar of strength became nonstop. After Van left, she no longer had anyone she could open up to. Her siblings knew of her love and faithfulness to them and to God, but she had to keep parts of herself locked away like her artwork.

Sharing some of her real self with Andy

had come as naturally as wanting to paint. Before today she'd stood on the threshold of opening all of her heart to him. But now . . . "It's been a Jonah day, that's all."

Naomi's eyes sparked with humor. "You're certainly wet enough to have been thrown overboard or swallowed by a whale." She embraced her again.

Naomi's husband and Michael hurried to them. Anna moved across the wet grass much more cautiously.

"Jolene's fine," Naomi assured them. "She needed time to reflect."

Willis skidded on the wet grass as he came to a stop. Of the numerous men interested in Naomi when she was single, he had not been the most handsome or the one with the best-paying job. Nonetheless, he alone had stolen her sister's heart. Willis steadied himself. "Is this connected to why you needed money?"

The man was generous to a fault. When Jolene said she needed money without explaining why, he offered to sell his home, saying they could live in someone's carriage house or move in with her. Maybe tucking away the forbidden parts of who she was helped anchor her siblings' faith in the truly important aspects of life — God and family.

Despite feeling muddled and scattered,

Jolene found a few words. "No. That has to do with Ray, and we'll discuss it later."

Naomi put her arm around Jolene's shoulders. "Josiah and Ruth are on their way to your house too. We wanted to celebrate your much-needed day off with a fun gathering, and we have some good news. We're all bringing food and games and . . ."

The whole family getting together on the spur of the moment wasn't unusual, and her siblings liked surprising her with a fun piece of news — a ten-cent-an-hour pay raise, a new-to-them horse or carriage, a better hand-cranked ice-cream maker purchased at a yard sale. It didn't take much for them to celebrate with food and games. As a sister-parent, she knew their minds and hearts, but who knew hers? Van had. But that had been long ago.

"Oh," — Naomi ducked her head, making eye contact — "and Josiah invited Glen. He believes Glen is your best chance of marriage."

Why were her siblings suddenly matchmaking? And how did Josiah know that if she wanted to marry, Glen was the man to consider?

"You don't like the idea of Glen coming, do you?" Naomi asked.

She shrugged. "It's fine. Seems a little odd

that you guys invited him without asking me. This is a first."

"You've been gone a lot, and it's been on Josiah's mind. Now that two more of us married this past year, we're ready to push you a little to start considering possible beaus."

Their good intentions were undeniable, and she stood a little straighter. "The best part of tonight is that all of you will be there." Being surrounded by her family brought a special encouragement, one that renewed her hope. But it wouldn't wash away the ache of loneliness this time. Today had thrown the truth in her face — she was locked in an attic.

Was Glen the answer?

Michael frowned. "I don't like that look in your eyes. You're scaring me, Jolene. Are you . . . ill, something serious you're afraid to tell us?"

Chiding herself for the pity party she'd been having, she silently asked God for forgiveness. "Not at all. Just wallowing in disappointment rather than remembering all the wonderful times God's given." She looped her arm through Naomi's. "What is this good news?"

Michael grinned, holding out his hand for his wife. Anna slid her hand into his.

Their news dawned on her, and a smile spread across Jolene's heart. "Congratulations!" She hugged each of them. "When?"

"Around Thanksgiving." He grinned, and Jolene was pretty sure Anna might have to sew the buttons back on his shirt if his excitement kept swelling his chest.

After hugging Michael and Anna again, she insisted they head for the rigs and get out of the rain.

As they began the trek back, Naomi stopped. "There is more."

"More?"

Naomi patted her flat stomach. "Around New Year's."

Jolene laughed and hugged her sister. This was exciting, a day she'd believed in and prayed for since her brothers and sisters became her children. Still, thoughts of Andy cinched her heart. He would understand the euphoric intensity of this wonderful news . . . and the sense of isolation and melancholy that came with it.

But she had to put dreams of Andy Fisher behind her. That thought caused an odd tingling in her chest. Was she thinking about the situation wrong? She had to give up all hope of their being a couple. Allowing herself to imagine what it would be like to hold his hand or kiss him was off-limits.

She knew that, but . . .

Would it really be against God's will for her to continue helping at Lester's until Andy no longer needed her?

19

After Jolene left, Andy took off walking, needing to collect himself. Now, soaked and hungry, he reentered his uncle's yard. Van's rig was still in Lester's driveway, and through the dining room window, he could see Van, Lester, and Tobias at the table eating. Andy went into the phone shanty.

He was sorry he'd come here. Hadn't Jolene experienced more than enough pain and disappointment in life without this happening? And embarrassment. How ridiculous that Van was there to hear everything.

He dialed his home number and waited while it rang.

Long ago he'd buried all hopes of having a fulfilling relationship with a woman. Not only was he in an impossible situation he couldn't get free of, but he'd been unable to imagine loving a woman enough to want to marry again. Years ago whenever a sprig of hope about good romantic relationships tried to take root, he shoveled dirt and moved boulders onto it until that dream was buried and his hands were callused and unfeeling. In his circumstances the action served him well.

But in the blink of an eye, Jolene had dismantled it.

He didn't mind so much for himself. But for her sake he regretted not letting Levi and Sadie come here for the summer in his stead.

He wouldn't do to Jolene what Van had done — stay close and make life even harder for her. And now that he knew how Jolene felt, he would be too pulled to her if he stayed. He had a marriage to protect — an invisible one, to be sure — but he'd taken a vow before God and family, and he couldn't act as if he hadn't.

Lester expected her to help with meals and horses, but Andy needed to take Tobias and go home. Levi could do this work, and now that the horses were much more settled, maybe Sadie or Andy's Daed could help, freeing Jolene from working with the horses. Neither Sadie nor his Daed would be as intuitive about the horses as Jolene was. Sensing their needs came naturally to her. But Levi and Sadie or his Daed could make this a workable situation.

The phone on the other end clicked as if someone had picked up, and then it sounded as if the receiver had fallen to the floor. Boisterous laughter from a woman and a man filtered through the line, and he could imagine Levi and Sadie scuffling and playing. Everything went silent for a moment, and Andy thought he'd been disconnected, but then he heard, "Where'd the phone go?" Sadie's cackles made it difficult to understand her.

"It doesn't matter." Levi chortled, sounding as if he could hardly breathe for laughing. "I pressed the button and hung up on the person."

His brother only thought he'd hung up. Their laughs faded, and Andy assumed Levi was kissing her. It's what those two did — played, laughed, worked, and took full advantage of the perks of being married and in love. They were quite discreet in their displays of affection when Tobias was around and only a little less so when Andy was there. Having the farm to themselves was probably a nice treat, and Andy hated to bring that to an end.

"Hallooooo?" Andy called.

"Did you hear something?" Sadie asked.

Andy cupped his hand around the mouthpiece and his lips. "Levi, pick up. Hallo?"

257

After a bit of scrambling on the other end, Andy heard his brother on the line. "Hallo?"

"Hey, it's me."

"Andy. Oh. Uh, sorry about that. If I'd known it was you . . . I mean . . ."

If Andy was in a mood to tease, he'd tell his brother, "Spare me, Levi. I know exactly what was going on. You and Sadie were playing, and you followed her into the phone shanty, where you were stealing kisses from her — for starters." Instead Andy cleared his throat. "I need a favor, a pretty big one."

"Name it."

This was Levi, and Andy was grateful for it. "I would appreciate it if you'd come here to finish the job with the horses and let me bring Tobias home. Sadie could come too." He was sure Levi preferred the privacy of being on the farm with Sadie to sharing a home with Uncle Lester. At least the house Andy and Levi shared was separated into wings, much like an attached *Daadi Haus.*

"Is Tobias sick?"

"No. I just . . . I need this."

"Sure. Okay. When?"

They would finish shoeing the horses today. It was against the *Ordnung* to hire a driver on a Sunday, but Andy would do it anyway. Maybe no one would notice. Maybe they would. He didn't care. Sometimes the legalistic views, like the ones about traveling on a Sunday, wore thin. Besides, his goal was to be gone so that when Jolene arrived Monday morning, she would be free of having to see him. He'd write her a letter, an apology along with words of encouragement, and he'd let it end there. "Would you be willing to travel tomorrow, on a Sunday?"

"If that's what you need, and I . . ." Levi's voice faded, and Andy heard Sadie talking in the background.

"Then let's plan for tomorrow afternoon."

"Uh, ya, sure. But Sadie can't stay more than a week, and a horse stepped on Daed's foot the other day, so he's laid up."

Andy heard the reservations in Levi's voice. Whatever Sadie had said to him had him rethinking how much time he could spend in Winter Valley. "Is this an issue?"

"No. Sadie and I have been discussing coming for a visit anyway. We'll work something out. We always have, right?"

"True." But it sounded as if trading places would come at a cost. "You see if you can find a driver, and I'll do the same." If Andy found one, the driver would take Andy home and bring Sadie and Levi back on the return trip. Or vice versa if Levi found one. Surely they could locate someone who could make the drive on a Sunday.

"We'll work on it and call you later. Anything you need us to be praying about?"

Andy squelched saying Jolene's name. He'd take every nuance of the incident to his grave. "I'll tell Lester that I need to be there more than here." That was certainly honest. For Jolene's sake and his, Andy needed to be anywhere but here.

"Sure thing. Talk to you tonight to confirm the plans. I'm sure we can find a driver for tomorrow."

"Denki." Andy hung up. As he left the phone shanty and headed for the barn, Van came out of the house. Puzzle was still tied to the post and still missing shoes on his hind legs.

Van descended the porch stairs. "You want something to eat before we start again?"

Andy shook his head and kept going. Other than leaving here, could he do any damage control with Van to prevent gossip about Jolene? Was Van capable of keeping his mouth shut? When Andy got to the barn, he murmured to Puzzle and eased the horse into being comfortable with his touch again.

Van grabbed a long lighter out of the toolbox, turned the valve to the propane gas tank, and lit a fire under the green coal. "I expected you and Jolene to talk longer than you did."

Andy wasn't surprised that Van brought up the subject. He didn't mind talking. Too bad he hadn't used some of that boldness years ago to ask Jolene about the best way to marry Donna without causing hardships for Jolene. He led Puzzle to the shoeing area. "I would appreciate it if you wouldn't tell anyone what you overheard."

Van paused, studying Andy. "What happened between you and Jo had to feel like getting hit by a train or something."

Was that his answer? Andy didn't think it qualified as one.

Van grabbed the file from the toolbox. "When I realized that Jolene and I were never going to marry, I thought I'd go crazy. Maybe she knew early on after the tragedy what was happening to us. I don't know. If she did, it was buried under her grief and steely determination to keep her siblings together. But I went from the most important person to her to the least . . . or that's what it felt like. I needed to talk about it, and Donna seemed to need to listen."

Andy stroked the horse's neck. How could he extract an agreement from Van? "You like for people to listen and understand you, and I get that. We all appreciate being understood, but —"

"I feel like such an idiot not to have seen Jolene's perspective." With the file in hand, Van bent the horse's leg, ready to finish the job they'd begun earlier. "No wonder she's tried to avoid me all these years. I'm an unforgivable jerk, and I didn't have a clue."

"You've made mistakes and thoughtless decisions." Andy grabbed a brush off a nearby shelf. "But you're not a jerk."

Van released the horse's leg and stood. "I expected you to feel different."

Andy brushed the mane. "I've put on blinders and acted on pigheaded motivations too, so I have no stones to throw. We often see what we want to see." From the second or third date with Eva, he'd caught glimpses of red flags about her mental health. But he had wanted her to be the one, and he'd plowed ahead, confident he could fix or make up for whatever instability she had.

As it turned out, by the time he realized she needed professional help, he didn't have the power to make her get it. He'd tried time and again. He'd managed to get her to see a psychiatrist twice, but she'd refused to work with the woman or take the prescribed medications. What was the saying — "You can lead a horse to water, but you can't make it drink"?

Using a set of tongs, Van grabbed a horse-shoe and submerged it into the hot coals. "I guess we have more in common than one might think. We both know what it's like to be married to one woman while caring entirely too much for another."

Was Andy that transparent to Van, or was the man assuming how Andy felt? And wait . . . Van had just admitted to caring for Jolene while being married to Donna. "That must've been hard on your marriage."

Van pulled the horseshoe out of the coals, flipped it, and pushed it back in again. "When I first started seeing Donna after Jolene and I broke up, Donna was like a drug to me, and I became an addict. About four months after we married, I realized I was still in love with Jolene. I tried to hide it from Donna for a while, but it became obvious that we had to deal with it honestly. So we slowly worked our way through those dark days."

Van took the horseshoe to the anvil and began hitting it with a hammer. "One night after another stilted, cold evening between Donna and me, we started talking and came to the conclusion that building a good, solid relationship is like forging metals. Life and emotions are the fire, but it's our vision of what we want to create and our willingness to pound with determination that give us a sturdy, useful end product." Van paused. "Doesn't exactly sound romantic, does it?"

"Being in a relationship that's honest, where both are dedicated to making it stronger and better, sounds really nice to me." Andy would gladly have taken that over what Eva did.

"Ya, I guess it does." He stuck the horseshoe in the coals again. "I have a reason for telling you this personal stuff. If you're looking for a guarantee that I won't tell anyone what I overheard between you and Jo earlier today, I just gave you the power of blackmail."

"That's good of you, but I'll have to take your word that you won't say anything. I'm leaving Winter Valley tomorrow, and my brother will take my place."

Van pulled out the shoe, banged on it some more, and went toward the horse. "Without talking to Jo one last time?"

"There's nothing else to be said."

When Jolene was talking to Van, she'd made it really clear that she would've been a lot happier if he'd not been around. Perhaps more important, Andy had reputations to protect — hers and his. He wouldn't ruin her chance of someday finding a good spouse by tainting her reputation, and Tobias already had the heartache of a missing mother to contend with. Andy would do nothing that might burden his son with additional gossip.

20

Ray's fingers still trembled. It had begun Tuesday and continued even now as he sat on a hard pew during a church meeting at Uncle Calvin's place. Today was June 1, and the muggy, hot air only made the service more unbearable. Other single men his age were on the same bench, all of them sitting on the last row according to the Old Ways. His thoughts turned to Teena.

Did the other single guys have someone who meant a lot to them? Girls they weren't dating and had no plans to date? Or was he just strange? Now, after paying Yoder, he didn't have the money to visit her. He didn't know when he would have enough money for that.

A chant kept circling in his mind — *Yoder cheated me, and now Jolene's paying an unfair price.* He wanted to make the chant stop. It would help if he could get up and do something. Church lasted entirely too long, making him constantly wish it was time for last kneeling in front of the church bench. Sometimes he liked praying, but mostly he liked that the last kneeling time signaled the end of the three-hour service.

One of the boys on his row fidgeted with a lighter, making a flame appear and disappear as Preacher Glen read Scripture in High German. Ray had a hard enough time understanding the Bible when someone translated it into Pennsylvania Dutch. Most of the guys on the bench with him were wriggling as if their britches were on fire. On the row of benches across the aisle were the single Amish girls, all in their rumschpringe and none who were very nice to him. Some of them were passing notes.

Jolene sat one row in front of those silly girls, because it was mandatory that, as a nonmarried girl, she sit near the back rows with the other singles. In another year or so, if she was willing to say she never intended to marry, she could move out of the single section. It seemed cruel to him that she had to sit with the teens and twenty-year-olds, watching one after the other leave that section as they married. She could've moved from the singles years ago if she had accepted a marriage proposal from a widower. As Ray saw it, his sister was picky and stubborn. No amount of personal embarrassment or social pressure from the Amish was going to sway her. He was proud of her for that. How many women would've rushed to marry someone because it would've made all of life easier?

But those thoughts only made him angrier. He'd added to her troubles by losing his temper.

Everyone shifted to kneel to pray, and he did too, but he didn't breathe a sigh of relief this time. He interlaced his fingers, trying to stop them from trembling.

If only his mind would quit pondering how he'd invited Yoder to empty his bank account and make Jolene's life harder. At least he hadn't embarrassed her in front of the community this time. Unlike when he'd vandalized the school, only a few people knew of this latest outburst.

Unfortunately, Ray had to return to work tomorrow and act as if Yoder hadn't swindled him out of his money. The old man had been pretty quiet the rest of last week, but how long would it be before he started yelling at Ray again? A day? Maybe two?

The service ended, and all he wanted to do was slip out the side door. Instead he helped turn some of the benches into tables and put others at the table for seating. Jolene caught his eye and smiled at him.

Glen approached and patted him on the shoulder. "I don't know about you, but I could use some of that homemade ice cream from last night."

"Ya." Whenever Glen went out of his way to talk to a Keim, Ray immediately looked for Jolene. She was in the kitchen removing plastic wrap from plates with slices of ham and bowls of cheese and peanut butter spread. She glanced his way, saw Glen, and returned her focus to getting lunch on the table. How did she feel about Preacher Glen? He'd come to last night's family gathering and joined them for food and playing games, but Ray couldn't recall seeing Jolene so quiet before.

Was that Ray's fault, or was something else going on?

Before long the ministers and older men were being served a sit-down family-style meal while the others waited. The house was crowded, so Ray went outside. The sun was almost directly overhead, and the place smelled of livestock and honeysuckle.

James was under a huge shade tree adding hay to the back of a wagon. Numerous horses were tied to the sides of the wagon so they could munch on hay while waiting on their owners to go home.

When James was finished, he sat on the back of the wagon with his legs dangling. A couple of cute girls went over to talk to him. Girls and guys weren't supposed to socialize until the mealtime was over, but sometimes while waiting to eat, the singles talked until an adult intervened. Every Sunday, whether a church day or a between Sunday, was supposed to be devoted to keeping one's mind on God for at least the first half of the day or until the mealtime was over.

James looked past them. "Hey, Ray. Kumm."

Ray's insides wadded into a nervous ball. He usually avoided the girls, especially in this district. It was like they'd taken classes on being snooty. James motioned for him again, and he went to the wagon. "Excuse us." James nodded at the girls. "We've got things to talk about."

The girls looked Ray over, disregard evident on their faces, and he relaxed when they walked off. James bent his knee and propped one foot on the wagon. "I've been thinking about this thing with Yoder, and I got some ideas."

Ray sat next to him. "What kind of ideas?"

"Good ones. The kind that could earn us some extra money."

That sounded odd. "I can't figure you out." Sometimes Ray thought James had his best interest in mind. At other times it seemed James was trying to lead Ray into trouble. So which was it? "Why did you get involved between me and Yoder?"

"You were going to get caught, Ray. There was no way around that, so I got Van to jump in the middle and keep you from going to jail. *If* you want someone to pay for doing you wrong, you don't smash his windows in broad daylight . . . or ever."

"Ya, I got that one figured out."

"You looking for revenge?"

The idea lured his emotions. "It's crossed my mind, but it backfires every time." And it hurt Jolene in the process. If it was true that his Mamm gave him the name Ray, what would she call him now?

"Maybe your definition of revenge is all wrong, Ray. There's a saying I agree with — 'The best revenge is massive success.' "

"To me, success is not ruining something at work."

"No, that's coping with a job you hate. No wonder we mess up. Our minds and hearts ain't in it, so while we're escaping through daydreams, we make mistakes. But maybe if we did something we liked, we'd actually be good at it."

"You're not any good at being a black-smith?"

"I'm okay. But the point is I hate it, and it shows." James eased a wad of cash to the edge of his pocket and then shoved it back. "I got an idea, and if it pays off, we can give up these jobs we hate."

"I'm not doing anything illegal ever again."

"Gut." James almost seemed to smile. "That's a relief."

So whatever the plan, it was legal, and James had the money to do it. Hmm. Ray liked the idea of being able to pay back the money Jolene had returned to Van. "Why not ask Urie or Alvin?"

"I could, but I'm keeping your secret about the smashed windows, and I thought maybe you'd keep mine."

Ray's gut told him to run. "I told Jolene everything."

James's eyes bugged out. "About us steal-ing the dogs too?"

Ray nodded. "Had to. It was eating me up inside."

James sighed. "I guess it took guts to confess it, although if she was unsure of me before because I'm Van's brother, she prob-ably doesn't think too much of me now. And she won't like the idea of us earning money doing something unusual for Amish men. If we aren't breaking the law, does she have to know what we're up to?"

Something unusual? Ray's heart skipped a beat. "Probably not. We keep good stuff from her — Christmas and birthday type things."

"Ya, that's what it'll be like — keeping a good secret." James showed Ray the money again. "Only if we don't earn any money at it, it'll be like sparing her feelings, right?"

"Ya, and I like that. So what are we doing?"

"It's just a Saturday thing, but I met an Englisch guy a few weeks back, and he says if it's done right, there's good money in it."

"What's good — something that would give me enough to hire a driver to visit Teena?" He would have his regular paychecks, but he'd give all that money to Jolene until they paid back everyone she owed.

"Ya, I think so. If we don't make enough in one Saturday, then we will in two."

Earning extra money doing something with a friend sounded like a piece of heaven. "Tell me the plan."

21

Church had been over for nearly two hours, and Jolene was ready to go home. Aunt Lydia drained water from her sink as Jolene dried the last few dishes. She hadn't slept worth anything last night, and her mind continued to race with questions regarding what to do about Andy. She missed him already. Why did they have to be punished when his wife was the one who'd left? How trapped did he feel? She at least had the constant hope of finding the right man and marrying him. What did he have?

Besides entirely too much of her heart.

Another reason she wanted to leave early today was that she could feel Van and Donna watching her every move. Maybe Preacher Glen too. How many times had Donna approached her today, started to say something, and then was interrupted? Had Van told her and others about Jolene saying she wanted Andy to ask her out?

Women were all around them, talking and laughing while cleaning up from serving a hundred and forty people a simple meal. Children ran in and out as they played. The menfolk were in the living room, placing benches and folding chairs in a circle for the afternoon fellowship. The teens had scattered, some playing baseball in a field, some watching. Others had gone for buggy rides as a respectable way to get a bit of freedom from the adults. With Donna seeming determined to catch a moment to talk to her and Glen glancing Jolene's way every little bit, she'd been tempted to hop in a rig with the teens and go for a joy ride. It had to be less embarrassing than remaining here wondering who knew about yesterday's incident with Andy.

She hung the dishtowel on a hook and turned. Glen was heading toward her, an empty glass in hand. Maybe she should've told him and her family last night about the incident with Andy. As a potential man in her life, Glen was due no explanation since he'd yet to ask her out. But as her minister, he probably should have been told. While Glen tried to work his way toward the sink, people intercepted him, and he smiled politely and spoke to each one. He glanced at Jolene, and she turned to Lydia. "I'm pretty tired, so I won't stay."

"Okay." Aunt Lydia hugged her. "It seems we hardly see you since Lester roped you into helping him full time."

When gossip began swirling, close relatives were the last to hear it. Her aunt wouldn't know that Jolene had shown interest in a married man. "I'll come by later this week." Should she simply return to her routine work that she'd done before Andy had arrived in Winter Valley? What had seemed a fine job this time last month sounded like lonely drudgery now.

While Glen was engaged in a conversation, Jolene eased around people and went out the back door. It was customary to say good-bye to the church leaders, their wives, and the host family, but Jolene wasn't up to it today. She shielded her eyes from the glaring sun and looked for Hope and Ray as she went across the yard. It was unseasonably hot for the first of June, and she hoped it wasn't a sign of the summer to come.

Ray and James were helping hitch someone's horse to a carriage. She'd seen them talking a couple of times today, including during the meal. What kind of influence was James?

"Ray," — she crossed the yard — "have you seen Hope?"

"She and some of the girls were in the hayloft playing with kittens last I saw."

"Would you mind getting her and then hitching the rig?"

"We're leaving already?"

She nodded and continued to walk until she was in the shadow of the barn.

"Gut."

James looked unsure of himself as he gestured. "I can get your horse and hitch it up . . . if you don't mind."

"I would appreciate it, James. Denki."

He looked pleased, perhaps relieved that she showed no wrath over his involvement with Ray's theft of the dogs. It was all she could do to judge the motivations and behavior of Ray, Hope, and herself. She certainly wouldn't venture into judging James, although being leery of his influence over Ray came naturally. But Ray wasn't a child. If James wasn't a good friend, her brother had to figure that out for himself. She'd kept him close for a lot of years, needing him to mature before he bonded with others, but at eighteen years old if he couldn't become friends with those raised in the Amish community, who could he be friends with?

"Hey, Jolene," Glen called as he hurried toward her.

She paused. It wasn't like him to be so bold as to call her out. Would this be enough to raise curiosity and cause some to hope they'd become a couple?

He hurried across the lawn and, once out of the sun, stopped short. "I . . . I wanted us to talk. Would it be okay if I came by your place tonight around six?"

Ah. He apparently had church business on his mind. Since he'd arrived for church service, he must have heard she made a pass at a married man. Did all the ministers wish to speak to her? "Just you?"

"Sure. If that's what you prefer."

Relief worked its way through her. If the church leaders felt the incident warranted more than one of them speaking to her, he wouldn't be free to let her choose. "Your coming alone would be preferable."

He smiled. "But last night with everyone around was *quite* enjoyable."

She chuckled. He'd won a round of Scrabble based on the points in his word *quite.*

Perhaps the upside of Glen's need to talk to her was that he now knew she'd wanted Andy to ask her out. Maybe he was only interested in being a good minister and a friend. He and his wife had come to her home at least once a month to lend a hand with whatever needed doing once Jolene began raising her siblings. Maybe that's all he wanted now.

He reached into his pocket. "I have something for you." He pulled out a tile to a Scrabble game and held it up. It had a *Q* on it, one of only two tiles with the highest point value.

"Preacher Glen," — she used her best parental tone — "did you steal a tile?" Last night he kept magically coming up with *Q*s and knew so many ways to work them into words.

He shook his head, humor in his eyes and dimples showing above his dark beard as he squelched a smile. "I would never steal anything." He held it out to her. "I would, however, bring extra items to your home. It is the charitable thing to do."

She pursed her lips, muffling her laughter as she snatched it from him. She'd forgotten how easily he could make her laugh, regardless of the grief she carried. "You cheated."

"No. During the game you clearly said all tiles in your home could be used, whether they came from that Scrabble box or another."

This was a side of him she hadn't seen in a really long time — fun loving, teasing.

"But I only said that because you found a stray one on the floor. Was it a stray tile, or was it this one?"

"Both."

"Both?" Had he brought a tile with him, knocked it onto the floor, and then called it a stray tile? "It sounds to me as if you have some confessing to do."

"Then we will make it a night of being honest with each other."

"Ah." Was he trying to make her comfortable with her need to confess to him? If so, it was working. It wasn't as if she'd done anything wrong. Her action had been a little bold, and among the Amish any gesture toward a married person was considered the sin of all sins, but she hadn't known Andy was married. Since Glen was being the same warm and friendly man he'd been last night, maybe he understood the situation for what it was — a mistake on her part.

She tossed the tile in the air ever so slightly and grabbed it again. "I won't be returning this. You can bank on that."

Amusement danced across his face as he pulled another tile from his pocket and held it up. It had a Z on it, which was the other tile worth ten points. "I don't need it back."

She laughed and tried to snatch it from him.

In a flash he raised his hand out of her reach, grinning. "Oh no. When it comes to you and your ability to devise words, I need to keep an ace up my sleeve to prevent total humiliation."

"Evidently you need a ten-point tile in your pocket."

"Whatever." He mocked a sarcastic roll of his eyes. "As long as I have the upper hand when it comes to winning."

"Preacher Glen, you do know I can simply refuse to play the game with you ever again, right?"

Without a moment of hesitation, he threw the tile as far as he could, which wasn't more than ten feet due to its lack of weight. He then pulled his pants pockets inside out. "No tiles."

She chuckled. "It's good to see some of the old Glen again."

His smile faded, but the peace in his eyes did not. Just as he opened his mouth to speak, his attention focused behind her. "Van." He nodded. "Donna."

Jolene turned. They stood on a knoll in the blazing sun about twenty feet back, out of earshot, but clearly waiting for a break in the conversation. Donna had her hand resting on her protruding stomach. This would be their fifth child. Thus far they'd had children like clockwork. The first arrived fourteen months after they were married, and each of the others had come less than two years apart.

Glen nodded. "Do you need to speak to me?"

Van and Donna joined hands and moved forward. "To Jolene."

Van hadn't singled her out to speak to since they broke up. They'd been distantly polite during church gatherings, and if they passed each other on the sidewalk, they spoke and kept going. Donna grimaced, supporting her stomach with one hand as they approached.

Would Jolene ever know the joy of having a child of her own?

Van and Donna stopped not more than a foot from her and Glen.

Glen took a step back. "I should probably return to the fellowship circle."

Van shrugged. "It might be wise if you stayed . . . if Jo doesn't mind."

Ministers were often brought in for conversations between people who had baggage between them, and if a minister had to listen to whatever Van and Donna had to say, she preferred it be Glen.

She clasped the tile, hoping the levity of the last few minutes would help her respond in a way that would please God. "Glen can stay. What's on your mind?"

Donna put her hand on the small of her back. "After you confronted Van yesterday, he came home and told me how wrong he'd been about certain things. But he also asked me a lot of hard questions."

Van put his arm around Donna's shoulders. "Whether we acted out of ignorance or selfishness, we should've done better by you than we did, Jo."

"It was more me than him," Donna blurted out. "I've known for a very long time that I needed to ask you to forgive me. He didn't realize the slights concerning timing or where we chose to live or how you might feel about any of it, but . . . I did."

Finally. Donna's declaration confirmed what Jolene had thought all along. Those few words released years of pent-up frustration at what Jolene had believed was sheer hypocrisy on Donna's part, mostly during the first few years of their marriage. After that, Donna's attitude seemed more humble.

The regret reflected on Donna's face and in her eyes said her remorse went deep. She had carried full knowledge of her actions for a lot of years. Jolene had no doubt that until she confronted Van yesterday and he went home and questioned his wife, Donna had been unable to share her guilt with anyone, even Van.

It would be easy to hold this confession against her. It'd been a nightmare to cope with Donna's smugness as Jolene muddled through those first few years. She'd forgiven them even then, but just as there were different kinds of love, there were different kinds of forgiveness. The type Jolene had given was between her heart and God's. She had let go of her anger and given the unfairness of the situation to Him. But Van and Donna were now asking that she give direct forgiveness to them. All these years had God been applying pressure on Donna to stop playing games? Looking at them now, Jolene knew they needed more than her forgiveness. They needed encouragement and hope. Jolene hugged her. "Completely forgiven," she whispered. She simply nodded at Van. "Denki."

Van smiled at her before focusing on his wife. He hugged Donna and whispered something. She kissed his cheek and then tenderly wiped the spot. Van turned to Jolene. "You may never know what today meant to us."

Donna excused herself and went inside. James was leading the horse and carriage toward them as Ray and Hope came out of the barn. "Glen, could you run some interference and give me a minute with Jo?" Van asked.

"Glad to if Jolene doesn't mind."

"Denki, Glen." She'd wanted a minute with Van.

Glen soon had Ray, Hope, and James preoccupied.

Jolene folded her arms and took a step back. "If I discerned correctly something you said yesterday, you've been giving money to Uncle Calvin to help us over the years, and I want to thank you for that." Since she was unsure if Donna knew about that part, Jolene thought it best not to mention it in front of her.

"I'm glad I was able to help."

"We needed every penny in those early years. I thought the saying about eating people out of house and home was a silly exaggeration until I faced the task of keeping those boys fed."

Van smiled, looking as if she'd lifted more weight from him. But then he rubbed the back of his neck as if worried. "Look, I could be really wrong to say anything, but I won't know until I tell you."

"Tell me what?"

"Because you made it clear that your life

was much more difficult when I stayed close after our breakup, Andy thinks the respectful thing to do is to return to Apple Ridge. He's leaving today."

"What?" She wasn't ready for that. She needed more time to think, and she hadn't yet decided whether they could work together until the horses were adopted. How much hardship would this put on the Humane Society and the Fisher family? "But what about the horses?"

"I don't know. He and his brother are trading places for at least a week, but I don't think they know what they'll do after that. Last I heard, they were trying to get a driver to make the swap sometime this afternoon. Maybe his plan is right, Jo. He's married, and you have to respect that."

"Of course we do but to the point that we can't work together until this job is done?" She'd been asking herself that question since yesterday, and now she knew the answer. They didn't have to burden Levi and Sadie with trading places. What harm could it do to keep the current working arrangement?

Could she catch him in time?

"Denki, Van." She hurried toward the rig. "Ray, Hope, get in. We need to go."

Glen opened the door for her. "I'll see you

tonight."

"Ya." Would he be disappointed in her if he knew where she was headed? Since it was after three now, she needed to set Glen's arrival time for a little later than they had originally planned. "Let's make it seven."

"Seven?" His brows furrowed momentarily. "Okay. See you then." He closed the door and held up the Scrabble tile with the *Z* on it.

She took the reins in hand and clicked her tongue at the horse. *"Geh."*

22

Andy rested his forearms on the split-rail fence as he waited under the shade of the dogwood for Levi and Sadie to join him. They'd arrived twenty minutes ago. After a warm welcome and a low-key conversation, they were being shown to their room by Tobias and Lester. But they'd asked to talk to Andy privately before he and Tobias left.

Four half-tame horses grazed peacefully. Andy's work here wasn't done. He'd never left a job before completion, and he hated to do so now, but he had no choice.

His thoughts about Jolene swirled like August winds, kicking up blinding dust, fanning burning embers. Andy wasn't sure how he was supposed to carry on with his heart this heavy. Since the ache couldn't be satisfied with a few comforting words of hope, he would have to get used to this sickening feeling.

Until Jolene confronted him, he'd found

it reasonably easy to ignore how fond he'd grown of her. She cared. An amazing, giving woman he truly connected with cared about him.

Stop, Fisher! Just shut up, already. The demand echoed inside him. He was a fool who longed to have what was outside his prison cell.

"Hey." Levi and Sadie moved beside him.

Andy hadn't heard them walking his way. "I appreciate your coming." But they could only stay until next Saturday, although they had yet to say why. Whatever their reason, Andy would have a week to find someone to take over his responsibilities with the horses. But who?

Sadie leaned in, peering around her husband. "We had intended to make this trip in about two weeks" — she grabbed the top of the split rail — "for the same reason that we can't stay." Her smile radiated the type of contentment Andy could only dream of.

Levi put his arm around her shoulders. "We're expecting."

Andy hugged his sister-in-law and shook his brother's hand. "Congratulations." He'd been anticipating this news.

"Denki." Levi pulled Sadie closer and kissed the top of her forehead. "But her days of helping with horses are over, and she has a doctor's appointment a week from Monday."

There was no need to ask why they weren't using the local midwife in Apple Ridge or why they couldn't reschedule the doctor's appointment. The answer was apparent in removing Sadie from helping with the horses. They would be cautious in every way concerning her health and the baby's health.

Andy wouldn't question their intensity or ask them to rearrange their health-care plans to meet his needs. Sadie and her unborn child came ahead of every other scheduling need.

"There's a young woman named Jolene Keim. She'll assist you in Sadie's stead. In the meantime I'll do all I can to find a replacement for us here."

"Any chance you want to talk about why we need to change places, why you're determined to find a replacement for yourself?" Levi asked.

He shook his head. "No, but I appreciate it." He stepped away from the fence. "Kumm. Tobias and I need to go. The driver's waiting."

Andy carried Tobias's and his bags to the driver's car, but he was convinced his heart weighed far more than their luggage. He tossed the items into the trunk. Lester,

Sadie, Levi, and Tobias were on the porch.

"I don't get it, Daed. We were enjoying it here. Hope's coming tomorrow, expecting Lester to take us fishing. He promised he would."

"You'll need to take a rain check." Maybe at some point Levi could bring Tobias here to fulfill that promise. Andy winked at his son. "I need you at the farm to help me. Your Daadi hurt his foot, and no one knows his way around our barn and the training centers better than you."

Tobias's countenance changed from distressed to pleased. "That's true. But shouldn't we call Hope or something?"

"She doesn't have a phone. But Sadie can give her our number, and she can call you from Lester's phone."

Tobias's eyes grew large. "I've never got a call of my own before."

This visit to Lester's had been good for Tobias. His temperament seemed more like the son he'd always known and less like a preteen. Since Tobias was only nine, Andy hoped all surly teen-ness stayed at bay for several more years — or forever. "Give Sadie and Levi a final hug, and let's go."

Andy closed the trunk, thanked his brother and Sadie one last time, and got in the car. Tobias hopped in the back. The driver put the vehicle in reverse and began to back up.

He pressed the brakes hard, jolting the van to a stop.

Andy fastened his seat belt. "Something wrong?"

The man adjusted his rearview mirror. "A rig pulled in behind me."

It was a wide driveway, designed to hold numerous carriages side by side. Andy removed his hat and leaned his head against the rest. "They'll move when they realize we're trying to get out."

"I don't think so." The driver elongated every word. "She left it there and is walking this way."

She?

Andy got out of the car.

Jolene looked exasperated as she thrust her hands palms up. "What are you doing? You have work to do — a commitment you made to the Humane Society and to those horses — and you're leaving?"

Andy glanced at his family on the porch. Did she realize they were standing there? "Jolene, you remember my brother, Levi." Andy gestured. "And this is his wife, Sadie."

Jolene seemed to come back to herself. She spoke to Levi and went up a few stairs to shake Sadie's hand. "It's really nice to meet you. I've heard so many good things about you."

Sadie studied Andy for a moment, and Lester's scowl indicated he was putting things together that he didn't like.

Tobias got out of the car. "Daed, Hope is here too."

Sadie descended the steps, introducing herself to Ray and Hope. But when that was done, no one seemed to know what else to do or say.

With the aid of his cane, Lester maneuvered off the porch. He deadeyed Andy. "You got things that need clearing up?"

Andy tried to stop looking at Jolene, but he didn't manage it. "It appears I do."

Lester motioned angrily toward the fence. "You all show Andy's driver the horses. Andy, Jolene, and me need a few minutes." Even the driver got out and headed toward the fence without questioning the old man's bark. Lester leaned on his cane with both hands. "What's going on?"

Jolene pursed her lips, shaking her head. "I can't believe you would consider leaving without talking to me first."

"I thought we'd said all there was to say. I'm trying to do what needs to be done for your sake and mine."

"Whoa." Lester made his way to the porch

steps and sat on the third one. "What exactly took place between you two?"

Neither of them answered.

"I want to know now!" Lester raised his cane, shaking it at Andy. "Have there been any melting moments between you two?"

Disbelief registered on Jolene's face. "What? Goodness no."

Andy wasn't sure what Lester meant by the phrase. Was he accusing them of holding hands, kissing, or sleeping together?

Jolene fidgeted with her sheer white Sunday apron. "I didn't realize he was married, and I . . . I let him know I would like him to ask me out."

"Oh." Lester lowered his cane. "I thought I made it clear he was a grass widower."

"You mumbled because you had food in your mouth, and I thought you said 'trace widower.' "

Lester's brows knit. "Trace widower? I've not heard of that."

Jolene shrugged. "It's something my Mamm used to say. I thought it was a real term."

"Oh." The old man's shoulders slumped. "Sorry, Jo. I was distracted by everything — the company, the horses, and the baked goods. I should have taken time to explain it all." Lester shook his head. "Andy, I knew something was odd about you asking Levi to come out here. Since he can only stay a week, what is your plan for after that?"

"I aim to find someone to replace him."

"That won't do." Lester shook his head. "I don't want just anyone working or sleeping at my place. You asked if I would loan you my property, and I was willing to allow you and Levi. If anyone else had made that request, I would've said no. You know me well enough to realize that's true." Lester turned the cane around, his brows furrowed as he seemed to ponder the issue. "Besides, it'll take Levi weeks to figure out everything you already know about these horses and about that same amount of time to get them used to him. And you signed the papers with the Humane Society, not Levi."

The papers he signed were a formality that could probably be changed, but Lester was right about everything else.

Lester held out his hand. "Help me up."

Andy gave him a hand.

"Here's what I think needs to happen. You two take a couple of days apart, and when you start working together again, do so with your heads on straight. I see no other solution." He jabbed a crooked finger toward Andy. "But if you cross a line with Jolene, even a little, there won't be an end to the grief I'll cause you. We clear?"

Andy wanted to assure his great-uncle that he wasn't a teenager, but out of respect he simply nodded.

"Talk it over, and let's not have any more issues." Lester turned and made slow, sure steps toward the fence.

Feeling a bit shaky, Andy sat on a step. What could he say to her? He felt responsible for the awkward situation she was in — having told him how she felt and now having to continue working with him. He wasn't sure it was a good idea. "He's right that I need to finish the job I began, but he can't insist that you keep coming here."

She crossed her arms. "I'll be fine. We'll get our thoughts and hearts in the right place and tame the horses. We're adults, and I'm pretty sure *one* of us can act like it." The slight curve in her lips was the only indication she was teasing.

"Jo, are you sure?"

She took a deep breath, her shoulders relaxing. "Van and Donna came to me today. Donna offered a humble, honest confession of her past behavior, and they both apologized."

He didn't know how that connected to his question, but he was so pleased for Jolene. What healing that must have brought her for Donna to stop playing games and to own up to her attitudes and actions. "Incredible."

"Ya, it was." Jolene sat on the same step as Andy but about five feet away. "See, you get it without me fighting for the right words to explain what their apology means to me. Do you know how many people in my life would even begin to be able to do that?" Without waiting for an answer, she held up her index finger. "One." She slowly pointed that raised finger at him. Her eyes bore into his. "I don't want you to go, Andy. And when the work is done with the horses, I want you to return when time allows. We can do this . . . be just friends, can't we?"

She probably could. She appeared to mold her will as surely as Van forged pieces of iron. Did Andy have that kind of willpower when it came to her? He needed to.

"It seems we need to try, Jo."

He hoped they could shape their feelings into an effective friendship, but regardless what anyone wanted to believe about themselves or relationships, time had a way of revealing the truth.

23

Jolene wavered between embarrassment and confidence as she stood at the fence near the dogwood tree. She had done the right thing to come here, hadn't she? Andy, Levi, and Sadie were at a round pen talking privately, trying to hash out what to do now.

Ray was in the pasture trying to make friends with Misty, a skittish yearling, while Hope and Tobias watched from this side of the fence. Interestingly enough, Misty could bolt to a far corner of the large pasture and avoid Ray, but she hadn't. Misty and Ray were in a standoff. He moved forward a few feet, and she backed up about the same amount.

What a mess Jolene had caused. First, she was too forward with Andy yesterday, resulting in a humiliating revelation. Then after he planned to put distance between them, she arrived here looking desperate for him not to leave. She sighed. How could a person who spent most of her life trying not to cause a scene or trouble for others create so much bedlam? With Andy backed into a corner, how much would he have to tell Levi and Sadie?

Every cell within her longed to go back in time and do something differently — an awful and all-too-familiar feeling. It'd taken her a long time to stop obsessing over the desire to return to the moments before her parents got in the buggy. If she could've gone back, she would've stopped them. And now if she could go back, she wouldn't have told Andy how she felt.

Regardless of opening Pandora's box, she was here, trying to make it right for every person and horse concerned. She'd learned the hard way that life required people to accept the facts, lift their chins, and move forward.

She glanced at the three — Andy, Levi, and Sadie. They were a family, and despite Jolene's weeks of daydreaming, she knew the truth as she stood here today. When it came to the Fishers, she was an outsider, and she would be for the rest of her days.

It was going to take real effort for her to stop her daydreams, but she could do it. She'd done it before. How long had it taken her to fully accept that she couldn't go back in time and keep her parents from leaving the house that night? How long had it taken her to stop hoping Van would break up with Donna and return to her? Actually, she knew the answer to that question. She'd completely accepted that Van wouldn't change his mind the day he married Donna.

Trying to shake free of the overwhelming emotions pounding her, she focused on Ray. He appeared to have something in the palm of his hand as he wooed Misty. The horse lowered her head, sniffing toward his hand. She then tossed her head and whinnied, a sure sign that the horse wanted what was in his hand but still distrusted him.

Tobias and Hope were sitting on the fence. Lester and the driver were in lawn chairs under the dogwood tree, talking and watching Ray.

Sadie walked across the yard and joined Jolene. She gestured toward her husband and Andy. "I'm not sure we came to any conclusion, but their conversation shifted to work and horses on our farm, so I thought I'd take this opportunity to talk with you." Sadie's beautiful red hair looked like shiny copper in the afternoon sun, and her freckles gave her a fresh glow.

Jolene wanted to say something elegant that would wash away the discomfort between them but wondered if such words existed. "I'm sorry about all this."

Sadie turned, her hazel eyes reflecting gentleness. "I'm sure there's a good reason for it, and the scenery between home and here was lovely, so if we need to return, I won't mind. But . . . it isn't like Andy to ask a favor, let alone change his request. I'm guessing you're single, right?"

"Ya."

Sadie blew a long stream of air from her lips. "I figured. It's the only thing that makes sense of today's upheaval."

Jolene recalled dozens of conversations with Andy, and he'd indicated complete trust in Levi and Sadie. Could it hurt to be open with her? "I had hopes of me and Andy . . . and then yesterday I learned he wasn't a widower, only a grass widower. I didn't know what that meant."

A faint grimace flashed across Sadie's face. "So we're here because he thought he should go, and you came today to let him know you think he should stay?"

"Ya."

"Sounds like thin ice for both of you . . . emotionally speaking."

Jolene thought it sounded worse than it was. "It could be, but it doesn't have to be. I let my feelings for Andy go too far based on a misunderstanding. Isn't that what truth does — redirects a person's mind, heart, and body?"

"Ya, it does. I usually don't share this, but I had a fiancé before Levi. I found him in the arms of my cousin the day before my wedding. Discovering *that truth* certainly redirected how I felt and responded to him after that. But this between you and Andy is different."

"Ya, I know. The moral issue of him being married."

"Ethics and morals are a different topic for another time, in my opinion. My fear is for Andy, for his heart." She folded her arms while looking at her feet. "Saying that his marital situation is tough for him would be a huge understatement. But everything would become unbearably harder if he were to fall in love with someone."

The word *love* skittered through Jolene, making her feel as if she held a flashlight in a dark room, searching until the beam illuminated just the right item. Was she already in love with Andy? Interested — definitely. Admired him and was attracted to him — no doubt. But would they have to work at not falling in love? If so, how? "We won't let that happen, and if it did, it wouldn't be worse only for him. It would be equally hard on me."

"Would it?" Sadie focused on her, looking skeptical. "You're free to get over the heartache and find new love. He will never be free, Jolene. But his situation can become *more* unbearable."

Sadie's heartfelt plea worked its way into every part of Jolene. Sadie loved Andy like a brother, and she was desperate for Jolene not to be naive about the situation. Only fools allowed themselves to fall for someone they could never be with.

"We won't be foolish."

Tears brimmed in Sadie's eyes. "Denki."

Looking for ways to change the topic, Jolene recalled one of her earliest conversations with Tobias. "The first morning after I met Tobias, I shared a memory from my childhood with him, and he said that my Mamm must've been nice to me like you are to him."

Sadie closed her eyes, and Jolene noticed the goose bumps on her arms. "I hope he always feels that way. I'm more of a stickler about him doing his homework, cleaning his room, and helping with dishes than his Daed or uncle. Sometimes I worry he'll look back and begrudge that I stepped into his home acting like a bossy Mamm."

Ray had Misty eating out of the palm of

his hand. How had he managed that?

Levi strode toward them while Andy went to the driver.

Levi moved to his wife's side. "We have a couple of choices. We can head back now, or we can release the driver and hire another one tomorrow around lunchtime."

"What about tending to the horses?" Sadie asked.

"I've pulled some favors from friends." Levi slid his hands into his pockets. "They'll tend to them tonight and tomorrow morning. The horses can go tomorrow without anyone training them."

Jolene backed away, giving Sadie and Levi time to talk in private. She walked to the fence a section down from where Hope and Tobias sat so she didn't appear to be hovering over Hope. Across the way Andy paid the driver and shook the man's hand.

Ray backed up from Misty, cooing, "What did they do to you *draus in da Welt?*" The phrase *draus in da Welt,* "out in the world," was used often among the Amish. Misty moved forward, wanting attention from Ray. He welcomed her, patting each side of her face simultaneously.

"Hey." Andy smiled as he joined her at the fence. "Sadie and Levi would like to stay the night."

"It's my fault they came all this way for nothing."

"We'll have a good visit." He propped his forearms on the fence. "And please don't be sorry. It was a good thing you came when you did. We ironed out far more wrinkles concerning the situation between us and the workload with the horses than we caused." He laced his fingers, never looking away from Ray and the horse. "How are you doing?"

As strange as it seemed, Andy felt like a safe person to be honest with — at least about this. Who else could she tell? "Relieved we got things back on track. Nervous about how we'll move forward from here. Embarrassed over yesterday."

"So basically you're an emotional mess."

"Ya, pretty much. You?"

"You clearly don't know men very well. If you did, you'd know we're rock solid and rarely feel a thing." He popped his knuckles, and a hint of a smile mixed with his lighthearted tone. "If you believe that, I have a herd of calm, well-trained horses here that would make perfect pets for you."

His smile and sense of humor soothed her raw nerves and eased the tension in her back and shoulders. The good news was they had known each other for only three weeks. How hard could it be to get her emotions and daydreams back in line with the reality that he was married?

Andy glanced her way, his eyes reflecting friendship and yet a distance between them. She'd seen that look many times over the last few weeks, but until this moment what was hidden behind those baby blues had eluded her. Why would any woman leave a man like Andy?

She had to stop those kinds of thoughts cold. It didn't matter. His marriage was his business.

Ray had Misty by the harness, murmuring to her while leading her toward Hope and Tobias. The flighty horse ambled beside him as if they were old friends. Levi, Sadie, and Lester surrounded Tobias and Hope while Ray introduced them to Misty.

"Wow." Andy stood straight, brushing fence debris from his forearms. "Did you know he was good with horses?"

"No. I mean, I saw a little of his working with animals when he brought home two old dogs a couple of weeks back, but that's it."

"He may be like you, naturally intuitive, which makes sense, because much of our gifting is passed from one generation to the next."

After Ray let the others pet Misty, he walked her to Andy.

Andy leaned in, letting Misty sniff his hand before he petted her. "Do you have a sort of sixth sense with horses, Ray?"

"Doubt it, but I'm starting to realize I like animals. They're easier to figure out than people."

Andy nodded. "That's often true, but only if you care enough to learn to read them."

"Remember this, Ray?" Hope asked, her voice raised to carry the fifteen or so feet between them. "There is no religion without love, and people may talk as much as they like about their religion, but if it does not teach them to be good and kind to man and beast, it is all a sham."

Jolene had a moment of motherly pride.

"That's a beautiful way to think," Sadie said.

"It's from my favorite book, *Black Beauty,*" Hope said.

"I remember." Ray smiled at his little sister.

"Hey, Sadie, can we read it one day after I get back home?" Tobias asked.

"I'll read it to you," Hope offered. "But it's got some really sad parts, and you'll never see a horse again without wondering what its life has been like."

Ray glanced at Jolene. "I thought you were coming here just to earn money, but working with these creatures is pretty neat."

Andy propped his foot on the bottom rail of the fence. "You're welcome to come here with Jolene anytime. Right, Lester?"

"Ya. I thought Jo told you that already."

"She asked if I'd help, but I thought she just wanted me to clean the barns and feed the horses."

Andy chuckled. "There's plenty of that too."

"Only horse I've ever really messed with is ours." Ray flashed a teasing look her way. "And that mare is older than Jolene."

"Hey." Jolene chuckled. "I'm standing here minding my own business, and you find a way to insult me."

Ray grinned, looking more serene than she'd seen in at least a year. He walked the horse back to the others.

Andy nodded toward the round pen, and Jolene went with him. "Maybe you should let him quit the cabinetry shop and work here for the summer."

"In a few months I'll help him find a job he likes, but to let him quit now would reward him for vandalizing Yoder's home."

"He's paying plenty for that, don't you think?"

"It was an outrageous thing to do."

"Agreed. But it sounds as if Ray is miserable at work and Yoder is provoking him."

"Regardless of what triggered Ray's outburst, he is responsible for his behavior."

"Ya, you're right about that too." Andy gave a half shrug.

"Yet you sound as if you think I'm wrong."

"Maybe it's time to reassess the situation. On a scale of one to ten, with ten being the worst, how much does Ray hate his job, and how much is Yoder trying to push his buttons?"

She heard Lester say that the horses needed to be fed. The group began to shift in that direction, starting with Hope and Tobias climbing off the fence.

Jolene stayed put while Ray led the horse toward the barn. "A seven, maybe. To both. I'm never there to see or hear what goes on, but I try to balance what Josiah tells me with what Ray says. I've never felt I could talk to Uncle Calvin about it because he gave the job to Ray out of the goodness of his heart. Yoder is his right-hand man, running everything when Uncle Calvin has to miss work."

"You challenged me on day two, and you've yet to challenge Yoder? Seriously?"

"Are you kidding? Can you imagine a big

sister walking into her uncle's cabinetry shop and giving an older man a piece of her mind? I'd embarrass Ray, Josiah, and my uncle."

Levi, Sadie, and the children walked toward the barn.

"Your points are valid, Jo." Andy started to follow the others.

"Hallo," Lester called, and everyone paused. "I'm going to the house to fix some sandwiches."

"Oh." Sadie spun around, smiling. "I'll help with that. It's a beautiful evening. Can we eat outside?"

"Sure."

But Jolene wasn't ready to mix with the others. She wanted to continue the conversation with Andy. "You didn't finish saying what you believe, Andy."

He returned to her. "I'm not sure where the boundary is between us on sharing opinions."

"Say what you think. I'll let you know if it's out of line."

"Okay. I know Van and Ray gave their word that nothing would be said to anyone in authority about the deal they made with Yoder, but I've got some ideas about that too — all fair and in line with the agreement. We'd need to get Glen involved." He studied her as if still leery of stepping on her toes. "That aside, is it possible that making Ray work at the cabinet shop is letting Yoder do to him what Donna did to you?"

His question hit hard. She hadn't considered that possibility. Is that what she was allowing? She'd learned a lot of valuable lessons throughout that time, and apparently Donna and Van had too, but maybe it was time to give Ray a chance to learn new lessons . . . like ones about shaking the dust off and getting free of Yoder. But how could she?

"Let's just say you're right about Ray, and Lester is willing to pay Ray some. We need Ray's full salary from the shop to pay back all the people I borrowed money from — my brothers, brother-in-law, and two uncles."

"Let him quit, Jo. I'll pay his salary for the summer, and —"

"You will do no such thing. It's very generous of you, but no."

"If Ray likes the idea, it could be the answer all three of us need. It might help him discover he's a horse trainer by nature, and it would keep us from working alone. Maybe in a week or so, he could begin working next to me in your stead."

His ideas surprised her. Why hadn't she

seen any of that? "Okay, that makes sense, and it's tempting. But we need his paycheck, and I'm not accepting your money."

"I don't want to sound flippant or like I'm bragging, but money isn't that big an issue for me. Starting at nineteen, you've had to pay rent, plus feed and clothe yourself and five others. Me? I was older than that when I married, and I have a thriving business with only one child to provide for — the only one I'll ever be responsible for. Let me do this."

"You're spending your summer doing volunteer work, and I'm supposed to let you pay my brother to do tasks he's never done before? You're being too generous. It's not happening." She still saw no sign of resignation in him.

"What can I say? I can be a patient man until it does happen." Despite his words his tone was filled with jesting.

"You're trying to be charming and disarm me, aren't you?"

"Well, ya, but you probably wouldn't realize that if you didn't have so much experience raising teens."

"Your suggestion wouldn't strap you for cash?"

Hope radiated from his calm demeanor.

"Isn't that what I just said, more than once?"

An odd feeling came over her, one from deep inside, and it dawned on her that Andy needed her to let him do this.

They had to start distancing themselves from each other, but she could allow him this desire . . . and enjoy the benefit of giving Ray the chance to quit the cabinetry shop. It was a little haphazard since she didn't know what Ray would do after the horses were gone, but she recognized that Ray had worked for Yoder far longer than he should have. She felt at fault because she hadn't noticed his distress and had pushed him to keep a good-paying job. This was her chance to make up for her mistakes concerning Ray.

"If Ray's willing to work here, I'm willing to let you pay him, and denki."

He grinned. "Excellent." He held up one hand. "Just one more thing. May I ask how you got the money to pay Van?"

She explained it quickly, wondering why he was asking.

"And your plan to pay them back?"

"Tomorrow I'll go to the bank and start the process of getting a loan." The problem was she didn't own anything to use as collateral, but Andy didn't need to know that.

313

"Sounds logical. If you need a cosigner, I'm sure Lester would be honored. Apparently he's got more money than half the Amish put together. I would be glad to cosign also but two issues: I can already tell how you would react to that suggestion, and it wouldn't look right if anyone learned of it."

She hadn't thought of asking Lester. "I appreciate it, Andy."

"If Ray is good at working with horses, I could take him to some auctions this fall and show him how to get started. It's good money if he has the patience and property. I bet Lester would rent out his stables."

Apparently Andy was quite the businessman, and a generous one. "I'll think about it. Now stop offering stuff before you make me permanently uncomfortable around you."

He made a locking motion on his lips. Levi, Ray, and the children returned from the barn and began washing up at the pump.

"I should go." She went to the house and helped get food ready. When she and Sadie stepped outside with trays of food, the men had started a bonfire, brought out more chairs, and set up a makeshift table for the food.

They set the trays down, and everyone ate.

Soon enough dusk began to settle over them. Hope and Tobias chased fireflies. Sadie and Jolene chatted about little things, while Ray sat with the men, talking as if grown. At the moment he looked like a young man who'd made another step toward returning to himself — a journey that began the day he'd been hit by lightning. What wonderful news she had for him. He could turn in his notice tomorrow and be done at the cabinetry shop within two weeks. In case the news caused tears of relief, she would wait until they were home to tell him. Would he sleep a wink tonight — or all week — for the excitement?

Despite her disappointment about Andy, peace floated around and through her like the beauty of the evening. When was the last time she'd felt this good about the life ahead of her?

However, something nagged at her that she couldn't place. Had she forgotten something? Did she need to be somewhere? Andy looked her way, appearing pleased that they'd worked through the issues.

"I love this tree." Sadie poured water into icy glasses. "How tall is it?"

Jolene peered up. "About thirteen or fourteen feet."

"We need one of these in our front yard,

Levi. There's no shade on one side of the house."

"My Daed gave my Mamm a dogwood for their wedding, and I've grown almost a dozen trees with cuttings from that one. I have a tree in our yard for each sibling, and I've given each married couple a tree for their wedding. Then I grew this one and planted it here for Lester. They take about eight really healthy years to reach this height."

Andy stared up at it. "That story is just too amazing, Jo."

"Ya," Lester agreed. "Who'd have thought your grumpy old uncle would get a gift like this?"

Several of the group chuckled.

Jolene already had two trees growing in containers at home to use as gifts for Ray and Hope when they married. She could give the Fishers the tree she'd been growing for Ray, which was a good size already. Then years from now when Ray married, she would give him the one she had been growing for Hope. Since Hope was so young, Jolene had plenty of time to grow another one for her. The plan brought a sense of peace, but it seemed inappropriate to mention it now. Later, when the time was right, she'd give the dogwood tree to the Fishers.

Hope and Tobias moved to the front porch and sat in the swing, holding their jars of lightning bugs. All seemed right with the world, and Jolene exhaled, feeling as if she'd been breathing shallowly for ten years.

A rig pulled onto Lester's driveway. Pinpricks skittered across her skin from her face to her feet. She was looking at what had nagged at her this evening.

Glen.

24

Andy's head pounded as he watched Glen dismount from the rig. Why was he here? Had Van told Glen after assuring Andy he wouldn't tell anyone?

"Goodness." Jolene clutched the ends of the armrests of her lawn chair, her cheeks pink and her face stricken. "I forgot he was coming over tonight. Wouldn't it be reasonable to think I could get one thing right this weekend?"

"Why again?" Ray asked. "He arrived before dinner last night and stayed until his sons' bedtime."

"Glen!" Hope skittered across the lawn toward him, clearly as excited to see him as Jolene was uncomfortable. Hope obviously liked him, and Andy supposed the gentle preacher filled some of her needs for a Daed.

"Who is he?" Sadie asked.

"Our preacher and a good friend of the

family." Jolene closed her eyes and took a deep breath before standing. "But I think he's here to have a serious discussion about boundaries."

If Van had kept his word, Glen shouldn't be here for that reason. But Andy realized he and Jolene couldn't live with the fear of wondering whether Van would keep his word or not. They had to take control of the situation.

"Jo." Andy stood and motioned for her to go with him. They walked toward Glen, but Hope had him hemmed up inspecting her Mason jar of fireflies. Glen looked their way.

Jolene waved. "He looks frustrated, doesn't he?"

"Maybe he feels like you stood him up."

"Glen?" Disapproval filled her eyes. Apparently the concept wasn't totally foreign to her, but she didn't like it. Hope and Tobias were both at Glen's feet now, talking to him. He helped them loosen the lids on their Mason jars, and the children removed them simultaneously, releasing their lightning bugs.

"All right, guys." Andy clapped, then turned to Jolene. "Van said he wasn't going to tell anyone."

"Really?" Her eyes reflected pleasure and maybe a bit more respect for Van. "You think he meant it?"

"I do, but . . ." The fullness of Jolene's future hit Andy. She had love to give, and she deserved a man free to receive it. She wanted a family. Glen was a good man who needed a wife.

Andy hated where his thoughts were leading, and yet he knew the bond between Jolene and him needed to be broken — or at least weakened by the addition of Glen into their workdays and off time. They had a full three months ahead of them, and considering they'd grown to like each other this much in three weeks, what would months do?

His head spun. The air vibrated with the sounds of tree frogs. The old chains of the porch swing squeaked, and Hope's words to Glen were indistinguishable murmurs. For a split second he felt as if he'd stepped into a new dimension — one where God wooed him to keep his vow and help Jolene find her future.

A plan took shape in his mind, and he knew how Glen could help free Jolene of the debt she owed her brothers and uncles because of Old Man Yoder. "Let's be honest with him, Jo. About everything, including what Old Man Yoder did."

"But Van and Ray gave their word. I

especially can't tell a minister."

"First, you didn't give your word, and, second, if you can't tell a church leader, can you tell a close family friend?"

She seemed reluctant.

"We need Glen for my plan to get the money back from Yoder to work. He has no right to Ray's money and certainly no right to enslave you in paying that kind of debt."

She nodded. "I'd like to get that money back."

"Another thing. If you tell Glen what happened between us yesterday and if months from now news of it does get out, you would've already done the right thing by confessing it to a minister. He won't tell the other ministers."

"How do you know?"

"Trust me." He knew that when a good man had hopes of marrying a good woman, he would protect her reputation, especially if she confided in him. His heart revolted at his plan, and he wiped sweat from his brow. "Go for a walk with him and tell him everything."

"What if he refuses to let us work together?"

"Explain the situation, and invite him to join us as often as he can."

She didn't seem in favor of that idea. Was

she still holding on to romantic notions about him?

He had to be blunt with her and assure himself of the truth. They both had to realize the finality of his situation. It broke his heart. If it broke hers, it would be the beginning of accepting their reality. Her heart would mend, and then she would be free to fall in love with someone. If she never cared for Glen in that way, surely God would bring the right man across her path. But he wasn't sure Jolene would recognize him until she was free of their alleged *friendship*. Friends didn't have to fight against their attraction to each other. They didn't want to date.

"When I leave here after the horses are adopted, I won't return. We won't exchange letters or phone calls."

"Why?" Her screech caused Glen to look their way. He put the lids on the children's jars, and Andy knew he was wrapping up with them and would send them on their way shortly.

"Because I'm married, Jo. She could return tomorrow or never, but her behavior toward me and Tobias doesn't change the vows I took."

"Maybe God has more grace than what the letter of the law states. If so, would it be so wrong to stay in contact?"

"Even if He does, the Amish don't. That's the reality, and we have our families' feelings and reputations to protect. I've got to think of Tobias above all else." He was also thinking of Jolene, but she would accept his stance more easily if he placed the sole responsibility on Tobias.

Jolene bit back tears, but she nodded.

"*You'll* be okay." The emphasis was meant to assure her of the strength she had, but he realized there was a double meaning. *She* would be okay. When he left here, he would enter a never-ending winter, the harshness of which he'd only read about. "I'm sorry." But he'd been right that she was harboring feelings of hope about their relationship. Clearly, he was too.

"I get it." She nodded. "I do."

"Hey." Glen closed the gap between them. He glanced at Andy before focusing on Jolene. "Did you forget I was coming by tonight?"

"I did. But I'm glad you found me, because I need to tell you some things. And then the three of us need to talk."

Andy eased away, neither of them seeming to notice. He watched as they walked toward the road, talking.

Would Glen understand and help with

Andy's plan to get the Keims' money back, or would he be offended by what Jolene was about to tell him? Would he do everything in his power to pull Jolene off this farm and out of Andy's life immediately?

Ray hummed, and the dim glow of a kerosene lamp lit the way as he climbed the stairs to the haymow. The dogs watched him from below as he tossed a bale onto the ground. His feet longed to dance. Yesterday had been his last day at the cabinetry shop. Uncle Calvin had questioned his leaving, and Ray had said he'd appreciated the job and hoped he'd done it justice for his uncle's sake, but the truth was, he had a new job for the summer and prospects for the fall. It seemed rude to tell him he didn't like the work.

His uncle had smiled, nodding and looking pleased for Ray. He then said that Ray only needed to give a one-week notice . . . if that's what he wanted.

The week was over, and today Ray was a free man. His brain was clear of the fog, and no matter what had gone wrong last week, his thoughts never reverted to choppy, immature sentences, and now he wanted to swing from the rafters of this old barn. Instead, he scurried down the ladder and finished his chores.

He'd used their new phone and called Teena last week. If all went well today, he might get to see her for a few minutes tonight. While he finished filling the water trough, the dogs began barking. Ray made several fast kissing noises, and the dogs returned to him, scrunching close to the ground as if they feared him. Would they ever get past that behavior? He turned off the water and hung the hose before he patted them. "Good job, guys. But I can't let you wake Hope."

Jolene was up baking before she had to leave for Lester's farm. Starting Monday, he'd go with her. He blew out the lantern and walked out of the barn. An oversize pickup truck was in the driveway. The sky had turned a dark purple with streaks of orange as daylight crept onto this side of the earth. The cool summertime air carried the aroma of honeysuckle and Jolene's baked goods. The sugary smell reminded him of a lifetime of waking up to baked goods. A mourning dove cooed, and the dogs wagged their tails as they walked beside him. Would all mornings from now on feel this beautiful?

The driver cut off the truck engine, but Ray didn't recognize the man. Made sense, he guessed. James didn't want anyone around here knowing they were going to sell flowers on an empty lot a couple of towns over, so he'd probably found a driver from outside these neighboring districts.

James got out of the vehicle but stayed at the door of the truck. "Gut. It looks like you're ready."

"I just need to put the dogs inside. Don't want them getting hit."

When Ray opened the back door, the aroma of pastries washed over him. As he shooed the dogs inside, Jolene came toward him with three brown lunch bags in hand.

"Perfect timing." She stepped onto the porch.

Ray closed the door and followed his sister down the steps.

James shrank back a few steps. Was he afraid of her? She held up the bags. "Pastries and coffee in to-go cups. One bag for each of you." She walked to the truck. What was his sister up to? She could've just handed the bags to him.

"Wow. That's really nice of you." James took the bags.

"You're welcome."

He reached into the truck, aiming to pass one bag to the driver. He almost dropped it, and when he did hand it to the man, he banged his head before standing up straight. "S . . . s . . . sorry."

What was he apologizing for — hitting his head?

The driver ducked to see Jolene while opening and sniffing the bag. "Thank you!"

She grinned. "You're quite welcome. I hope you like it." She focused on James. "I make you nervous, and that makes me nervous." Jolene searched his face. "Care to help me understand?"

James set the other two bags on the truck seat. "Well . . ." He removed his straw hat and held it with both hands, fidgeting with it. "I just figure you don't much care for me . . . you know, since I'm Van's brother, and he . . . well, you know."

"Ah." She nodded. "And maybe because I know of your hangout in the woods? And taking Yoder's dogs with Ray wasn't the wisest thing you've done lately."

Why did his sister feel a need to say all that to James?

"That too." James inched his hands along the brim of his hat, slowly turning it round and round. "But those dogs weren't being treated right."

Ray figured this was why he and James got along. They thought alike, which Ray found comforting . . . and scary since his thinking tended to be skewed at times.

"Remember the first time Van brought me to Ohio to meet the whole family?" Jolene asked.

"How could I forget? I was about ten, and I lived for fishing. You and Van took me, and you helped me reel in the biggest fish ever caught in that creek."

She shuddered. "Ew."

He laughed. "Ya, that's what you were like then too, but you waded out into the creek with a net and got wet up to your waist making sure that fish didn't get away. It's mounted on my wall."

"That was a fun time, including the picnic that was overrun with grasshoppers."

James held up two fingers. "There were only a couple, and after one hopped onto your dress, you danced around squealing for nearly a minute." He laughed. "I told Van you were a little too girly about lots of things for my taste." His eyes got large. "Sorry, I didn't mean . . ."

She chuckled. "I'm still a lot like that, but since God made me a girl, I intend to use the rights of that license as needed."

"That's funny." James relaxed a little.

She lowered her eyes for a moment. "Ray said that whatever you're doing today is private, and he's not supposed to tell me. I suppose you're both old enough to have that right, but when I find out — and I always find out — will I mind?"

"Some will laugh at us, but I doubt you would mind what we're doing." James shrugged. "We're going a few towns away to set up a stand and sell flowers. I've been told we can make good money at it, but I don't want any of the other guys to know. That's all."

"Oh." She gave James a familiar lopsided, you're-okay-kid smile. Ray knew that smile well. "I won't tell anyone, and I hope you sell every flower you've paid for. It may be a little unusual for a young man to sell flowers, but you should be pleased with yourself for being willing to venture into something that takes guts."

James's eyes bugged out.

Ray elbowed her. "You're pretty cool."

"Almost," she mumbled and pointed at the truck. "Get. What time will you be home tonight?"

Ray paused. "Depends. But I'd rather not say on what."

Jolene drew a deep breath and folded her arms. "You and James sticking together?"

"Ya."

"Then that's fine. Home by eleven."

Ray's day just kept getting better, and it

was early morning! "Will do."

Ray crawled into the truck and waved to his sister. The sky had turned lavender, and the top of the sun peered through breaking clouds. He couldn't recall seeing this side of Jolene before. Then again, they'd talked a lot since the incident with Yoder, and he understood himself better, so she trusted him more.

James opened his bag and got out the coffee. "I thought she hated me. But she's pretty cool, Ray."

"Ya, I know." Ray opened his brown bag. "I thought she was as strait-laced as a body could get."

James put the drink between his knees. "But she's like your Mamm. Don't all children think that of their parents when they're young? Maybe you'll see more of the real Jolene now that you're eighteen." He took a sip of his coffee. "Do you know where Teena lives, you know, for after we're done selling flowers?"

"I have her address."

The driver pointed at the GPS. "If you have an address, I can find it."

Ray wasn't ready for a serious girlfriend. He didn't have a job past summer. He was only eighteen, and he'd vandalized Yoder's place out of anger. Maybe Teena didn't think of him that way, but he was ready to see her again and ask what was new in her life and tell her what was new in his.

25

Jolene stopped her pastry-toting wagon in front of the bakeshop. Glen was on the sidewalk, waiting for her, not a hint of a smile on his face. He had treated her in this manner since they'd talked a couple of weeks ago. She opened the door to the rig. "Morning."

"Hi." His tone was even and kind but almost void of friendliness. But he held out his hand and helped her down before he tethered the horse to the hitching post.

Two weeks ago when he'd come to Lester's place looking for her, she did as Andy requested and walked with Glen, explaining about her mistake of thinking Andy was a widower and her forwardness in letting him know she cared. Glen was clearly disappointed, maybe even hurt, although he said little, perhaps because she immediately launched into explaining what Ray had done and how Yoder had taken advantage of the situation. That angered him, and her revelation about caring for Andy seemed to move into the background. When she mentioned Andy had an idea to right the Yoder situation that would require Glen's help, he wasted no time crossing the lawn to talk to Andy.

Straightening her black apron, she gathered her thoughts. Glen followed her as she went to the back of the wagon and opened the pastry case. He held out his arms, and she loaded several boxes into them. Before she released the last one, she looked into his eyes. "I appreciate what you're doing, and I admire that you're helping me even though you're disappointed in me."

Gentleness overshadowed his stoic face. "I should've been more understanding when you said what you did. But I'm not disappointed *in* you. It was reassuring that you confided in me and that you and Andy want me to come to the farm as often as I can and help with this plan. I just . . . Well, now that I'm ready to date, I thought, or maybe hoped, that you would feel differently toward me than you have other widowers."

"I do!" She hadn't meant to sound that enthusiastic, but, goodness, she'd had nothing in common with any widower thus far except the awkwardness between them.

Glen was in a class all his own. That didn't mean she cared for him as a girlfriend would. Yet Andy wanted her to try, and she would do exactly that. She cleared her throat. "We're friends, Glen, and becoming better ones as we go along. We've known each other forever, but you didn't have any desire to date me until you began to heal from losing your wife. Your life changed, and at some point after that, you began to see me differently. My life hasn't changed, so I haven't had the same aha moment."

Thoughtful questioning lined his brows. "That's really profound and quite helpful." He smiled. "I feel better now. I suppose I should've known you would take some real wooing or you'd be snatched up by now, right?"

She hadn't thought of it like that. Andy certainly hadn't done any wooing. He simply showed up, and on day two, *bam,* her heart hoped it had found a home.

"So you meant it when you and Andy invited me to spend as much time at Lester's farm this summer as possible?"

"Ya."

He smiled before turning to go into the bakery. After they'd delivered the goods, they sat at a table in the bakeshop with a cup of coffee. Glen had a pastry, but as much as she enjoyed making pastries, she wasn't one for eating them. She was more of a homemade ice cream kind of girl.

Glen pulled out his pocket notebook and flipped through the pages. "You have your lines memorized?"

"I know what needs to be said, so that's enough. I just hope I can keep my cool. This may sound ridiculous, but I'm a mix of emotions. I'm angry at Yoder and want that money back, but I feel guilty because Ray and Van gave their word, and I'm not abiding by it."

"Deceitful people often get away with stealing from others because good people don't want to get dirty in the fight. The dirt in this instance is your guilt that you can't be completely forthright. I don't like it either, but I like giving the Yoders of the world the upper hand even less."

"Basically that means my conscience is haunting me far more than Yoder's is weighing on him."

"I'm sure of it." He tightened the lid on his to-go cup and took a sip of coffee. "How did your uncle end up with someone like Old Man Yoder as his second-in-command guy?"

"According to what my Daed told me when I was a little girl, Uncle Calvin and

Old Man Yoder went into business together when they were young men, early twenties."

"But Yoder doesn't own any of the cabinetry shop, does he?"

"Not anymore. Daed said about seven years in, before you and I were born, the two had a falling-out, and they parted ways."

"What happened?"

"According to my Daed and Lester, Uncle Calvin never said, so it's only speculation."

"Kumm on, Jolene. Tell me what the rumors were. It might help us pull off this plan."

He might be right, but she couldn't resist teasing him. "You just want in on the gossip."

His eyes flashed with humor. "It's one of the perks in the nonpaying position of having been chosen to be a minister. I know today's gossip, and I have the power to learn what took place before I was born."

"Lester once told me that Yoder was stealing from Uncle Calvin. Lester called it cooking the books. Once Uncle Calvin caught him, he paid Yoder for his share of the business, minus what he had stolen, and ended the partnership. Yoder left the church and moved away. He returned ten years later, repented, paid the price of being shunned, and got right with the church.

Then he went to Uncle Calvin with his hat in hand, flat broke. Calvin hired him, but he doesn't let him do any banking or bookkeeping."

Glen nodded. "The bishop had told me Yoder once left for ten years. He said that no one felt he was even a decent Amish member, but to turn him out to the world when he came back repentant would have been too cruel."

"I understand how they felt, but in hindsight I don't think it was a wise decision." She rose and tossed her cup into the trash. "Let's try to set things right for Ray. I'll go first. See you in ten?"

He pulled a pocket watch from his jacket. "In ten."

Jolene stopped by her rig and took out a beige file folder. She walked down the sidewalk and into her uncle's cabinetry shop. But rather than pause at the door, she went to the first work station, appearing rather lost. It would be the best way to get the buzz started. A few of the men stopped cold.

Nate, a man from her district, walked toward her. "Hi, Jolene. Can I help you with something?"

She lifted her head, trying to speak loudly over the room while pretending to search for him. "I need to speak with my uncle. It's official business." Did she look as silly as she felt?

Yoder came from a back room, and on cue she dropped the folder, hitting the corner of a work station, which sent the contents flying farther across the floor than if she'd let the folder drop straight down. Several of the men helped gather the items, including Yoder. He barely glanced at one paper when she tugged on it. "Denki." She eyed him, doing her best to look suspicious of him. "My uncle, please?"

"What's this about?" Yoder asked.

She put the items in the folder. "It's a private matter." She looked around. "I haven't been inside this shop since I was a girl. Where is my uncle's office?"

"He's really busy today. I don't think —"

"Jolene." Her uncle appeared from a door behind him. He grinned. "What a wonderful surprise this is."

Yoder pulled his focus from the folder. "I was just telling her how busy you are. I'm sure I can help her with whatever —"

"That won't be necessary." Uncle Calvin embraced her, but when he backed up, he grew serious. "Something wrong?"

Her uncle couldn't be doing a better job if he'd known what trick she was pulling.

She studied Old Man Yoder and then turned to her uncle. "Can we talk in private?"

Yoder looked desperate as she disappeared into her uncle's office.

Calvin held a chair for her, and after she sat, he went behind his desk. "What's going on?"

"Would you mind looking at these?" She wanted to tell him the truth, but the whole point of this charade was to keep the confidentiality Ray and Van had promised.

Calvin held out his hand for the folder. Once the items were spread out on his desk, he put on his glasses and then got out a magnifying glass. "I'm confused. At first glance these bank statements look official, but Yoder's name has been added over someone else's, so these are bogus papers."

"Ya, I know."

"Then —"

"Would you do me a favor and call the blacksmith shop and ask for Van Beiler to join us here?"

Her uncle frowned, but he did as asked without prying for information. It was one of the perks of having both the love and trust of her uncle. While he was still on the phone, someone tapped on the door.

Calvin lowered the mouthpiece. "Kumm."

339

Preacher Glen entered and closed the door behind him.

Calvin's eyebrows rose when he saw the preacher. Someone must've picked up, because Calvin asked that Van be sent to the cabinetry shop right away. "He's on his way." He put the receiver in its cradle. "I'm getting more confused by the moment."

Preacher Glen took a seat. "Are you a deer hunter, Calvin?"

"Not much of one, why?"

"Back in my twenties I used to keep the family fed throughout the winter with deer meat. A good hunter prepares well, gets to his tree stand early, and waits."

"You're expecting a deer to enter my office?" Calvin's dry wit took over. But they chatted about various things while waiting for Van. They immediately became silent when someone else entered the shop.

"I got a call at the blacksmith shop from Calvin Keim." Van's voice echoed throughout the shop, ensuring Yoder heard it wherever he was. "Anybody know where I can find him?"

A few moments later Van entered Calvin's office and closed the door. They continued the casual talk of weather and such, keeping the conversation going for about ten more minutes. Why hadn't a very curious, guilt-ridden Yoder come to the office by now? Jolene squirmed. "Is this going to work?"

Glen shifted. "He might be harder to flush out than we expected."

Calvin tapped the folder. "The person is Yoder, right? What's he done now?"

The three of them shrugged. Calvin stepped out of his office. "Yoder! My office, now!"

A red-faced, nervous Yoder stumbled into the office.

Calvin held up the file and used it to motion to Jolene, Preacher Glen, and Van. "You want to explain your side of this?"

Jolene bit her tongue as Yoder said horrid things about Ray. Then he launched into a denial of everything. She reached across the thin armrest and poked Glen's hand, prompting him to speak up. He grasped her fingers, keeping her hand still while barely shaking his head. As Yoder continued to justify his actions, she dug her fingers into Glen's hand.

Calvin rocked back in his chair. "Interesting take on it, Yoder. By your denial you've just confessed to events that I knew nothing about."

Yoder spouted more excuses and lies, but Calvin had experienced enough of the man over the years to decode all Yoder said and deduce the truth. Yoder ended up begging to pay the money back if Calvin wouldn't call the police.

Calvin looked disgusted and furious. "After all these years and the second chances I've given you, we find ourselves in the same basic place we've been before." Calvin bounced the end of his pen against his desk. "Write them a check for the money."

"Sure. Just don't call the police. But I don't have all of it. I'm five thousand shy."

"Imagine that." Calvin sighed. "I'll go with you to the bank, and you'll write a check for all you have left of their money. I'll turn over to my niece the pay you're due later this week, your vacation pay, and your upcoming bonus." He looked to Jolene. "If that doesn't square things, we'll figure out the rest later." He returned his focus to Yoder. "While you clean out your locker, I'll get the papers for you to sign, and you're done here."

Yoder blustered, "You need me."

"Not that bad. And if I'd known you were treating anyone like this, especially Ray, I'd have fired you immediately." Calvin looked to Jolene. "This incident tells me a lot about Josiah I didn't know. He's got honor, and the only reason he's not been promoted is that when Ray was here, Josiah needed to be his shadow. Do you think Ray would like to return?"

"Denki, Uncle, but nee. He doesn't like cabinetry work, and he has some skills working with horses."

"Good for him." Calvin scratched his forehead. "I think it's time Josiah received the promotion of a lifetime."

Jolene squeezed Preacher Glen's hand. They would get their money back, and Josiah would be promoted — all without breaking the oath Ray and Van had made. She felt sorry for Yoder and hated that he was now without a job. But as Calvin said, he'd been given numerous second chances. If allowed to stay, Yoder would curtail his behavior for a while and then prey on someone else.

A noise echoed and Calvin rose. "Excuse me for a minute."

When the room became quiet, Jolene realized she and Glen were holding hands. He turned to her, glanced at their hands, and winked.

How had it been so natural to simply let her hand remain in his?

26

The back door slammed shut, and everyone's voices faded along with the creaking of horse-drawn cutters and a wagon. Jolene stood in Lester's old farmhouse shrouded by silence.

The house was eerily still — a first in two and a half months. The mid-July air was sticky, despite that it was barely past breakfast. There were dishes to do and laundry, but the attic whispered her name. She'd been forced to ignore her quiet space since the second week of May. No wonder it was calling to her. Before the horses arrived, she'd spent at least a few hours here every week for the last decade.

Sweat trickled down her back as she pulled the key to the attic out of her apron pocket and headed that way. Lester had rounded up everyone except her to help mow a hayfield. It was her job to tend to the house and fix a small lunch for the workers. Lester had invited guests for tomorrow night, including Levi, Sadie, and Glen, to name a few. Glen was a regular.

If having Ray and Glen between her and Andy was supposed to keep her from growing fonder of him, it hadn't worked. A hundred people could be between them, and she would still see him for who he was and be drawn to him. Whether they were working with the horses or she was setting a cold drink on the table in front of him, sparks flew inside her.

But she was careful not to say anything else on the matter while aiming to be as dutifully void of daydreams as she knew how. She carried out her responsibilities while treating Andy as the married man he was. Did Glen have a clue that, despite her best efforts, her feelings for Andy had yet to obey her will? Did Andy?

She slid the key into the brass padlock on the door that led to the attic. As the cool metal lock in her hand opened, her skin tingled with excitement. Although she trusted Andy above all others, she hadn't told him about this secret. Their goal was to avoid anything that gave them freedom to get emotionally attached, and for her this topic was too personal and private to share with him.

Slowly tiptoeing up the stairs as if it were hallowed ground, she breathed deep, smelling the delicious scent of old wood in a hot attic . . . and the faint aroma of canvases and oil paints. The stairs moaned and creaked, and the air carried a hint of an unfamiliar smell. Did years of memories have their own smell?

She and Andy had done all the right things to break the bond between them. Despite that, she had stored away a dozen memories from every day she'd seen him. Was he experiencing a similar reaction by unintentionally doing the same thing? They would never talk about it — in part because it would be wrong and in part because they'd fashioned their days so that it was a fluke for them to be alone with each other.

Topping the stairs, she paused and surveyed the room: five easels each with a canvas on it, tubes of paint sealed and waiting, and stained but clean paintbrushes. A large red windup clock sat on a long table filled with paint cleaners, thinners, and rags.

Painting had once been vital for her sanity. Then it slowly became like her comfortable old nightgown and favorite house shoes — things she cherished in a world of strict rules held together with straight pins and tightly tied aprons. This attic world now felt like a hobby, one she enjoyed but didn't need for her sanity. Were those days behind her forever?

She went to the tray holding the paint-brushes her Daed had given her. She lifted the largest one, remembering how pleased he'd been to give her this gift. Looking through the small window Lester had installed just for her, Jolene's eyes misted. "Denki, Daed." The view from the attic wasn't much, just a rutty pasture that was seldom used but now had horses in it. She could also see the phone shanty and the dogwood she'd planted. But much like life itself, she felt the scenery wasn't about its beauty; it was about how it stirred her faith.

A desire to paint tugged at her, and she got out a pallet. Surely if she took only a few minutes, she wouldn't need to set the clock this time, and she could still get everything done and have the sandwiches for the crew as needed.

Her thoughts turned to Andy again. Without knowing it, he influenced her thinking. She watched him from afar, seeing the same steady integrity for humanity and beasts. She had a phone and Ray was learning that he liked training horses — because of Andy. When they took the horses for a walk to the creek, they were accompanied by Tobias and

Hope and usually Ray or Glen as well. But despite Andy's patience, she'd had little success going down the bank of the creek or sitting on the log above it. Panic stole her breath every time. Ray or Glen would try to get her to ease toward the water as Andy stood by. But each time she returned to the lawn chairs, feeling panicked. She would sit there, eyes closed, listening to the sounds of the creatures and smelling the aroma of the woods until her breathing became normal. During those times with her eyes shut, she could sense Andy's presence, could almost hear his heart pounding, despite his chatting casually with the group around her. His inner man was pulling for her to get past her panic, and they didn't need words for her to know it. That didn't mean he felt for her all she did for him. It meant he cared about her successes or failures. She used to think love and romance were magnificent goals to attain. Now . . . she'd grown to hate the very idea. Why Andy? Why did she have to care for a married man? It was like a cruel joke.

But they kept to their schedule, involving every available person to work beside them. Although others were around them, every conversation she had with Andy imprinted words on her soul. The group, which often included Glen in the evenings and on the weekends, talked freely while working or eating dinner, sharing serious things as well as hilarity and laughter. Despite all they'd done to put space and people between them, she'd fallen in love with him.

She had no choice but to put effort toward falling out of love with him. There was nothing that could clear the path for her connection to him to be more than a private matter of her heart. But Andy seemed completely satisfied to allow Glen to try to win her heart, and she wished Glen would. It had yet to happen. Before meeting Andy, she'd wanted to marry at some point, but now she could barely imagine actually doing so. It seemed impossible. As she ran her hands down her flat stomach, an odd yet peaceful melancholy stirred within her. Wasn't it better not to bear a child than to marry someone she could never fully give herself to?

It seemed she'd barely begun painting when the echoes of someone coming up the porch stairs caught her attention. Any noise on the wooden porch echoed into the quiet attic.

She laid the pallet aside and opened a jar of paint cleaner and put her brushes in it. The warning bell Lester had installed rang, meaning someone had entered the house. Trying to tiptoe and hurry at the same time, she glided down the stairs, closed the door behind her, and squeezed the padlock until it clicked. She rushed along the back wall as Lester had showed her, stole down the second stairway to the main floor, and went out a little-used side door to the clothesline. But it was empty.

She and Lester had a plan for unexpected visits. But after all these years of putting out at least a string of towels before each visit to the attic, she'd completely forgotten to do that this time. So she had no way to explain where she'd been.

"Jo?" Andy called.

The sense of panic eased. It wasn't the bishop who'd entered the house. He was the man most likely to cause her issues and one who let himself in whenever he visited Lester. The two men were about the same age and had grown up together, so the bishop thought nothing of welcoming himself into Lester's home. He wouldn't think anything of shunning Lester either, because no one came above God's Word, and that's what the bishop thought he was doing by denying art — keeping God's Word.

"Jo?" Andy called again.

"Coming." She went back through the

side door and eased out of the tiny storage room. "Hi."

"Hey." His eyes searched hers, and her knees became weak. "You okay?"

She looked beyond him and saw no one else. "I wasn't expecting anyone to return this soon."

His eyes narrowed, focusing with concern. "We've been gone more than four hours."

"What?" She went into the kitchen and looked at the clock. *Oh, my.* "I'm so sorry. You all must be famished."

"We're fine, and Lester assured me you were too, saying it isn't unusual for you to lose track of time if no one is around. I didn't know that about you, and it seemed to come as a surprise to Ray and Hope too. But he convinced them of it and took everyone into town to eat."

"But you needed to check on me." She liked that.

Did she really want to know how he felt about her? His eyes moved across the sink and countertops. It was apparent she hadn't washed a single dish in those hours. "Whatever is going on, I find it unsettling. Are you sure you're okay? Because you look pale and shaken."

It was time to tell him. "I have a secret, and I get lost in it if I don't set a clock, but

I neglected to set one this time." She longed to hold out her hand for his, but she grasped handfuls of apron to occupy her wanton fingers. "Kumm."

He followed her up the first flight of stairs to the second story of the house. She fidgeted to find the key in her hidden pocket.

"I've wondered why he keeps this locked."

She didn't answer. Every sound seemed magnified. The echo of the padlock scraping against the wood, the key clicking inside the bolt, and their footfalls against the wooden treads as they climbed the stairs.

Once the paintings came into view, Andy seemed unable to budge. Slowly he edged into her sanctuary. "Jolene . . ."

"They aren't much, but I —"

He studied one, his reverence unmistakable. "Don't belittle it," he whispered. As he quietly moved from one painting to the next, she went to the jar that contained her paintbrushes and began cleaning them.

He went to the stacks of paintings that stood along the walls, looking at each canvas. He held up one of her earliest paintings. It had ominous clouds and rain pouring into a river that disappeared into the horizon. "It's your soul." He went to one she'd painted years later — a picture of sunlight from heaven filtering into a home as benches of faceless Amish women sat at a church meeting. "Everyone has a secret, Jolene. Few have one that carries such beauty and depth."

"If the wrong person finds out, Lester will be in as much trouble as I will, and my siblings will be humiliated when I'm shunned for it."

"This would be allowed in Apple Ridge." He sounded distracted, as if his conversation were an afterthought while the rest of him was lost inside her paintings. "If you were allowed to do this art, my cousin Beth and her husband would be thrilled to sell these in their store. Actually, Beth and her husband met because he carves items out of wood, completely allowable in his district in Steubenville, Ohio, and she wanted to carry his work in her store. Bishop Omar is a kind and loving man, but it took some effort for him to see the work as art and not as an idol. He eventually did. Maybe that will happen here one day."

"It's a nice thought."

"It's as if I could crawl right into this art and live there." He patted his chest, then picked up another canvas. "This has to be one of the best secrets I've ever been privileged to know about." He held up a canvas painting, letting the afternoon light fall across it.

"Everyone has secrets?"

"Sure they do."

"Even you?" Her imagination ran wild. Did he know where his wife was and he'd refused to go after her? Had Eva been expecting his child when she ran off, and he had a daughter or another son somewhere? She wouldn't ask.

"My secret . . . is you." His low tone rumbled through her like the roar of rain against a tin roof.

She knew it would continue to do so forever, and she knew something else — they could no longer be on the same property. They'd done all they could to squelch their feelings.

It hadn't worked for either of them evidently.

Several moments passed before Andy looked up from the painting. When he saw her, confusion flickered through his eyes, and then his face mirrored shock as he seemed to realize what he'd let slip. "Jo, I . . . shouldn't . . . I didn't mean to . . ."

"I know." She managed only a whisper. But they both knew that despite their determination, their love had shown itself, and now they had to go separate ways.

27

With a thirty-foot lead line in hand and a longe whip, Andy walked through the barn alongside Ray. "After a horse is used to and trusts the human working with it, we spend time with it in the round pen, attached to the line. Never before that."

Ray seemed invested in learning all he could about horses, and with his savings back he was talking to Lester about going to an auction and buying a few horses to house on this farm. Ray had a lot to learn, but if Lester took him under his wing and Ray went with Andy to a few auctions come September, Ray would have a two-man team to help him learn the ropes.

It was the end of July, and Andy had two horses trained and ready to go. A driver and horse trailer would arrive soon. Andy gestured. "Until the truck arrives, we'll work with the filly today." He'd begun working with the filly a few weeks back, and it was time Ray tried his hand at it. But she was too young to be saddle broke.

Ray opened the gate to the filly's stall and eased inside. "Hey, girl. Jolene says you're something special."

Jolene. It'd been a week since that day in the attic. Andy thought he was braced for moments like this, but the mention of her name caused disappointment to burn his skin. She still came to the farm when it couldn't be avoided, but Naomi often came in her stead. Hope arrived with Ray each day and helped watch Tobias, not that his son realized she was his baby-sitter.

What was Jo doing with the long summer days now that she wasn't spending them working next to him?

It seemed crazy to think he loved her, but he did. It didn't matter that there really hadn't been enough time together to fall in love. It had happened anyway. From their second day together, it was as if he could catch glimpses into her soul, and the wealth he saw there turned him into a man with gold fever.

"The longe whip" — Andy held it up — "is mostly used for showing the horse. To begin with, you may have to flick the horse's rump a few times, but if a horse trusts you, it won't require more than a tap as a means of instruction. If the horse doesn't respond well to gentle commands and light flicks, we've missed a step in the process and need to reset." Andy prattled on, trying not to think of Jolene.

"Jolene had a question she thought I should ask you." Ray took the horse by the harness and led her out of the barn.

Andy's heart about stopped, but he kept his feet and body moving. "Ya, what's that?"

"She read that auctions aren't the best place to buy horses."

"That depends on what a person is looking for. A lot of horses at auction have issues, serious ones. But if your goal is to buy them for a song and to train them well, then you can sell them for ten to fifteen times what you paid for them. Of course overhead on a horse is expensive, and some require months of intense training."

They'd barely entered the round pen when Jolene pulled onto the lane, driving Naomi's wagon and horse. She stopped at the hitching post. His best guess was Naomi couldn't bring dinner since Jolene got out of the rig with the large box that had been used to carry their meal before.

She paused, looking their way, and their eyes locked. Moments later she gave a nod before going into the house. His heart thudded like crazy. A truck pulling a horse trailer drove up and stopped twenty feet shy of where Andy had the horses tied. He left the round pen. These horses had been some of the oldest and easiest to train of the group, which meant they'd had good owners before going rogue from abuse and neglect. They had settled quickly and were quite at ease being ridden bareback or with a saddle. Neither was trained to pull a rig, but they wouldn't be used for that.

The driver got out of the truck. "I'm here to pick up two Morgans."

"Ya." Andy gestured. "You have the paperwork?"

"Uh." The man looked around as if the stuff might float from the air and into his hands. "Let me check on that." He pulled a cell phone out of his pocket. A minute later he talked with someone, and then he nodded at Andy. "Yeah, I got it." Still on the phone, the man got back in the cab of his truck.

As Andy waited, Jolene came out of the house, floating down the steps like a dream.

"Hey, Jolene." Ray motioned for her. She hesitated, but then she closed the gap between them. "It's your favorite. Look." Ray grinned and gestured to the horse. "She likes me."

"You're just trying to make me jealous." She smiled before looking to Andy. "Hey."

"Hi, Jo." His palms sweated. "How's the new schedule working for you?"

She slowly rolled her eyes. "It's doing its job." Hurt reflected in her eyes, but he knew there was nothing they could do about it.

"Here you go." The driver of the truck handed Andy a clipboard with papers to sign. Andy read over the notes, trying to focus on them. He tapped the papers on the clipboard. "The tag numbers for the horses don't match your paperwork. Should start with a zero, not a nine or eight."

The man took the info. "Give me a minute, okay?"

"Not a problem."

Jolene stood at the fence, watching Ray, her expression somber. How had her limited time with Andy blossomed into a miserable desire to be free to be together?

Ray secured one end of the longe line to the training post. "Glen said he'd like to adopt this one when the time came."

Glen. Andy was tired of thinking about him. He swallowed, and it felt as if sand was stuck in his throat. Glen was many things. Andy could make a list, and the words *good* and *patient* would be at the top of it. *Careless* or *clumsy* when it came to

Jolene wouldn't be on the list. Glen intended to win her heart, and he trusted her sense of boundaries. As a preacher, he could've stirred up trouble for Andy, but he hadn't. Did Andy feel like a rash on the man's skin, one that would disappear along with the prickly heat of summer?

Andy untied one of the horses and walked him into his metal box and closed the door. He felt as if someone were loading him into a compartment and locking it. He returned for the second horse, all too aware of Jolene's presence. After closing the trailer, he dusted off his hands, determined to sound upbeat. "The first ones on their way to a new home."

"Congratulations." Jolene's words matched his, empty and yet aiming to sound upbeat.

The driver returned with fresh paperwork. Andy read over it and scrawled his name on it before passing it back. The driver got into the cab of his truck, and Andy moved out of the way as the vehicle slowly backed up.

When the horse trailer and truck separated Andy from Jolene, he took a breath. It would be easier once he left Winter Valley, wouldn't it?

The truck pulled out, and Andy was surprised to find Jolene looking right at him.

His eyes met hers, and just as their summer had faded, so had the spark he would normally see there.

He'd leave here in a month, and he could see her future as clearly as he saw her standing there. A month, maybe two, after he left, the ache of missing him would dull. Traditional Amish gatherings and the holidays would roll around. Family and church get-togethers would replace the wearying awareness that Andy was out there somewhere, married. She'd have days, then weeks when she didn't think of him. One of the Keims, perhaps Naomi or Hope, would invite Glen and his sons to Thanksgiving. During the feast Glen and Jolene would revel in the supernatural power of family and love. Jolene would realize that Glen might not ever own her heart as fully as Andy once had but that he didn't have to. He was there, touchable and obtainable. A week or so later Glen would ask Jolene to go with him to watch his children in the Christmas play at school. The lure of it would tug on her, and she would go because his sons were adorable. Moreover she would long to feel light and love stir within her once again. Reality would swell within her heart, bringing peace and hope. With Glen she could have the joy of an instant family and conceive that longed-for child of her own and could even step into a high-esteem position within the community by marrying the widower preacher.

In a year Andy would be dead to her.

He swallowed hard, fighting with himself to remain on his feet and go about his day. He pulled his attention from her and focused on Ray. "Okay, she's feeling skittish. Her feet aren't moving, but see the prancing of her leg muscles. You need to . . ."

The mid-August sun was brutal as Jolene stood on the bluff staring at the current in the murky river some ten feet from her. The stone bridge her parents had tried to cross was in her peripheral vision. Andy wasn't here, but she imagined him standing on the sandy part below, his hand extended toward her, his blue eyes assuring her she was safe.

Her rib cage and stomach ached from the muscles quaking inside her.

Voices belonging to Glen, his sons, Ray, Hope, and Tobias floated from behind her. Glen had cut the grass and some of the brambly bushes so they could picnic here today. He and Ray had created a makeshift area to play baseball, and Jolene had spread a blanket and put a basket of food on it before meandering to this spot.

For the past several weeks she'd barely seen Andy, and she still missed him. She'd caught glimpses of him, and they'd exchanged just a few words here and there.

She folded her arms tight, fists clenched as she stared at the river. She couldn't catch her breath.

Glen eased next to her. "How are you doing?"

"I . . . I feel weak and dizzy."

He put his hand around her elbow. "I could go with you."

"I . . . I've changed my mind."

"You haven't changed your mind." His tone hinted at amusement, and she didn't appreciate it. "Your fears are changing it for you."

Whatever. She sat. "I think I'm done trying."

He sat beside her. "Okay." He dangled his feet over the edge.

Andy's voice washed over her. *Jo, close your eyes and breathe.*

Am I safe?

Absolutely. I promise.

The imagined conversation soothed her somehow, and she allowed her senses to be filled with the sunlight and sparkling water of summer. The river had a muted roar, a sound she hated. It reminded her of the distant noise of traffic on a highway. She listened closer and heard the small patches of woods bustling with nature. Humid air brushed against her skin, cooling it, and she realized the August sun wasn't bearing down right now. It had to be hidden behind clouds. An acrid smell of muddy water and decaying wood filled her nostrils. She breathed in deeper, searching for something beyond what she didn't like, and with that breath she relaxed even more. Something about this moment was familiar, perhaps a little like the indistinct feel of the attic. Waiting, she felt the breeze rush past her and heard the treetops rustling while birds of all kinds chirped.

Quietness filled her, and she felt so alive.

A hawk cried out, and for a moment it seemed she was the one in the sky looking down on the river. The water didn't appear frightening from the sky. In her mind's eye she soared over the field where family and friends played ball. She unfolded her arms, tilted her head back, and released her clenched fists.

Everything her senses picked up on seemed to swoosh together and sweep through her soul, filling her with peace and love. She opened her eyes. The shadows of the trees were long on the water now. Glen was gone. How long had she sat there with her eyes closed?

She turned and looked behind her. Glen was pitching, and he had his five little boys, Tobias, Ray, and Hope all playing softball.

What was Andy accomplishing on the farm today by himself? Ray said that he was sending off four more horses today and that he had stacks of paperwork to do for the Humane Society. She closed her eyes again. Odd as it seemed, she actually enjoyed the sound of the river this time.

Jo. Andy's voice washed over her again, and she opened her eyes. A bright-red male cardinal was at the edge of the water, dipping his beak in and then stretching his neck, drinking. He hopped in farther, little by little, until he was bathing in it. The female swooped onto the dirt a few feet away, tilting her head as if watching for danger.

As she breathed in the beauty of God's creation, verses from Romans chapter eight came to her, and a peace she had never experienced before became a part of her — a peace that appreciated that as beautiful as life could be, it also groaned under its slavery to corruption.

She was tired of being held captive by an unreasonable fear of rivers and creeks.

While she was removing her shoes, a bee buzzed past her face, and when she swatted at it, both birds flew off. She eased down the side of the bank. The sandy dirt was cool against her feet, and she inched toward the river until her toes were touching the warm water.

It felt like freedom, and she stepped in farther until it just covered her feet. She wished Andy were here.

"You did it, Jolene."

She looked up to see Glen smiling.

"I did."

He glanced behind him, probably making sure Ray and Hope were watching his sons. Then he skidded down the bank and held out his hand to her. She took it, and he kept her steady as she stepped back out of the water.

He motioned to a large rock, and they sat on it. "I, uh, have some news, and since no one can hear us, now is probably the best time."

"What's up?"

"Some rumors have started about you and Andy."

"What?" Had her siblings already heard them? What about Andy's family? Could he keep Tobias from learning of them? "Who —"

He shook his head. "Not completely sure. It's not as bad as it sounds, but the bishop and his daughter dropped by Lester's a few days ago. Maybe Tobias said something that caught their ear. His daughter is known for asking lots of nosy questions and putting a picture together."

The bishop's daughter was over fifty. She should be more mature than to stir up unnecessary trouble. Jolene's fairy-tale moment of having victory over the river drifted away with the water rushing downstream. And clearly Glen was disappointed. Again.

"So now what?"

"I'm not sure. The fact that you've not been going there nearly as often lately helps. I was in and out a good bit before then. I say we keep our mouths shut and hope the community ignores the rumors. The last of the horses will be gone in two weeks, and Andy will return home."

Her chest constricted so tightly she felt unable to breathe.

He started to reach for her hand, but he pulled back. "Maybe one day you'll tell me why you aren't going to Lester's much anymore. My fear is something specific happened between you and Andy."

If she wanted to confess to Glen, she would tell him that seeing Andy less and him more had done nothing to dissipate her feelings for Andy. Rather than sharing a meal with the family, they exchanged glances as she walked in or out of the home. But he was in her heart, and Glen deserved the truth. "Nothing happened, Glen. Not in the physical sense. I . . . *we* realized that we cared too much, and we knew we needed more separation. But I have trouble imagining my life with any other man, and I know that's not right because Andy isn't mine to imagine life with. Shutting out the possibilities of love and family may be refusing God's best for me. But it's where I am."

"I appreciate your honesty. And if there is one thing I do understand it's wishing the one you love were here with you. But life isn't what we want it to be. It is reality, and I think we're meant to accept our limits and make the most of what we have." He stood. "I need to check on my boys."

She stared at the river, thinking of her parents. Glen was right. Life was about reality and learning to accept what was. But if she spent time with Glen for another year, would the reality of how she felt about him change?

28

The cicadas chirped, and a mourning dove cooed as Andy loaded the last horse onto the trailer, at least the last one that was leaving by motorized transportation. His work here was almost done. His bags were packed, and a driver would pick up Tobias and him in two hours.

Jolene was here . . . to say good-bye. She'd come an hour ago and stayed too long. It bothered Andy for her sake, but he couldn't make himself discourage this final visit.

He signed the papers and kept the needed copies. The rumble of the truck leaving barely registered.

Jolene sat on the porch steps, and he wished they could go for a walk — simply to talk freely and say a proper, respectful good-bye. But she shouldn't be here without her siblings or Glen. Was the presence of Lester and Tobias on the nearby porch swing enough to keep the rumors at bay?

Apparently not or there would be no gossip going around. The last thing either of them needed was a minister to charge them with inappropriate behavior.

Andy clutched the papers and paused at the foot of the steps. Of the four horses still on this farm, Lester had adopted three, and Glen was adopting one.

"You're a good horseman, Andy Fisher, and I'll miss your being here." She spoke with a strained nonchalance, a valiant effort to conceal what was reflected in her eyes.

He appreciated her desire to strengthen him for the winter ahead — the lifetime of winter ahead. "It's been a good summer, ya?"

She nodded. "Ray's so excited to have found something he's decent at."

"He needs to keep studying, and he can call me if he has any questions." Andy leaned toward her and kept his voice low. "Emphasis on *he* can call. No asking for trouble, okay?"

Tears brimmed in her eyes. "I know." She cleared her throat, and soon the tears seemed to evaporate.

Did she really understand? It seemed after coming here tonight that she needed a good lecture. He couldn't give it, not without being a hypocrite, because he was glad they'd had a few minutes to chat, even if it was on the porch with an old man and a boy.

Glen pulled into the driveway.

And Glen.

Andy suppressed a sigh. Glen's horse pranced as he pulled the open carriage, and his little boys waved excitedly at Jolene. Glen brought the rig to a halt near the front porch. "I thought I'd pick up the filly tonight."

Before Jo stopped coming here, Glen usually brought only two or three of his sons with him at a time. Andy wasn't sure why. Maybe to keep down the rowdiness or maybe because the boys would rather stay with one of Glen's sisters and play with cousins. Or maybe to give Jolene time to bond with each one rather than feeling overwhelmed by all five. But regardless of which sons were where, Glen wasn't here for the filly. He'd already signed the paperwork, and he could pick up the horse anytime. He was here because he'd somehow known Jolene would be here.

Andy walked toward Glen. "Sure."

Glen lifted his youngest sons from the rig, and when he set the littlest boy's feet on the ground, he didn't release his Daed's hand. "Let's see about tethering the filly to the back of my carriage."

371

Was there another way to get the horse to Glen's place? Andy knew his patience with Glen was wearing thin. Ya, he wanted Jolene happy, and Glen was a good man, but right now it felt as if he was being a buttinsky. "Okay."

Glen's older son slid his hand into Jolene's, talking excitedly about the new horse. All of them walked toward the barn. Glen removed his hat and put his youngest son on his shoulders without even pausing. "Would you like to go with us, Jo? You know, to help keep the filly calm while she's following the rig and to help get her settled? I'm sure she'll do better if you're a part of getting her home."

"I . . . I suppose it's a good idea, but I hadn't planned on . . ."

Andy couldn't resist looking around Glen to see Jolene. She glanced at Andy, seeming torn. She'd avoided coming here for the last six weeks, and yet they couldn't have even a little time to talk with Lester and Tobias nearby?

But Glen's request was legitimate. She had bonded with that filly since mid-May, and in two days it would be September. So he understood her desire to settle the filly in her new home. Or maybe her only desire was to keep from causing trouble.

Glen moved his son onto his hip. "You can leave your horse and carriage here. Andy will tend to the horse, and I'll bring you by here Monday morning to get it. Or we could do it tomorrow afternoon. Your choice."

Feeling territorial, Andy wanted to tell Jolene he could find a reason to return in a month. It would be easy enough since he and Ray were planning to attend some auctions together, but Andy wouldn't say anything that would hold her back from bonding with a good man.

He got the filly, and after the awkward minutes of attaching it to Glen's carriage, Andy stood in the yard and waved as Jolene rode off with Glen and his five sons.

The kitchen table had at least four-dozen folders strewn across it. Ray had not been this confused since the last time Yoder yelled at him. Ha! Those days were behind him. That part was nice, but it was midweek, and Ray wasn't working. Andy and Tobias had returned to Apple Ridge. They'd left just the way they'd arrived — quietly with no fanfare. Ray had wanted to throw them a party or at least invite them to dinner here, but Jolene declined his idea, mumbling about how it could cause an issue with some in the church. He wasn't sure that made sense, but she hadn't wanted to talk about it.

Silky pushed her nose against Ray's elbow, and he patted her. She was the needier of the two dogs.

James set some papers to the side. "We have to make some decisions."

If Ray could see into the future for just a moment, he'd know what answer to give. James wanted Ray to partner with him, and Ray didn't mind working part time, but his main goal right now was to focus on training horses. Lester was going to let him use his facilities, which was too amazing an opportunity to pass up. But James was looking to make a go of some business that would eventually get him out of the blacksmith shop.

James handed Ray another set of papers with pictures attached. "Not sure you saw this one."

Ray looked at the information. "Maybe we should've stuck to the corner lot where you made flower arrangements and I sold them."

"Maybe. But a man has to dream." James smacked the table. "Now focus and help me dream!"

"But we made good money."

"I want to start a landscaping business. Selling flowers from an empty lot is not the answer." James had the guts to go after what he wanted, only as it turned out, he didn't enjoy it like he thought he would. But if he hadn't followed that dream, he wouldn't have discovered his real one — running a plant nursery.

Woofy barked and went to the back door, and a moment later Hope entered. She must've already finished cleaning Mrs. Pinson's house. He glanced at the clock. Jolene had probably already left from her half day at the bakery and gone straight to Lester's. That's what she'd done regularly for the last ten days, since Andy and Tobias had returned home.

"Well, hello." Hope spoke to the dogs without noticing Ray or James.

James watched her before focusing on the folders. Ray recognized that half-interested, half-embarrassed look on James's face. He liked his little sister? She was barely fifteen years old.

She set a stack of books on the old linoleum floor. Either she'd gone by the library, or Mrs. Pinson had loaned them to her. Hope knelt and patted Woofy. Silky went to her too. "Do you need to go out? Ya? Okay, then, let me get a drink, and I'll walk out with you." After a final rub behind each dog's ears, Hope grabbed her books and stood. Her eyes got large. "Goodness, guys, you startled me. You should've spoken up. I had no idea anyone was home."

"The dogs went out recently." Ray drummed his fingers on the table. "But it's good to know you're nice to the dogs when I'm not around." He was only teasing. Hope had been gentle and sweet all her life, which should help make it up to Jolene for all the trouble he had been. But those days were in the past. If the temptation to rip something apart came over Ray again, he'd go to someone immediately and talk. Jolene would be his first choice and Preacher Glen his second.

Hope ambled into the kitchen and put her books on the counter. "What's all this?" She got a glass from the cabinet and filled it with tap water.

"Information on the properties I told you about. You know, the ones James is considering as start-up places for a nursery."

"I remember." She moved to the table and stared down at the mess. "But I'm surprised you're seriously looking already."

"We're daydreaming mostly." James fidgeted with the edge of a stack of papers.

Hope lowered the glass and wiped the

back of her wrist across her lips. "That's cool."

James barely looked up from the papers and toward Hope. "Is it?"

"Sure it is." She shifted some of the papers, glancing at the images. "So which ones are in the lead?"

"No idea," James mumbled. "Hopefully, I'm better at running a nursery than I am at choosing a location."

"You'll find that out soon enough, won't you?" She went to the head of the table and sat.

When did his little sister start sounding so much like Jolene?

"But first you gotta get the business started." She sipped on her water as she glanced through several portfolios of properties. "What's the budget?"

Ray dropped a folder on the table. "More than zero but not by much."

James rolled his eyes. "I have fifteen thousand saved, and I can get a loan for thirty more, but that's not much when you're talking about a business."

Hope set one portfolio on the table and slapped it. "You should toss that one out of the running."

"Really?" James picked it up. "Why?"

She waved another one under his face.

377

"Because it's no better than this one, and it costs twice as much."

"Gut. One decision made." James pulled out a chair and laid the portfolio in it that Hope said to discard.

Hope passed him another one. "This one should go too. Look at it. It's in the middle of nowhere. Finding something in Winter Valley would be better than that."

"True." James put it on top of the other discarded one. In less than an hour, Hope had the number of properties to consider down to five. "Okay, men," — she stood — "I've done my part. Maybe it's time to call the Realtor who gave you all those."

"Denki, Hope." James patted the stack. "We were feeling overwhelmed. Next thing on our list should be to talk to Amish businesspeople who live in those towns. They'll be able to tell us things the Realtor can't."

Hope put her glass in the sink. "For a man bumfuzzled by a stack of folders, you're pretty smart."

"Even a blind squirrel is right twice a day."

Hope broke into laughter. "Uh, I think you mixed two different sayings. It's 'even a blind squirrel finds a nut once in a while,' and 'a stopped clock is right twice a day.' "

James never looked up from the folder in his hand. "So you're saying a squirrel is never right?"

When Hope said nothing, he peered over the top of the folder. Ray knew James had on his poker face and was teasing Hope, but would she realize it?

Hope shook her head. "The squirrel is right twice a day if it squirreled away a broken clock."

"I reckon so." James lowered his eyes to the folder, never cracking a smile. But Ray could tell he was doing his best to keep a straight face.

James nodded toward her stack of books. "Read much?"

Hope grabbed her books. "Never read at all." She went up the stairs.

"You like my sister."

James's cheeks turned pink. "Does it show that much?"

"She's six years younger than you. That's too young for you."

"Uh, ya, I know that. But she'll grow out of being young. Maybe if I'm lucky, I'll have become a real grownup about that same time and will be running a successful business. I have nothing right now. I live in my brother's carriage house with a job that's been handed to me. I probably need six years to get my act together enough to be worthy of her." He shuffled the folders.

"Speaking of girls, I've hired a driver to take me to see Teena next weekend."

"It's about time you visited her by yourself."

"That's what she said."

29

Andy walked beside his son on the path through the woods. The mid-October leaves were almost at peak color, and the air smelled of fall as they returned from the creek. Tobias held the lead to his horse, patting her while walking beside Andy. He had no doubt he'd done the right thing to give Tobias a horse. It was the very one he'd wanted before they went to Lester's, the solid black one with an irregular, T-shaped blaze on her face. As Jolene and Hope had read him the novel *Black Beauty,* Tobias's heart had broken for the mistreated creature, and Andy knew his son was ready.

"Daed, you gonna answer me?"

Since Tobias had been a toddler, Andy had known the time would come when he'd have to tell Tobias nearly everything concerning his mother. But Andy had hoped to have better words than the ones he could currently find.

His sudden questions about his Mamm were sticky ones. Why had she left? Would she return? Didn't she love him or Andy? What was wrong with them that she ran off? "Sure, I'll answer. I just need a minute to think how best to word it." He rubbed his neck. Sleeping on the couch every night was rough on a body, but his bed seemed entirely too large for one lonely man.

Before going to Winter Valley, he had been content and at peace with his life. What had Jolene done to him?

"Your Mamm is sick. She —"

"Then we need to go to her, right? Sick people need someone to help them."

"Well, they do, but this is a different kind of sickness. Her brain has an illness, and she doesn't want my help."

"Doesn't want it?"

God, please don't let learning these things endanger Tobias's sense of well-being.

"You like walking to the creek, don't you, Daed?"

The quick change of subject seemed to be how Tobias's mind was working today. "Ya." Seeing the currents and hearing the rushing sound made him feel closer to Jolene, and it brought him some peace, as if assuring him she was fine. Was she?

He wasn't. It'd only been a few weeks,

and he was miserable.

"The horse in the book *Black Beauty* couldn't have been any prettier than my horse, huh? Miss T is a beaut."

Andy patted her. "That she is."

"I told *Grossmammi* about me and Hope sitting on that log feeding fish."

It would be safer for everyone involved if Tobias didn't mention the Keims at all, but how could Andy ask that of his son? "That was a fun day, wasn't it?"

"Ya." Tobias pointed. "Daed, look."

Bishop Omar and Levi were waiting at the end of the path where the woods met open pastures.

"Hallo." Omar sounded like his usual friendly self. "It's beautiful out, ya?"

"It is." Tobias waved. "Me and Daed have been all the way to the creek!"

Levi strode toward Andy and Tobias, leaving Omar at the end of the path. "Hey, little buddy, let's put Miss T in the pasture and hop in the rig. Sadie's waiting."

Andy's heart kicked up a notch. He and Sadie were getting Tobias off the farm as quickly as possible. "What's going on?"

Levi put the horse between Andy and Tobias. "Omar got a call from Jolene's bishop. There's to be a meeting."

Andy's head throbbed. "The subject matter?"

"Inappropriate behavior," Levi whispered. "Maybe adultery."

Adultery? The word made his heart race. How was it possible anyone thought that? He willed his pounding heart to slow. "Has anyone talked to Jolene to find out how she's holding up?"

"No, and the bishop said there's to be no contact from any Fishers. There's a gag order until it's settled."

"When's the meeting?"

Levi started to say, but Tobias came around the front of the horse. "Where we going?"

Levi smiled. "To get ice cream and visit Mammi and Daadi. Sound good?"

Tobias nodded, but he looked from Levi to his Daed, confused by what was going on. Andy winked. "You get an extra scoop for me and bring it home in your pocket."

Tobias laughed, and Levi and Tobias led the horse to the pasture.

Andy came face to face with Omar. The man shook his head. "I'm sorry, Andy. I tried to stop this . . . for Tobias's sake more than anything."

Sunlight streamed in through the windows

of the spare bedroom. Jolene's mouth was dry and her heart pounded as she aerated the soil around the containerized dogwood and put some fresh, fertilized dirt around the tree. Today she would face her bishop and Andy's.

What an awful spot to be in — for all of them. Guilt hounded her, but as odd as it seemed, so did a strong sense of faith. But both of those things aside, Jolene would return home with it imprinted on her brain that there could be no more contact between her and Andy. Ever.

She had to put him out of her mind and heart, but just as this dogwood tree would continue to grow, so would her respect for Andy Fisher. After dusting the dirt off her gloves, she removed them. This room was where she'd grown her dogwoods for the last ten years. Long ago, in another lifetime, it used to be the nursery. She remembered every sibling's birth, including Josiah's, even though she was only three at the time.

"Hey." Josiah's familiar voice pulled her from her thoughts.

"Hi."

In his eyes she saw worry, and yesterday he'd voiced that he wanted to go with her today. But the instructions regarding who could attend were very precise. Only those who'd witnessed Andy and Jolene together during regular work-hours, when they were the most likely to have their guard down from onlookers, were allowed. Thankfully, both bishops felt Hope should not come, due to her age. "Why am I not surprised you're here?" She ran her fingers over the leaves of the dogwood, and her faith in this gift steadied her beating heart.

Four months ago when Sadie had mentioned wanting a tree like Lester's, Jolene began praying specifically for Andy and Tobias while tending to this tree. She would have to give it to Levi and Sadie, but since the night she'd kept Andy from returning to Apple Ridge, she'd cared for this tree with the same depth of love and care she did each one she gave away. Well, this one might have received a few more fervent pleas to God to take care of Andy for her. She blinked, willing the tears away. "The driver will be here soon, so would you carry this outside for me?"

"Sure." Josiah picked up the heavy container as if it weighed no more than his son. "I want to say something encouraging. I can't believe you of all people are facing this kind of meeting with church ministers, from two different districts no less. It's just so wrong."

She had yet to be told what the exact charges were. Obviously they were related to her becoming too friendly with a married man, and she had mixed feelings about that — some guilt and some defensiveness. "I hate it for Andy and Tobias. It's my fault Andy didn't go home when he wanted to. He could've used those few days at home to try to find someone who could replace him for the summer while Levi and Sadie stayed here."

"I feel really guilty. Maybe if I'd been here for you, but I've been so busy with my own life —"

She held up her hand, shushing him, but before she said anything, someone knocked on the front door.

"Hallo? Jolene?" Glen called.

The plan had been that a driver would bring Glen here, and then Ray, Glen, and she would go to Apple Ridge. Her bishop and deacon had left earlier. She wasn't sure why. "Take the tree out, and make sure Ray's finished tending the horse."

As soon as Josiah disappeared, Jolene reached into her pocket and felt the key to the attic. She'd fallen asleep with it in her hand last night, holding it tight. When she woke, her first thought was to give it to Andy. Maybe because the attic was a connection between them, or maybe because it represented a secret room, much like the undisclosed feelings that ran between them. Would anything be a secret after today?

The floor squeaked, and when she turned, she saw Glen in his Sunday best with a Bible in hand. He walked to the much-smaller dogwood, the one she would now give Ray when he married. "I didn't say anything sooner because I was afraid it'd keep you from sleeping, but I don't want you caught off guard. I don't know what Andy's bishop has said to him, but our bishop says I'm not to tell you the specifics. I do know, however, that it's going to be a really tough day with a lot of hard questions."

"I've been pondering the possible questions, so I hope I'm ready. I get that someone doesn't like that Andy and I developed a friendship, but his wife is gone. How much mud can they sling?"

"Lester gave an excuse about being too old to go, not that I believe it, but who's going to question an elder? Personally, I'm not sure he's doing you any favors by staying home. It makes it look as if he has something to hide. He doesn't, does he?"

Lester knew about her painting. Her friend wouldn't chance being asked the wrong questions.

A horn tooted.

Jolene clutched the key to the attic. "That's our ride."

No matter how bad today got, she would remember her limited time with Andy as a good thing. Maybe that would keep her from losing her temper and making the situation worse.

They rode in a King Cab truck, Jolene and Ray in the back and Preacher Glen and the driver in the front. The scenery was pretty, but Jolene was exhausted by the time they arrived more than three hours later.

The beauty of Andy's farm was startling with its lush greenery, well-kept barns and home, a huge round pen, and plenty of horses in the pastures. She hadn't expected it to be such a pretty place.

Preacher Glen paid the driver and told him he would call him later today, possibly before dinnertime. It was an hour before noon now, so apparently Glen wasn't expecting the meeting to drone on too long. Jolene hadn't even considered who was paying for the gas or the driver's time.

Glen moved the containerized tree to a wagon sitting just inside the barn. Then he went to the front door and knocked. A man Jolene didn't recognize opened it. When they stepped inside, she saw people in chairs around a long kitchen table. Then she spotted Andy. Their eyes met, and despite the chaos she saw steady gentleness radiating from deep within him. He was simply a man who'd been young and had married a woman against his better judgment. She would not fault him for that.

How many misjudgments did each person make in a year? She had blindly kept Ray working in a place that was undoing all she was trying so hard to accomplish with him. She'd trusted her uncle and Josiah to look out for him, and they thought they were. Blind mistakes were as much a part of life as getting things right. They didn't make a person a fool or less worthy. They showed that people were human and in need of grace. Her parents were intelligent, loving people who made a foolish mistake, but that did not change the beauty or value of who they'd been.

Jolene searched Andy's eyes, and even now she could feel that there was something indefinable about him.

Ray bumped into her. "Oh, sorry about that."

She realized he'd done it to break her stare. She swallowed hard and tried not to look Andy's way again. Tobias wasn't here but was probably with his grandparents for the day.

Introductions were made, but her head was swimming. There were six ministers — three from Andy's district and three from hers — plus Levi, Sadie, and Andy. Bishop Omar motioned toward a chair. "You may take a seat."

After prayers Andy's bishop began. "Today will be filled with heated emotions, and I ask each of you, in the name of Jesus, to use self-control at all times as we work through this. The ministers have discussed it, and I will ask most of the questions. They have already given me many of their questions, which I've compiled into one list. But they may write down more as we go along and pass those to me as well. We'll begin at the starting point of the issue, which is, When did Andy tell Jolene he was married, and what was her response? We will come to a conclusion on each charge before we move on to the next one. When discussing the elements of the accusation regarding what took place between Andy and Jolene, we, the ministers, will talk to the witnesses privately so that the ones being charged cannot hear the accounts of the others before they answer the questions we have for them. We will aim to give a decision today on all accusations, but we reserve the right to meet again concerning the allegation of lust and breaking the seventh and tenth commandments."

A roar pulsed in Jolene's ears as the impact of the charges hit her like being trampled by a rogue horse. "The seventh commandment?" Her head spun. She and Andy had crossed a few ethical lines. Perhaps a marriage, even when a spouse was missing, should be protected in ways she and Andy hadn't honored, but . . . "We're being accused of adultery?" Each of her words was packed with emotion, and she could hear the shrillness in her voice.

Andy closed his eyes and rubbed his forehead. Why hadn't someone warned her about this? Jolene's stomach churned, and she feared she'd be sick. Where was the bathroom? She darted to the kitchen sink, turned on the water, and drew a handful to her lips. It immediately eased her nausea.

A dishtowel was held out to her, and when she turned, she saw Sadie looking mortified for her.

Jolene gasped for air while dousing her face. She pulled the crumpled towel from her shoulder and dried her face. "I'm sorry. I . . . I had no idea that . . ."

"Sadie, would you get Jolene a glass of

water?" Omar took a deep breath. "Jolene, please sit."

Jolene returned to her chair, embarrassed almost as much by her reaction as the accusation. Adultery! Maybe whoever the accuser was didn't understand the gravity of thinking such a thing. She'd spent her life wearing a cape dress, keeping her head covered, and praying every day. The claim was as harsh as accusing a peacekeeping, nonresistant woman of murdering someone for personal gain.

Sadie put a reassuring hand on Jolene's shoulder for a moment as she set a glass of water on the table in front of her. Then she returned to her chair, but she didn't look at Jolene.

Jolene tried to pay attention, but the pain was too much. What did God think of her misconduct? She didn't claim to be innocent, but there was an ocean between unintentionally falling for a man whose wife had left him six years ago and adultery!

Omar asked Andy a lot of questions and then turned the questions to Levi, Sadie, and Ray.

The questions and answers between Omar and the others continued for more than an hour. "So," Omar said, sounding ready to bring a conclusion to this issue, "what happened when Jolene realized you were married?"

"She said good-bye and left."

"Immediately?"

"Not in the first thirty seconds, but as soon as the shock wore off, and I explained the situation, ya."

"How long?"

"Within seven to ten minutes, I guess."

"What was your reaction?"

"Confusion. Disbelief. I thought she knew. I was also honored that she cared and surprised that such an amazing woman would be interested in me if I was available."

"So you wanted her," Jolene's bishop said.

"Wait." Glen waved both hands. "There's a huge gap between being flattered or honored and what you're suggesting."

"Is there?" the bishop asked.

Omar nodded. "I agree with Preacher Glen."

"My daughter thinks they were playing footsie under the table."

Glen's eyes flashed with anger at his bishop. "Your daughter never saw them together. Your daughter talked to a child, jumped to conclusions, and is threatening to damage two families. I told you yesterday that I will not sit in silence while hypocrisy slings its spite, and it is hypocrisy for a gossip to falsely accuse others and use her bishop father as the instrument!"

Guilt for the position Glen found himself in hounded her. If he wasn't careful, he would find himself facing charges for talking to the bishop in such a manner.

Did honoring a marriage demand that Andy and Jolene should've gone their separate ways as soon as they realized there was a spark between them? Or was that the letter of the law speaking?

But the real question was, What had they gained for their rare, intense moments together? The news of today's meeting had already spread throughout their districts, and no matter what the outcome was, their reputations might be dashed to pieces.

And this meeting had broken their hearts.

30

Andy sat on the edge of his bed, staring at the wood floor, waiting to be called back to the kitchen table. Probably for the first time in his life, he understood depressed people's desire to crawl into bed, pull the covers over their heads, and stay there.

The hopelessness eating at him made him want to do the same thing — give up. The gossiper had won. She'd hurt Jolene and her reputation. Why would anyone be so mean? What was the point? If not being able to marry Jolene wasn't bad enough, if having to give up their friendship wasn't bad enough, he'd had to stand by while Jolene's bishop cut out her heart. Andy's chest physically hurt. Could the severity of a heart attack be any worse?

He'd gone into a solitary room and testified concerning his relationship with Jolene. Then she went in alone. After that, Glen, Levi, and Sadie had done the same. Right now Ray was in there, answering question after question.

Voices came through the open window, and Andy went to it and looked out. Jolene and Glen were in the front yard, facing each other and talking. Jolene wiped tears from her face, and Glen put his hand on her shoulder. Andy returned to his bed and sat.

"Andy?" Omar called.

The hairs on Andy's arm stood on end. This was it. Whatever the ministers had decided would be carried out. He was fairly certain of their decision and his punishment — not guilty on adultery, but guilty of inappropriate behavior so a sentence of an eight- to twelve-week shunning and Bible study time with Omar.

But he prayed they punished him and not Jolene. Andy drew a deep breath and went down the hall to the kitchen table. Jolene and Glen were coming in the front door. Each person took a seat.

Omar shuffled his papers. "It's a grievous thing when a family is torn apart like Andy's has been because Eva left. It causes innocent people to be tainted by prejudice and opens their lives to unfair scrutiny — as seems to be the case here. The only just and fair decision we can come to is to clear Andy and Jolene of all charges brought against them."

Relief washed over Andy, and he could feel a weak smile tug at his lips.

Jolene stared blankly at the table. "I've been asked the most humiliating questions today. At one point my own bishop insisted I see a doctor to prove whether I've been with a man or not."

Outrage coursed through Andy.

"I came here feeling humble and contrite because I do have strong feelings for a married man. But we kept a strict distance between us, and now anger burns in me, and questions keep circling." She leveled a look at her bishop. "What is your part in the injustice that's been done here today? Do you have no responsibility at all, no sense of humility? Are you capable of feeling anything beyond your self-righteous indignation that we didn't handle our temptation in a way that met with your standards . . . or apparently those of your daughter?" Jolene stood, looking at every minister except her bishop. "I appreciate the justice you've given here today." With that said and without looking at Andy, she went outside. Glen followed her.

Seething, Andy got up and walked out. Ray went with him.

Andy went down the steps, and when

Jolene saw him, she walked toward him.

Glen came out of the phone shanty. "The driver is already on his way. He'd planned on waiting in the driveway for the meeting to end."

"That's fine." Jolene folded her arms. "May Andy and I have a minute?"

Glen looked from Andy to her. "Ya." He shrugged. "But I can't let you leave my sight. Ray and I will wait here."

"Denki." Jolene ambled toward the barn.

"I can't begin to tell you how sorry —"

"He's my bishop, so I'm the one who's the most sorry. He's been strict all my life, but this is not the man I once knew him to be."

"It seems he should've stepped down sometime ago."

She motioned toward a containerized tree. "I brought something for you." Her voice wavered. "Well, it officially has to go to Sadie and Levi, but you know what I mean." Tears welled. How hard had it been for her to keep them at bay throughout the questioning? She rushed onward. "Since it's mid-October, it needs to stay in this container throughout the winter. Then plant it early next spring after the last frost. It's strong enough to survive winter in the barn, except it'll need to be somewhere with good sun —"

"Jo," he whispered.

Her face crumpled into tears, and she turned away from him.

He took a step toward her. "I appreciate the tree from the bottom of my heart, and I always will, but this is our last time to talk."

"There isn't anything else to say" — she turned — "except . . . words we cannot speak."

Words of love, he knew. This was his Jo — as honest with him as the day was long. He released a deep breath, trying to stay in control of his emotions. He couldn't acknowledge what she was implying. It didn't matter that he adored her. His goal was to get her to grab on to a real future. "You need to walk away and let go. Do you understand?"

She shrugged, giving a slight roll of her eyes. "I've tried that."

"Try again."

Jolene fidgeted with something in her hand. "This may not feel like a good fit for your situation, but after my parents died, Josiah said something about keeping the family together that really helped me. He said maybe we're in this family — maybe we exist — for the sake of our siblings. I held on to those words many a night." She clutched her fist tighter. Was there something in her hand? "Maybe your marriage isn't about you. Maybe you're in it for Eva's sake, regardless of where she is."

That thought struck hard, and he could see why it had bolstered Jolene. A bit of faith stirred within him. "That helps, Jo. A lot. But the only way I can stand this situation is if I know you will be all right. So give Glen another chance. You saw him in there today. He cares for you, and he had a dozen chances to take a pound of flesh from either of us, but he never did."

She gazed out the barn door at Glen. He was doing his duty standing guard, but he was talking to Ray and only glancing their way. "He was at his best when I was being questioned alone."

"See, he could be the one, Jo, and you had to go through this to really see it."

She shook her head. "Now that I know what it means to have an inexplicable connection to someone, I don't think I can marry if I feel less for someone else."

The truck pulled into the driveway. "Tell me you'll try. Please."

"Okay." She held out her hand to shake his. It was the only acceptable way to say good-bye with Glen watching. But she'd put something in his hand, a warm piece of metal with edges.

She smiled and wiped away another tear. "Bye."

Andy stood rooted in place as she got into the truck. He waved, and soon the vehicle was out of sight. He looked in his hand.

A key to the attic. They both knew he wouldn't return to Lester's and meet her in the attic. The key wasn't for that. But the impact of what the key meant washed over him, and despite the value of its significance, he was certain the harshest wind yet swept across his soul.

31

Ray came down the stairs carrying an armload of wrapped presents. The home he'd grown up in smelled and sounded as it should on Christmas Eve. He paused on the stairs, enjoying the many noises. Snippets of several conversations. Laughter. Cabinets and drawers being opened and closed. Plates and utensils scraping against each other.

Love and family — that's what he heard.

When he'd first been injured, noises overwhelmed him, and Jolene would sit on these steps with him, covering his ears as he watched his siblings open their gifts.

Josiah's little one ran through the house giggling, probably for no other reason than excitement. Michael's newborn was happy in Jolene's arms as she cooed to him, her newest nephew. Michael and Anna were setting the kitchen table. Naomi was getting cookies out of the oven, her round belly very much in the way, and her husband moved already-cooled cookies onto a plate. Hope stood at the island, reading . . . when not jumping into the middle of a conversation. Apparently she could read and listen to others talk at the same time, because she lowered the book and hopped directly into a conversation and then returned to reading her book.

One thing about tonight stuck out — an old, familiar aspect that he'd sensed numerous times over the years. Jolene was deeply content, and her faith was intact, but her heart was broken. A person would have to know her to see that, and as far as he knew, she hadn't said a word about the events that had taken place at Andy's home. If Ray hadn't been there, he would only know what the others had heard through the district — that she went, answered questions, was cleared of all accusations, and returned home.

Glen had invited her to attend the Christmas play at school tonight, but she'd declined. Jolene hadn't missed attending the Christmas play since her own play when she was in the first grade. But she hadn't wanted to go anywhere tonight.

She glanced up. "Oh, look at you, Mr. Moneybags."

He laughed and finished descending the stairs. "Had some money. Now have none." He went to the corner and set the gifts with the others. Money didn't hold the power over him it once had. Anxiety crept in at times, but his obsessive concerns were manageable enough that he ignored the pressure when it began to mount. He'd discovered that diving into a job he enjoyed was the best possible medicine.

Josiah leaned against a counter. "So explain how your business-venture plans work."

"I'm working at Lester's with horses Andy helped me buy at the auctions. All my other business ventures are various jobs James comes up with. Since a bank wouldn't approve a loan so he could buy a nursery, I'm helping him get started by doing lawn care and landscaping without owning a nursery. Anyway, to get our names out there for lawn services in the spring, James got the idea of shoveling snow from sidewalks for free. One time per potential customer, and then we leave them our business card. But people liked us and the job we did, so they started calling us to clear snow and ice off their driveways and sidewalks for pay."

"Ray is also doing pet and house care for people who've gone away for the holidays.

He does that for two families of snowbirds, who won't return until May. And" — Jolene beamed at him — "he's boarding a couple of horses at Lester's for people."

Michael clicked his tongue. "Who would've thought you could make full-time pay doing a bunch of part-time jobs?"

"James." Hope lowered her book. "He's creative, and he's got more ideas than he's got time. He'll earn enough to buy a nursery one day. It might take two years, but you just wait and see."

Josiah frowned. "What you're doing is odd, Ray. It's like a Fruit Basket Turnover of small jobs. You train some horses and then dabble in a dozen other things. You can't continue living this way, can you?"

"Oh, let him be." Jolene brushed the back of her fingers across the newborn's rosy cheek. "He's eighteen and not looking to marry or provide for a family anytime soon, so why can't he do a hodgepodge of jobs if it makes him happy?"

His sister had changed over the last year, or maybe he simply saw her more clearly now. Either way, it appeared to him that she no longer felt a need to conform to set ideals or to follow a set way so that the Amish would perceive her behavior or her siblings' behavior as acceptable.

"Ya, I guess he's in a position to hold numerous and ever-changing part-time jobs." Josiah nodded. "It's just . . . different from what's expected among the Amish."

"It is." Jolene swayed the baby. "In case you haven't noticed, we, as a family, are different. It began with Daed, the most loving, non-rule-centered Amish person I ever knew, and Mamm, the most educated Amish person I've ever known. Apparently coloring outside the lines is in our genes, and we're carrying on the tradition."

"But" — Michael put the last butter knife on the table and walked to the island — "once sure of the right path, we follow our hearts without wavering."

"Michael," Josiah said, "remember the time Daed . . ." Ray's brothers started down memory lane.

Ray put his hands on Jolene's shoulders. "Look around you, Jo. You're surrounded by whole, happy, and faithful people, and you were the glue." He squeezed her shoulders and peered at his nephew. The only thing he knew to do to ease her heartache was tell her one encouraging thing each day. Oh, and make her proud of him.

Andy's attention focused on the barn as he drove the horse-drawn carriage toward his driveway. His miracle from God was in that barn — the tree Jolene had given him. The way one branch of that tree bloomed in winter might be a sign from the Creator that Andy would not lose his sanity as he ached for Jolene.

He'd discovered it one night in November. The ground was covered in several feet of snow, and Andy kept circling through the woods and barn, looking for a bit of peace that he couldn't find. How was he going to keep going? His mind and heart were screaming for Jolene, and he just wanted to give up. As he cried out to God, he climbed the ladder to the haymow to water the tree Jolene had given him, and that was when he discovered the miracle.

A secret he'd told no one.

"What a busy day." Andy had several sacks of groceries at Tobias's feet and even more in the back.

His son looked inside a grocery bag. After getting groceries and running errands, Andy had picked up Tobias from school. "The teacher said the groundhog saw his shadow yesterday. Did you know that, Daed?"

It'd been a long, bitter winter. The first snow had hit in October, and even though it was now the first week of February, there was no hint that the snowstorms would let up. "I read it in the paper this morning."

"It means six more weeks of winter. I'm glad. I like sledding and ice-skating." Tobias poked his Daed's shoulder. "Hey. Some of the guys are going sledding on Omar's hill this afternoon. Can I go?"

"Doesn't Omar get tired of you boys being over there?"

"Not at all. His wife, Lizzy, offers us hot chocolate and cookies almost every time. So can I go?"

Andy's attention never left the open hayloft window. He hadn't gone up there yet today. Time hadn't allowed for it. "How much homework do you have?"

"I did most of it at school, so maybe half an hour."

"Get that done while eating your snack, and I'll take you over there."

"Really?" Tobias grinned. "All right!"

Andy pulled the rig to the front door. He grabbed the handles of half a dozen plastic grocery bags and hopped out. "Tobias, as soon as you get inside, wash those hands, scrubbing off all the germs from school, and then take your homework to Sadie. She said to tell you that she made an apple strudel pie and that you may have a slice of it for your snack."

"Yum!"

Andy opened the back of the rig, passed bags to Tobias, and grabbed the rest. By the time Andy walked inside, Tobias was down the hall washing his hands. Andy unloaded the rest of the groceries.

The barn wooed him like the savory aromas of a feast drew a half-starved man. He drove the horse and carriage into the barn, his heart pounding in anticipation. He put the horse away, dried him well, and laid a blanket over him. After feeding and watering him, Andy got a container of water and climbed the ladder to the haymow.

The moment the tree came into sight, his heart palpitated. He walked to it and caressed the beautiful white flower. Who would believe a dogwood tree could have a single branch that had kept a bloom on it all winter? The current flower would fall off in a week or so but not before another flower bloomed on this same branch.

First and foremost, a winter-blooming dogwood branch meant God had performed a miracle just to be sure Andy knew the truth — that He was taking care of Jolene. Of course it also meant that in the midst of accepting his life for what it was, God had sent a message that He cared about Andy and what he was going through too.

32

The view of early summertime through Lester's attic window was stunning. The dogwood was in full bloom, and one of the horses was in the pasture right behind it. Jolene studied the view and had a loaded paintbrush in hand. But she knew this painting would be similar to all the others she'd done over the last eight months.

It didn't matter what the view was or what season the view reflected. The focal point of the painting would be Andy. Maybe the artwork was therapeutic, and one day she would paint something or someone else. Out of respect for the Old Ways and perhaps because she had no experience painting faces, she left him faceless, although she would shadow in his skin color and beard. It fit well with her impressionistic-style work.

She'd been down this path of grief before. The trick was to allow herself to paint whatever came from her heart. Eventually other forms of life would begin to bud and sprout inside her again, much like spring itself.

Lester wasn't here, and although he usually left a note for her, she didn't know where he was. She wanted to talk to him about one thing: Glen. Discussing Preacher Glen might take a little time. To keep her word to Andy, she'd invited Glen to family functions since October. She also saw him at church and fellowships, but he hadn't asked her to go anywhere with him since Christmas Eve. She'd told him then that she wasn't ready to commit to dating. It was a serious matter to date a widower preacher. One date with him and word would buzz through the community. People loved him and were protective of him. If she dated him, they would assume it was serious, and she had wanted to be sure how she felt before agreeing to go out. Now she knew.

When the warning bell rang, signaling that someone was entering the house, she jolted. Why hadn't she heard the *clippety-clop* of a horse-drawn carriage or car wheels on the driveway? She peered through the small window, seeing nothing.

"Lester?" Glen's voice made her heart

pick up its pace. It wouldn't do for him to discover her secret. As a preacher he was obligated to uphold the Ordnung. Desperate to hurry downstairs, she fumbled the paint pallet while trying to lay it on the desk, almost dropping it. As she grabbed the pallet, her foot caught the easel, causing it to skid an inch or so. The sound echoed against the wood floor.

"Lester?"

Her hands shook as she steadied the easel. Was Glen coming up the stairs? She scurried to the steps and tiptoed down as quickly as possible to the second floor of the house, where all the bedrooms were. She closed the door behind her just as Glen topped the stairs, but she had no time to lock it.

When he saw her, his face showed concern and surprise. "Jolene, I didn't realize you were . . ." He moved closer. "I came to visit, and then I heard odd noises, and no one answered my calls." He seemed baffled. "Is everything okay?"

She swallowed, trying to slow her heart. "Ya, sure." It would be easy to lie and simply say she was cleaning and had shifted the furniture, but she couldn't go that far to cover her secret. Silence was one thing. A direct lie was too much. "Lester isn't here."

Her breathing was rapid and her voice shaky.

"Jolene," — he grabbed her wrist — "you're bleeding."

She tugged her hand free, noticing the swath of red paint across her palm. "No I'm not."

He looked her over and angled his head. "Oh." Tension eased from his face. "It's paint," he said, pointing at her dress. She glanced at the blue and green splotches, the effect of having almost dropped the pallet. "What's going on?"

She shrugged.

"Jolene, you can trust me. You know that, right?"

Could she? Where was the line between his relationships and his duty as a preacher? But he deserved to know who she was. If he did, maybe he would decide on his own she wasn't the one for him.

She opened the attic door and waited as if that one action was more than enough for him to understand. He took her cue and went up the stairs. She remained at the bottom, hoping for the best. Once at the top he paused, looking across the room.

Andy had asked her to put effort into a relationship with Glen, and in her estimation she'd given him a fair try. But it seemed to make them more awkward around each other. Were they even friends these days? She couldn't build a future with him. That's what she wanted to talk to Lester about. She respected Glen greatly, and she liked him, but he simply didn't stir any romantic sentiments in her.

He descended the stairs, returning to her.

Did the look on her face match the emotions pounding her — embarrassment at having such a secret and dread of what he'd do?

He straightened his straw hat, looking every bit the preacher. "Who all knows?"

"Lester, Andy, and you."

"Andy," he mumbled.

She knew even less to say about that topic than about painting. On shaky legs she moved past him and went down the steps and into the kitchen, where a basket of laundry was waiting to be ironed. She set the flatiron on the stove and removed the wooden handle before she lit the gas eye. "May I fix you some lemonade or get you a glass of water?"

"I'm good. Denki."

What would he do now that he knew her secret? She got out the ironing board and set it up near the stove.

He leaned against the counter. "You

trusted Andy with your secret before me. I don't understand."

She froze, stunned. He'd not challenged her or asked questions about Andy since the meeting in October. She took a pair of pants from the basket and spread them on the ironing board. "I'm not sure what to say."

"When I first considered dating you, I thought, *I know Jolene Keim.* But this past year I've come to realize that you don't easily let people into the inner sanctuary of your heart. Even so, whenever I catch a deeper glimpse of the real you, I like you even more."

She started to reattach the wooden handle to the flatiron, but she turned off the eye instead. At the very least Glen deserved her undivided attention. "I'm sort of the same way. The more I get to know you, the more highly I think of you. You are a rare and remarkable man. But . . . I would like to be allowed to move out of the singles' section at church."

He eased into a kitchen chair. "We both know the pain of losing loved ones, and you've had enough loss to understand that all people have is today. Together, you and I could make every day as good as it can be, but you'd rather stay single?" He gazed up at her. "At forty I'm way too old to play the fool, but I've played it for you. I knew there was a spark between you and Andy. You told me that yourself. But has it faded at all since that meeting last fall?"

"Glen, I am truly sorry. You've been good and kind, and you deserved better. But I'm not the one for you. I've had months to make my decision, and moving out of the singles' section is the right thing for me."

It didn't mean she couldn't ever marry, although it was a clear statement that she was no longer interested in marriage or being courted. But if she discovered a single man who had the power to own her heart like Andy had, even if it happened when she was fifty, sixty, or seventy, she would marry him.

Footfalls echoed on the front porch, and the door flew open. Lester entered the house holding a small paper bag with artist paintbrushes sticking out of the top. Lester spotted Glen and lowered the bag. "Preacher Glen, how are you today?"

"You and Jolene are good at keeping some pretty big secrets, aren't you?" He walked out of the house, got in his rig, and left.

Glen was hurt and angry, and he knew their secret about the attic. Was Jolene about to see his less-than-noble side?

■ ■ ■ ■

Ray slit open the last bag of mulch, and Teena surveyed the pots of flowers and the freshly mulched islands. They had added splashes of fall colors, but they were also preparing the ground for winter.

She passed Ray the shovel. "My Mamm usually does most of the fall yard work by herself. I do not want to miss the expression on her face when she arrives home in an hour or so from visiting her sister. She's going to love it."

"Gut." He wiped sweat from his brow. The long shadows of mid-September stretched across the yard, but the heat of summer had yet to break. Almost a year had passed since he'd sat in Andy's home and answered questions about his sister's behavior with a married man. How different this day was. "You've been a lot of help today."

"Ya, I began today hoping if I worked hard, you'd have enough energy left to take me out tonight. But now I'm too tired to care."

He chuckled. "Really? Even for a meal at Burger and Shakes?"

"I could manage that."

"Good, because James was frustrated that

he couldn't come help today. If you were too tired to go out with me after this, he'd be doubly frustrated."

"So I need to ask you a question . . . for my Mamm."

He pulled his leather-bound notebook out of his pants pocket. "I've been studying and taking notes on various yard plants for nearly a year, so maybe I'll know or have the answer."

"Are we officially seeing each other, or am I just someone you take out to eat when you're working in the area?"

Ray liked this question, but he remained studious and flipped through pages of his notebook. "I don't have an answer to that in here." He lowered the book. "But I do in here." He touched the center of his chest. "I'd like it if you saw no one else, and I never have seen anyone else, but at nineteen I'm years from being ready to marry."

"I haven't gone out with anyone in a very long time . . . except for our occasional dates. And I'm years away from being ready to marry too."

It seemed to him that every day he spent with Teena, though it wasn't often, was better than all the others combined. "Then tell your Mamm we're seeing each other and no one else. In the meantime get back to work."

"If we ever have children, I'm telling them about today. Completely lacking in romance but rich with demands to get back to work."

Ray removed his hat, bent low, and kissed her on the lips. When he backed away a few seconds later, her cheeks were red.

She looked around to see if anyone was watching. "That was really nice."

"Not bad," he teased.

She nodded. "You're right. We might need a little practice."

Ray slid his dirty hands over hers and squeezed. "I could manage that."

33

Andy finished the chores in the barn and trudged through the thick snow. It wasn't yet time for dinner, but night had fallen, and the stars twinkled. It was early January, and it'd been snowing a couple of times a week since mid-December, his second December since the summer he'd met Jolene.

He went to his beloved dogwood. He'd planted it in the front yard in a spot he could see whether he was in his kitchen, the barn, or the round pen. With his gloved hand he shook the snow off the branch, and let the warmth of hope and love wash over him. This one branch still continued to bloom.

He couldn't believe it, and yet he could stand right here and watch it for hours if he let himself. Each time he came to this tree, he prayed for Jolene, and it brought him renewed peace time and again. He also prayed for Eva and Tobias.

Sadie and Levi's little girl was a year old now. Had it been nearly fifteen months since he'd seen Jolene? She seemed so close to him. But soon enough he would blink, and fifteen years would have passed. He pulled off one glove and touched the cold petals. Several fell into his hand.

Odd as it seemed, he was at peace with his life now. He'd become content again, although he doubted he would ever stop missing Jolene. He'd learned that part of many people's journey on this planet was to accept a constant ache — whether of the heart, mind, or body — and to keep on going, giving, and loving as if there were no pain.

His family, church, and business life were thriving. He caught himself laughing while sharing meals and playing games with Levi, Sadie, and Tobias. Peace had never felt this good. Maybe it took losing all of something to be alive to it anew. He'd attended a few auctions with Ray, and each time, Ray had said Jolene was well but absolutely nothing else. Was that an edict from their bishop, or did Ray not want to tell Andy how well Glen and Jolene were doing?

Tobias now seemed to understand the situation with his Mamm, and he'd accepted her absence the best a young boy could. He was wounded but not critically so.

At the moment Tobias was with Sadie, doing his hour of homework. Even though she had a child of her own, Sadie didn't want to give up that time with Tobias. Andy had much to be thankful for.

A rig pulled onto his driveway, and Omar got out. "Andy."

"Hallo." Andy went toward him, his hand outstretched. There were so many ways that Omar could've mishandled the accusations against Jolene and him, but his bishop had trusted what he knew to be true of Andy. It was a shame that Jolene's bishop operated from suspicion of sin rather than grace. But Omar had gone through the steps required of him and had done so in a way that stopped the gossip from spreading. Most had set the issue aside, unwilling to form a judgment. "Care to come inside?"

Omar glanced at the dogwood tree and then did a double take. "It's blooming!"

"Only one branch, but ya."

"In winter." He went to it, inspecting the branch. "I've never heard of such a thing. Where did you get this tree?"

"Well, since you asked directly, Jolene."

The man gaped at him. "How long has it

been blooming?"

"About fourteen months. All the branches bloom in spring, but that one blooms year round."

Omar stood frozen, staring at it for several long seconds before he shook his head, apparently freeing his thoughts. He reached into his coat pocket. "A large envelope arrived at Feenie's early last week."

Feenie was Eva's favorite sister and the only one she ever contacted. Was Eva on the brink of returning? "Did Eva write to her sister?"

"Ya, sort of. She wrote to Tobias but addressed it to her sister. Feenie would have brought it to you herself, but she wanted me to verify its contents first," — he held it out to Andy — "which is what I've been working on nonstop since Feenie brought it to me."

Andy took the manila envelope and peered inside. The darkness of night prevented him from being able to read anything out here, so he lowered it to his side.

"I have some . . . disturbing news, and it will hit hard." Omar drew a deep breath. "Eva passed away more than two years ago."

Grief and remorse over lives poorly lived — hers and his — hit hard, and Andy sank to the ground and sat in the thick snow.

"Two years ago? How?"

"She was living on the streets, refusing medication for her mental-health issues. She died of pneumonia."

"But why are we just now finding out?"

Omar eased his hand under the flowering branch, gingerly cradling it. "It may be the second miracle you've received." He released the branch. "More than two years ago Eva wrote a letter to Tobias and addressed it to her sister. Before Eva died, she asked a street friend to mail it." He shrugged. "Apparently the woman was with Eva when she died, but in her confused mental state, she thought she'd lost the letter."

Mental illness was so cruel, making Eva choose to live on the streets as a poor homeless person rather than here in the warmth of their home with their son.

Omar cleared his throat. "Somehow two years later the envelope showed up in an old coat of Eva's street friend, along with the newspaper obituary, which described Eva as an unclaimed indigent person." Omar cradled the blooming flower again. "I never would've figured a homeless woman would have the ability or mind-set to mail the items. But with that information and with Feenie's help as a relative, we managed to get the death certificate. It arrived in the mail today, giving us the last piece of information needed to verify that the woman who died was Eva."

This new reality continued to pound him. After all he'd been through with Eva, he wouldn't have figured the news would rip out his insides like this. Their regrets were now etched in stone. Why did it have to be this way for Eva and him? And for his tender-hearted son?

Omar crouched. "It may be too soon to mention this, but perhaps this is God's way of opening a door for you and Jolene."

"No, it's not." That time had passed . . . if it had ever existed.

She and Glen were together now, and he wouldn't mess up that. Even if Andy knew she'd rather be with him, if he made one step toward her, it would confirm people's suspicions that they'd been inappropriate or, worse, had an affair.

"I'll share the news with my family and hers if Feenie hasn't already done so. If the letter is coherent and nice, I'll give it to Tobias, but I'd rather keep this development as low-key and quiet as possible."

"I hope it isn't an inappropriate time to mention this, but Jolene's bishop contacted me. Preacher Glen has been gathering information about various church districts who have changed their position on the creation of art from impermissible to permissible. The bishop seems to think Glen is pushing hard for him to relent on that topic because of something to do with Jolene. I'm not sure if the bishop has valid reasons for thinking that or if his daughter is putting ideas into his head again. But the situation has me curious."

Even though Andy trusted Omar, he wouldn't share Jolene's secret. But this news did confirm that Glen was a good man who wanted to free the captive. That alone was reason enough to stay away from Jolene. Anything Andy did to renew that friendship would only serve to make Jolene a prisoner of gossip and confusion concerning them.

"Do you want me to come in for a while so we can talk?"

"I appreciate it, Omar. I do. There's a lot to think about and sort out, but there's nothing to discuss."

"Okay." Omar shook his hand before heading to his carriage. He paused and turned. "Maybe you know this, and maybe I'm out of line for saying it, especially right now, but while I was talking to Glen about ways to get artwork approved, he said that Jolene removed herself from the singles' section late last spring."

The impact of that for Jolene cut deep, but Andy would end his days on this earth as he'd been living them for nearly nine years — as a single Daed with one son. If one looked at it the right way, it was more than enough.

Jolene held the squishy orange football firmly, running as her three nephews squealed loudly and chased her. The eldest one, now four, grabbed her legs. She willingly fell to the ground and swooped him and his cousins into her arms while tickling them. Lying on the soft green grass, facing the gorgeous spring sky while kissing their chubby, soft cheeks, she felt whole.

The grill had smoke billowing from it as Michael and Josiah cooked hamburgers and hot dogs. Mother's Day. She loved it and her little munchkins.

Teena was here, sitting next to Ray. Her youngest brother was quite the horseman and businessman, and he'd asked Teena to marry him. They were joining the faith this fall, but they would wait until the next fall to marry.

Hope, at seventeen, was now fully in her rumschpringe and had her sights set on James Beiler, not that she'd told him yet.

James had yet to ask her out, but he came to family gatherings. He and Willis were on the porch hanging her newest Mother's Day gift — a swing like Lester's.

With the little ones wallowing around her legs, Jolene propped up on one elbow, viewing her family.

James glanced at Hope, who sat on the steps reading. Jolene wasn't ready for them to date, not with the age difference between the two. Her little sister needed more time to mature, but Jolene hoped they would marry one day. They had such a good time together. They were true friends with sparks of romance between them. Didn't romantic love based on first truly liking the other person make the best marriages? It seemed so.

Hope had a love of writing, and Jolene wasn't sure what to do about it. Her sister was far more talented at writing than Jolene was at painting, but their bishop didn't allow novelists either. Maybe Jolene should move to a district with a more lenient bishop, but she'd have to go at least thirty miles, which meant her family wouldn't be able to drop by easily.

A rig pulled onto the driveway, a normal occurrence around here. She had a busy household with loved ones in and out all the time, but who was joining them? She sat upright, holding a lapful of wiggly children.

Glen got out of his carriage. Jolene squinted against the sun, peering through the window. Inside was Glen's fiancée, a quiet, gentle woman who'd been married only three years when she lost her husband. She'd been widowed seventeen years ago and had one child, a daughter. She lived in Ohio, and Glen had met her while visiting other churches to preach. He grinned. "It looks like old home week around here."

Jolene stood, shooing her nephews to their Mamms before straightening her Sunday apron. She wore a black half apron with no bib for church Sundays now. The white aprons were for singles who intended to wed. "Hey." She smiled. "Would you and Lillian like to join us for burgers?"

"We can't. My Mamm is expecting us, but could we get a rain check?"

"I'd like that." She used her hand as a visor against the sun. "So what brings you by this afternoon?"

"I talked to Omar over in Apple Ridge yesterday, and he shared something I think you should know . . . if you don't already."

Her heart thudded. Were Andy and Tobias okay? What about Sadie and Levi? Had Eva

430

returned?

He shifted. "My understanding is Lester knows this, but Andy's Daed asked him not to say anything."

"What's happened?"

"About four months ago Omar learned and shared with Andy that Eva had passed away, apparently a couple of years earlier."

Why had Glen dropped by to tell her this? It might make sense if they'd bumped into each other in town and he took that opportunity to mention it. But no matter how she viewed it, this was really difficult news. She had meant no disrespect to Eva by falling in love with her husband. And how awful for Andy. Whether Eva was alive or dead, he was without his wife. How did a man grieve the loss of someone he'd lost so long ago?

"It was good of you to stop by and tell me. But I have my life back. People have finally stopped whispering about Andy and me. And I'm content." She had no doubt that Andy felt the same way, because she'd not heard anything from him. This information wouldn't change anything between them.

Their love remained, or at least hers did, but they had been washed downriver.

34

June humidity lay heavy on Andy as he sat on the back steps and reread the letter Eva wrote to Tobias. It wasn't long, but in it she assured Tobias that she loved him and believed in him. She apologized for not living with him like other Mamms did. Her few, simple words brought a lot of comfort to Tobias and to Andy. But one thing she wrote struck him as profound, and it kept churning in his heart: live life based on what you know to be true, not what others think is true of you.

She was speaking in the context of Tobias trusting that she was proud of him even though others might think she didn't care because she wasn't around. But was Andy staying away from Jolene because of what others thought their relationship had been?

He folded the letter. He had read it many times, and it sounded as if she'd returned to Apple Ridge at some point and seen Tobias, watched him even. It had given her peace to know he was a whole and healthy boy. Andy used to think that if he had the power to turn back time, he never would've married Eva. But then he wouldn't have Tobias, and Eva was right — Tobias was a gift.

"Daed, kumm look!"

He put the letter in his pocket. Tobias had Miss T in the round pen, training her to back up on cue, very useful for driving carts and carriages. "That's great, Tobias."

His son had grieved his mother's death and would continue to do so, but Tobias felt good about the letter. If Andy had only one word to describe Tobias, it would be *thankful*. His son saw the silver lining in everything. Andy watched him for a while, applauded, and then headed inside. It was time to put the letter away for good unless Tobias asked for it.

The full bloom of the dogwood caught his eye.

Jolene.

Andy couldn't make himself call or write or visit her. He longed to, but so much stood between them. He'd hurt her, damaged her reputation, and disappeared from her life.

What was he supposed to do? Go up to her and say, "Now that my wife is gone . . ."?

No. Contacting her would be wrong for a hundred reasons.

A pair of cardinals flitted in and out of the dogwood regularly these days, and when he'd investigated, he saw that they were building a nest.

He couldn't help but smile. He went to his bedroom and put the letter inside the top drawer. As he closed it, something small and metallic fell, and he instinctively reached out his hand.

The key.

How in the world?

It must've been on the very edge of his dresser, but he kept it in the same drawer where he'd just put the letter. When he'd taken out the letter earlier today, maybe the key had been stuck between the folds in the page and then had fallen onto the top of the dresser.

Just as quickly as it had fallen into his hands, an idea fell into his mind.

The attic.

The moment Jolene entered the attic, she knew something was different. But what? It was mid-June, and the air was stifling up here. The problem with waiting until night-time to paint was the lighting wasn't good.

She was glad now that Glen had come up

here and learned her secret. Since that day a year ago, he'd gathered information from other Amish districts and had asked bishops who did allow art to write letters, and Glen had presented the information to their bishop, asking him to change his stance. Glen was such a kind man, but she didn't regret letting him go.

What must it be like to paint out in the open or in a spare room?

As she reached for a paint pallet, an unusual piece of paper on her very cluttered desk caught her eye. She picked up the thick ivory paper that contained only two lines:

Willing, but unsure.
Let peace guide us.

Her heart jumped and skipped like sparks flying from a flame, and her internal reaction stunned her. But she knew it was Andy. Not only because she'd guarded the keys diligently, but because she could feel his presence. He'd been here. She closed her eyes and basked in the feel of it.

He must have seen her dozens of paintings. Embarrassment caused her cheeks to burn. She hadn't expected that Andy would ever enter their attic. It had to have been obvious to him that he was the man in the pictures and she was the woman.

She grabbed a fine paintbrush, dipped it in red paint, and responded. Under the phrase "Willing, but unsure," she wrote, "Timeless friendship." He was willing to step forward or stay away, and she felt that either way, they were timeless friends. What else they were remained to be discovered. Why was her heart pounding so? Was she happy that he'd contacted her, or was she terrified? Maybe both.

Beneath "Let peace guide us," she wrote, "Share more . . . but not in person."

What was he thinking and feeling? He was free to let her know, but she wasn't ready to look at his truth full on, not if she wanted to keep the peace she'd worked so hard to regain.

She left the paper there and picked up a paintbrush. It seemed like a very sky-blue-and-sunny-yellow kind of painting day.

35

Andy sat in Lester's attic, finishing another word game. The wordplay was so good for him, and it must be healing to her too. They weren't spoon-feeding each other information. He and Jolene had never been like that. In this game he had to search his heart to find the right words, and he spent hours contemplating in order to understand what she meant in the few words she responded with.

He breathed in the nighttime fall air. He came to Lester's house every other weekend, arriving right after dark on Saturday and leaving two to three hours later. His great-uncle had strongly questioned him about coming all this way so often, frowning at the cost of time and money.

Andy couldn't believe the old man didn't understand, didn't get that reuniting with Jolene outweighed all else. He had money. Was there a better cause to spend it on? And what good was time if it wasn't used to pursue love? Isn't that what people spent their lives doing — sacrificing in hopes of obtaining what really mattered? He loved Jolene, and that was reason enough to keep coming here.

Would they continue this type of correspondence for another month? Or year? She knew when he arrived every other week, but she'd yet to come. She responded to his words, but she'd yet to write "I'm ready to see you."

It reminded him of the struggles she'd had to leave the edge of the creek or riverbank. It had terrified her. In some ways this dance was the same. She was good at finding him and drawing him out, but she was more complicated, more hidden to herself as much as to him.

Since returning to the attic after news of Eva's passing, had Andy not yet found Jolene? She seemed hidden, which made sense. Heroically secretive was a big part of who she was. Yet with him she'd been vulnerable and honest, and it had cost her. As he thought back, he realized her life stayed shrouded in hiddenness. At nineteen she did her best to hide from her siblings the pain of losing Van. She boldly took care of her siblings while hiding from them the pressures of the task and her own dreams. She hid her anger with Van and Donna and trudged onward. She hid her paintings from everyone except Lester . . . and then Andy. He'd been the one to realize she was terrified of the creek and was uncomfortable having a phone. She'd hidden those fears from others but not from him. Despite how much she'd shared with him that summer, they'd had to keep the depth of their friendship hidden in order to work together.

Veiled. She didn't mean to be that way. Much of it had happened from the necessity to protect others. Some of it was out of the need to protect herself.

But had she not given him the key to the attic, the most hidden part of her life?

Andy rose and took the time to study every painting. What was it about Jolene that he was missing? Something was keeping her from being ready to see him. Each painting worked its way into his heart anew, and he felt so close to her.

Suddenly it struck him.

He picked up a thick, rounded paintbrush with a point to it and went to a blank canvas. Words teemed in his mind, and he intended to paint each one, using as many colors as he could.

Apparent actions
Disclosed hearts
Revealed souls
Visible lives
Unmasked fortitude
Vulnerable tenderness
Incomplete love

He laid down his paintbrush. It wasn't bad. She would like the colors and the honesty. If they were open with their relationship, some would take it as an admittance of guilt regarding what took place between them while he was still married. But those who knew them wouldn't, and that was all that truly mattered.

He went to the desk and found a pen and fresh paper.

My dearest Jolene, our love was undone, and we know that's how it had to be. Let's begin anew. Bold and open. Say yes, Jolene, and I will go to your church leaders. I will stand before your church and declare my intentions before our first date. Say yes, and let's find a way to live life together, being vulnerable and unflinching.

He went downstairs. His driver was visiting with Lester, and Andy sat and joined the conversation. Then a new idea struck.

He went back upstairs, grabbed his canvas painting, an easel, and the letter. He then gave the driver directions to Jolene's house.

As his first act of boldness, he would leave the letter and the painting on her porch.

Jolene closed her book and blew out the kerosene lantern. She moved her hair to the side, wrapped her shawl around her shoulders, covering her nightgown, and tiptoed through the darkness until she reached the porch. A streetlamp lit the yard and some of the porch. What a beautiful evening, although there was no moon or stars shining. But the air was crisp and smelled of fall. She went to the porch swing. A lantern and lighter sat on the side table for when she needed it. How many hours had she spent right here, reading to and rocking her nephews?

It seemed unreal that she had a chance to reconnect with a man she loved like no other, and yet she could not reach out to grab it. Why couldn't she step from the shadows and proclaim her love? She longed to, and yet every time she'd been on the brink of happiness in the past, tragedy ripped it away. Every chance at forever had been stolen. If she dared to reach out, hoping for a final forever, would it also be snatched from her?

Father, I don't know that I have it in me to lose him again. But loss, whether tomorrow or in sixty years, was inevitable.

A car pulled onto the driveway, probably someone needing to turn around. Then the passenger car door opened.

Andy!

Her heart ran crazy, sounding like a drum inside her. What was it about this man? Moreover, what was he doing?

Sitting at the far end of the porch, she was hidden in the shadows of a dogwood tree and an overgrown azalea bush in front of the porch — both blocking the lamplight from this spot. He couldn't see her, but she could tell that he was getting something out of the trunk. Was that a painting? He eased onto the porch, set up an easel just outside the front door, and put a canvas on it. He tucked what looked to be a letter between the painting and the tray of the easel. Then he studied the canvas and drew a deep breath.

Unsure whether to make herself known, she closed her eyes, feeling the quality of the man she adored. There was a force to him — a quiet, temperate way that wasn't silent or mild at all. Had she realized that before now?

He crept toward the steps to leave.

"Andy."

He jolted and wheeled around, staring at the darkness. She took the lighter off the table beside her and lit the kerosene lamp. He seemed speechless as he focused on her.

"What have you brought me?"

Using his thumb, he gestured toward it but said nothing. Instead, he picked up the canvas and folded paper, moved forward several feet, and held up the painting.

She extended the lantern, reading it. The words made tears sting her eyes.

"You paint words through pictures, and I'm hoping I painted pictures through words."

"You did." No one understood her or knew how to overcome her issues the way Andy did. Despite past rumors about them, he wanted to come and speak boldly to her district, proclaiming who he was and his intentions. "It's beautiful."

He stared at her. "*You* are beautiful." He jiggled the canvas. "This is hopeful." He leaned the canvas against the house and held out the piece of paper.

She set the lantern on the table, took the letter, and read the most beautiful sentences of her life. But they only made her feel panicky.

"I see the concern on your face, Jo, and I imagine that you feel as if you're on the edge of happiness, similar to the night your Daed gave you the paintbrushes. And then all your hopes, dreams, and joys were destroyed. It's terrifying to feel as if you're in that same spot again. There isn't a lot I can promise you, because I don't own a single day. But you own my heart, and you have since those first few weeks together. What I can vow to you is that whatever days we are given, I will cherish every one and do all I can to be sure they are filled with love and joy for you."

She closed her eyes, feeling much as she had when he began helping her face her fears of the river. He had wanted to help free her from her irrational fears, and even though they had to part ways before she conquered her fears, because of him she had been able to find peace with that river.

Isn't that what he held out today — freedom to be loved, to be herself, to fulfill her deepest desires if only for a short season? Or maybe until they had great-grandchildren.

She opened her eyes, tuning out the raging fears, and held out her hand. His warm palm was gentle and firm against hers, and he tugged so very gently.

She stood. "You may boldly make your intentions known to everyone. You let them know I am yours and you are mine."

Andy put his arm around her back and caressed her face before he lowered his lips to hers.

EPILOGUE

Contentment flowed through Jolene like a lazy river in summer.

Breakfast was over, and the house around her slowly grew quiet while she added fresh paint to the canvas. Sunlight streamed in through the three walls of windows. It was a far cry from her years of painting in an attic. Everything about her life was like a dream come true. Andy loved her deeply, and she him. They both seemed to bask in it.

Hope had driven Tobias to school because she was the substitute teacher for the day. They were the only two who lived with Andy and her. Levi and Sadie had built a home not more than a stone's throw away, and all of them had dinner together regularly. When Jolene moved out of her childhood homestead, Josiah and his family moved into it, buying it from Lester.

Ray, as well as the rest of her family,

visited here often, but he lived in Winter Valley, renting the barns and pastures from Lester for a pittance. He also rented a small house not far from Lester's, and he and Teena would marry next month.

Jolene and Andy enjoyed returning to Winter Valley often to visit Lester and her family. Hope would live with them for only a couple more years, but when she moved out, she wouldn't go far. She and James were in love, and he owned a very successful nursery not more than six miles from here. Her little sister had a contract with a small publishing house. She wrote children's picture books, and of all unexpected things Jolene illustrated them. The books sold well. It seemed so strange to go from hiding a gift to earning income from it, with their names listed on each book for the world to see.

When time allowed, she and Andy traveled some, taking Jolene's paintings to little towns along the East Coast and selling them. Such unexpected fun to discover new seaside ports where they could stay a night and sell paintings when it suited them.

She and Andy had married nine months ago, at the start of winter. Pennsylvania winter nights were long and cold when single, and she and Andy wanted to begin erasing years of winters from their memory.

Life kept moving along briskly, changing constantly as it glided on the warm winds of love and respect.

Jolene pressed her hand against her flat stomach and smiled. Pregnant but not yet showing.

The front door opened. "Hey, Jo?" Andy called, plastic bags rattling.

She put down her paintbrush and went to the kitchen.

"I needed to get some horse feed, so I picked up a few groceries." He pulled a half gallon of her favorite store-bought ice cream out of the bag. "For tonight." He put it in the freezer. He then pulled out a bag of peppermint sticks. "I know you haven't had any nausea yet, but this will help when or if that time comes."

"You are too good to me."

"No such thing." He winked. His expression changed, and he frowned, looking at the floor. "It's sticky."

She smiled. "My husband spilled orange juice on it. Then he swiped a wet towel over it, giving it a lick and a promise, saying the kitchen was too full of people right then to clean it." She shrugged. "His wife began painting rather than mopping."

"Good for her. It proves she's a smart

woman." After putting away the few other items he'd bought, he paused. "I've got a little time. Want to sit on the deck?"

She shook her head and moved in close. He wrapped his arms around her, and she kissed him, their kisses deepening by the second. "Everyone is gone," she mumbled around the kisses.

"It's rare," he whispered.

She kissed his neck. "Are you thinking what I'm thinking?"

"Ya." He paused, caressing her face. "We should take this opportunity to scrub the floors."

READERS GUIDE

1. The accident that claims the lives of Rosanna and Benny Keim creates a ripple effect in their children's lives with potentially devastating results. Do you believe Jolene softened the blow of that tragedy for her siblings? As time passes, it's apparent that she's failed her brother Ray in several ways. Was her sacrifice of giving up her future with Van worth it, or did her failures cause you to feel she should have let her siblings live with older and wiser relatives?

2. Describe Jolene. What is her greatest strength? her greatest weakness? Do you believe her relationship with Van has defined her life?

3. When Josiah says, "Maybe we were given life and are in this family for their sakes," he is referring to his siblings, and this becomes the foundation of Jolene's decision to keep the family together. What do

you think Josiah meant by his statement?

4. Andy's situation as a grass widower, a married man whose wife has abandoned her marriage and family, is more uncommon in Plain communities than in the Englischer world. The Old Order Amish don't condone divorce in such a situation. How do you view their position? If you were in Andy's shoes, how do you think you would react?

5. Jolene has an unusual friendship with Lester Fisher, a man who is difficult to get along with and is on unsteady terms with his immediate family. Why do you think Lester allows Jolene to use his attic for her painting, especially since it goes against the bishop's edict about creating art? Do you have any Lesters in your life? What are some of the positive and negative effects of the relationship?

6. Using a metaphor from horse training, Andy encourages Jolene to take back her ground. What did you think about Andy's advice to Jolene? Wise or intrusive? Is there an area in your life where you should apply Andy's advice?

7. When Jolene confronts Van with her long-buried hurt feelings, he then realizes his own offenses. How might you approach a similar situation where you have unre-

solved issues from the past? Have you found yourself in Van's position, having caused hurts and offenses you were unaware of? What did you do when you realized it?

8. Ray Keim feels powerless and useless to others, and much of his emotional distress stems from a childhood memory he doesn't really understand. As someone with challenges, is Ray responsible for his actions? What could Jolene have done differently to help him feel comfortable in his own skin?

9. Do you think Andy and Jolene were being reasonable to try to work together as friends even after she understood Andy was married and she was interested in him? Were they playing with fire?

10. How did you feel about Preacher Glen and his friendship with Jolene? Since he is a widower with young children, do you think his pursuit of someone as guarded as Jolene was wise? How do you think he felt when he found out about her painting?

11. Jolene's father gave his wife a dogwood tree when they married, and although the original tree hasn't survived, Jolene has grown new trees from the original cuttings, one for each of her siblings and a

couple for gifts. What do you think the dogwood trees represent for Jolene? What does it mean to Andy when he receives one from her?

12. Andy and Jolene make the hard decision to cut ties, believing God's plan for their lives is separate paths and trusting in His comfort. Have you had to make a similar choice at some point, where trusting God was hard but necessary to follow the path ahead? What was the result?

GLOSSARY

Daadi — grandfather
Daadi Haus — grandfather house
Daed — dad or father (pronounced "dat")
denki — thank you
draus in da Welt — out in the world
Englisch — a non-Amish person
geh — go
Grossmammi — grandmother
gut — good
hallo — hello
Kapp — prayer cap or covering
kumm — come
Mamm — mom or mother
Mammi — grandmother
nee — no
Ordnung —— means "order," and it was once the written rules the Amish live by. The Ordnung is now often considered the unwritten rules.
Pennsylvania Dutch — Pennsylvania German. Dutch in this phrase has nothing to

do with the Netherlands. The original word was Deutsch, which means "German." The Amish speak some High German (used in church services) and Pennsylvania German (Pennsylvania Dutch), and after a certain age, they are taught English.

rumschpringe — running around. The true purpose of the rumschpringe is threefold: to give freedom for an Amish young person to find an Amish mate; to give extra freedoms during the young adult years so each person can decide whether to join the faith; to provide a bridge between childhood and adulthood.

ya — yes

* Glossary taken from Eugene S. Stine, *Pennsylvania German Dictionary* (Birdsboro, PA: Pennsylvania German Society, 1996), and the usage confirmed by an instructor of the Pennsylvania Dutch language.

ABOUT THE AUTHOR

Cindy Woodsmall is a *New York Times* and CBA best-selling author of fourteen works of fiction and one work of nonfiction whose connection with the Amish community has been featured widely in national media and throughout Christian news outlets. She lives outside Atlanta with her family.

If you'd like to learn more about the Amish, snag some delicious Amish recipes, or participate in giveaways, be sure to visit Cindy's website: www.cindywoodsmall.com.